SET A COURSE FOR FREEDOM

*To my dear friend,
Betty
Wm K. Lewis
"Bill"*

SET A COURSE FOR FREEDOM

A Novel of the Revolutionary War

William K. Lewis

Copyright ©2000 by William K. Lewis.

Library of Congress Number:		00-190180
ISBN #:	Hardcover	0-7388-1498-9
	Softcover	0-7388-1499-7

All rights reserved. No part of this book may be reproduced or transmitted in any form or by any means, electronic or mechanical, including photocopying, recording, or by any information storage and retrieval system, without permission in writing from the copyright owner.

This is a work of fiction. Names, characters, places and incidents either are the product of the author's imagination or are used fictitiously, and any resemblance to any actual persons, living or dead, events, or locales is entirely coincidental.

This book was printed in the United States of America.

To order additional copies of this book, contact:
Xlibris Corporation
1-888-7-XLIBRIS
www.Xlibris.com
Orders@Xlibris.com

CONTENTS

PROLOGUE 9

CHAPTER I 13
CHAPTER II 30
CHAPTER III 47
CHAPTER IV 65
CHAPTER V 81
CHAPTER VI 98
CHAPTER VII 114
CHAPTER VIII 127
CHAPTER IX 141
CHAPTER X 161
CHAPTER XI 179
CHAPTER XII 192
CHAPTER XIII 196
CHAPTER XIV 211
CHAPTER XV 226

NOTES 231

This book is gratefully dedicated to those courageous men and women who set a course for our freedom.

PROLOGUE

The tall, thin man leaned back in his saddle and put tension on the reins to ease his horse down the slippery, muddy road to the river bank. Suddenly the rain turned from drizzle to downpour. He pulled his collar up around his neck in a futile attempt to keep dry, but he was already soaked through to the skin.

The road, such as it was, ended at an old, wooden ferry landing, but the ferry was not there. Thomas Owings could see he was in for a wait. He stopped his horse at the edge of the landing and leaned forward to scan the scene, but his eyes could not penetrate the gray curtain of rain, which obscured the Connecticut River. He could not even see the other shore.

Fortunately, off to the right, there was a shelter someone had been kind enough to erect for waiting passengers. It was only a three sided affair but it was a welcome place to get out of the weather, if only until the ferry returned.

Thomas tied his horse to the post beside the shed, removed his bag from the saddle and went inside. There was no one there. That was just as well for he would rather not have to dodge questions presented by well meaning but curious fellow travelers. Besides, his thoughts were of his home and family back in Annapolis and he wanted to dwell on them. As he sat down on the crude half-log bench he wondered what his wife, Matty, was doing at that moment. Probably tending to their newborn son, Michael, he guessed. He could picture them both and the image filled him with a warmth that made him forget how wet he was.

When he left Annapolis he thought the extent of his travel would be to Philadelphia. Little did he anticipate he would be given the opportunity to go to Boston, where the embers of revolt were beginning to take on a bright glow. There he could meet and talk to some of the most influential men in the Colonies. When he was asked to deliver certain secret dispatches to the Committee of Correspondence there, he leaped at the chance. Of course he sent a letter to Matty letting her know he would be gone much longer than planned; he certainly didn't want to worry her.

When the rain let up a bit he peered out and could just barely discern the dark shape of the ferry on the opposite shore. It looked like it was starting to return. He sat back down and let his mind wander back to his home and family. At first he did not hear the approaching horses, then one of them whinnied. He jumped to his feet and cautiously looked out; three British soldiers were approaching. A chill ran through his body but it was not from the cold rain. He knew he had to act nonchalant. If he aroused suspicion in any way they may search him. If they found the papers he was carrying it would not go well for him, not well at all.

It was one of those unfortunate situations in which patrols were out looking for someone else. A young private at a nearby garrison had decided he had had enough of life in the British army and so slipped off to make a new life with one of the local girls. As it so happened, this was not an isolated case, and the enraged commandant was determined to make an example of this deserter. He ordered patrols to scour the countryside and question every male they encountered—no exceptions.

As the three soldiers entered the shelter the sergeant gave Thomas a cordial greeting. He did not really think this man was the deserter; he nowhere fit the description. But, orders are orders. "I'm sorry, Sir, but there's been a problem and we've orders to check everyone's identification. Do you have any papers?"

"Why, yes," replied Thomas as he reached into his bag and pulled out the papers, which rightly identified him as a tobacco merchant from the Colony of Maryland. He handed these to the sergeant and waited for a reply.

"I'm sorry to have troubled you Sir, these look all right to me," apologized the sergeant as he returned the papers to Thomas.

Perhaps it was the inordinate look of relief on Thomas' face that drove the slightest dart of suspicion into the sergeant's mind. He thought for moment, hesitated then said, "If you don't mind sir, perhaps I should examine your bag."

"I do mind. The rest are only private business papers." Fright began to engulf him. He knew he dare not let them see the papers he was carrying, yet further resistance would only increase suspicion. Maybe he could divert the sergeant's attention. "Looks like the ferry's coming back," he said, glancing out over the river.

The sergeant was resolute now. "I'll take that," he demanded as he took the bag from Thomas' hand and began to examine its contents. He removed a folded, heavy document and turned it over several times before deciding to break its seal. Was he going too far, he wondered. "No, this colonial just doesn't look right to me," he said to himself. Thomas stood there, cold, numb, frightened, waiting. There was nothing he could do now that could alter whatever fate had in store for him. The sergeant read the document with intense interest. When he had finished, he slowly looked up at Thomas. A wry smile revealed the pride he felt for what he had discovered. "You're under arrest for treason against the Crown."

CHAPTER I

May 21, 1774

Wisps of early morning fog were beginning to stir and rise, lazily and reluctantly, from the still surface of the Miles River. The first few rays of a brilliant spring sun were just finding their way through the trees and scrub of eastern Maryland's lowlands. The air was already filled with the rising whistle of wood ducks and the low cooing of bitterns from the woodlands just beyond the river's banks. Great egrets tiptoed among the marshes beginning their day long search for food. For them and all the other small creatures that inhabited the shores of Chesapeake Bay it was just another day, a day like any other. For the people of the town of St. Michaels it was not, nor was it for most of the towns in the thirteen American colonies in 1774.

Turner Hall placed his large, callused hands against the edge of the table, pushed himself away, got up and stretched. For a moment he just stood there with his thoughts focused far beyond the walls of their modest gray cottage.

Ellen stopped drying the plate she held in her hand and turned to her husband. Her round and usually smiling face showed only concern this morning. "Is anything wrong, Turner?"

"No, I was just thinking I might keep the boat in tomorrow too. I'm paintin' the fish hold today but this might also be a good time to replace some of the lines. Really not much use in goin' out. What's the point in catchin' 'em if ya can't sell 'em. Guess I shouldn't complain though. Business is pretty bad all over."

"I can tell something's bothering you. Just look at that plate. Is that all the breakfast your going to eat?"

"Yup, that'll get me through the mornin' just fine. It's not like we were fishin' the bay today. It's like I've always said, land work's a might easier than workin' on the water."

"You fishermen aren't a little biased in your opinions are you?"

"Course not! Least not as much as some of our land folks are. I swear, if some of these hot heads don't simmer down with their boycotts and wild ideas of independence, Parliament's goin' to bear down even harder. Lord knows they've made thing bad enough all ready with their taxes and restrictions."

"Can't anyone bring the two sides to reason?" asked Ellen. "Where's it all going to lead?"

"Don't know, but if it comes to a fight there's goin' to be a lot of folks havin' to make up their minds which side they want to stand with."

"Oh, I pray it doesn't come to that. There was enough bloodshed in the last war. You don't suppose Christopher and Benjamin will have . . . ."

"Now look what I've done. I've set you to frettin' again." Turner chastised himself for saying too much and causing his wife to worry. "I'm sure cool heads will take over eventually. In the meantime what we need to worry about is keepin' ourselves together. We can't take the whole world on our shoulders."

Ellen walked with him to the front door. "Are you sure you had enough breakfast? You didn't eat much. It's not like the Turner Hall I've been married to for twenty-two years. Here, wait a second." She turned him around to face her so she could straighten his collar. "Are you sure you don't want more to eat?"

"I had enough. Not real hungry this morning. And it's been twenty-three years," he said with a smile. "Your memory goin' already?"

"Twenty-three and a half if you want to be so picky. I'll bring a lunch down to you later on. Are you sure you don't need Christopher to help? It's not all that important that he go to Annapolis today."

"No, Benjamin and I can manage. Besides, you've been mighty anxious to get the baby quilt over to Matty. I know, 'cause you stayed up half the night to get it finished. Who knows, maybe things will pick up soon and I'll need him more then." Deep down he had little hope for this to happen but Turner Hall's optimism was as much a part of him as his leathery tanned skin and graying hair. "No, you let him go on. He'll only be two, maybe four days at the most. He oughta see his sister. Besides, maybe he can bring back some good news from Annapolis. Tell him to allow himself enough time to stop by the boat before he leaves. I want to talk to him." With that, he leaned forward and gently kissed her as he had done every morning for those last twenty-three and a half years. He then turned and started off for the waterfront. As he closed the white, picket gate behind him he looked back, smiled and waved.

Ellen returned his smile, knowing his did not completely conceal his concern for the future. She stood in the doorway, her hands in the pockets of her faded green apron, watching the man she loved walk from his one love to the other—from his family to his boat and lifelong work. His wooden tool box, hanging from his left shoulder, hardly swung as he walked along. He shouldered this with the same strength and responsibility with which he provided for his family. When he turned the corner and disappeared from her sight she stepped inside and closed the door.

Christopher Hall stooped before the oak framed, oval mirror on the wall of the room he shared with his younger brother, remembering how he once could look straight into it. He had just had his twenty first birthday the month before so it had been several years since he had not had to stoop to see himself. Once more he ran his comb through his brown and unruly hair, then dropped it into his duffel along with enough clothes for two or three days. While securing the drawstring with a square knot he thought, "Guess that'll be the only knot I'll have to tie today."

"Christopher," his mother called from the kitchen. "Get your brother up. He needn't be sleeping any longer. There's things to do."

Christopher walked over to the feather bed that engulfed Benjamin. He grabbed a part of the mountain of covers not knowing what part of his brother it represented and shook it vigorously. "Get up, Ben. Ma says to get you up." A low muffled grunt was the only response. Christopher got a good grip on the edge of the quilt and gave it one great pull, removing the haven of comfort that Ben was so reluctant to give up.

"Aw gee, Chris! I was gettin' up."

"Sure, I know. But today, or some time next week?" With that, Christopher picked up his duffel and went into the kitchen to the breakfast his mother had put on the table for him. He was surprised to see there were johnny cakes as well as the usual bowl of oatmeal and stewed apples.

"Go ahead and eat. If you wait for Benjamin you'll be late," his mother said. "Don't forget to give Matty my letter. Do you have it?"

"Yes, it's in my duffel. Where's the quilt you made?"

"I put it right there on the chair next to the door so you wouldn't forget it. Make sure you find out how they're doing. Your sister married a fine man but these are hard times and Thomas is young and not yet got himself established very well. Just make sure they know that if they need anything they should let us know."

"Yes, Ma," Christopher said as he sat down to the meal that awaited him. He quickly finished the breakfast, saving one of the three cakes to eat on the way down to the waterfront.

"You'd best be getting along now. Your Pa wants to see you before you leave. He's already down to his boat working on it."

"What's he want?"

"I don't know. He just said he wanted to see you. Tell him Benjamin will be down shortly. Now give your mother a kiss and be off with you."

Christopher picked up his duffel and the package containing

the quilt, gave his mother a peck on the cheek and started toward the door.

"Wait a minute," she said. As Christopher turned back to her she gave him the kind of hug only a mother can give when she has that unexplainable feeling of foreboding at seeing an offspring depart from home, even if it's just for a few days. "Be careful Christopher," she said slowly and deliberately, "be careful."

Christopher then followed the same footsteps as his father's but cheerfully eating his last johnnycake as he made his way down to the waterfront.

Turner Hall was not the only fisherman that remained in port that day. Four others were using this day to make repairs or improvements to their boats. These were men whose attachment to their boats was more than economic. It was also emotional, for the many years working on them made the vessels an integral part of their lives. It was a personal relationship. If they were not in their boats fishing the waters of the Chesapeake they would be working in or about them in port. It was something others could never understand.

As Christopher approached the *Elizabeth*, it had been named after a topsail schooner Turner had once seen and admired, he didn't see his father anywhere about. But sitting on the wharf was Ol' Put, town sage, town bum, mentor to some, fool to others, never without an opinion and strangely enough, seldom wrong.

"Good mornin', Ol' Put. See Pa anywhere? Ma said he wanted to talk to me."

"Mornin', Chris Lad, Your Pa's up to the store gettin' some paint. Said to tell you he'd be right back. Hear ye're goin' over to 'Napolis."

"Yes, sir. I'm goin' over on the mail boat to see Matty. It's been a while. Pa says might as well take advantage of the chance. Fishin' business is so poor, hardly pays to go out."

"Ye're right there, young man. And things could get a might bit worse 'afore long. Hear trouble's brewin' up the coast in the New England colonies. Stupidity! That's what it is, just downright stupidity."

"What's stupidity?" asked Christopher.

"King George, of course! Young man, if you'd seen as much as I've seen in my time you'd know what's stupidity and what aint. You'd see what's comin'." Ol' Put took a long deliberate draw on his pipe and turned to look out over the river but with eyes that seemed to be focused far beyond anything one could see from the waterfront. Then he slowly turned back, looked down at his pipe that he held in both hands. The blue exhaled smoke circled his gray head. He then looked up and straight into Christopher's eyes. "Yes, sir, you'd see what's comin'."

Christopher listened intently for he had always liked Ol' Put and as a youngster thought Ol' Put knew just about everything worth knowing.

"Ol' George keeps on pushin' and a pushin', a squeezin' and a squeezin'," retorted Ol' Put with his clenched fists portraying the increasing pressure being imposed upon the colonies by Great Britain. "If he'd half the sense of a Maryland gray squirrel he'd know he can't push the colonies around forever. There's trouble comin', Lad. Mark my words, there's big trouble comin'." Then Ol' Put said no more. He just sat there staring down at his cracked and callused hands as Christopher pondered the old man's words.

Finally, the silence was broken by the sound of Turner's voice. "Christopher, give me a hand."

Christopher turned to see his father coming toward him with both hands full. "Here, let me have the rope. I thought you were just going to do some painting."

"The shrouds are starting to look pretty frayed. Thought it best to replace them while I have the chance."

"Where do you want the rope, on board or here on the pier? Are you sure you don't need me?"

"I'm sure. Just set it there by the tool chest. I'll be using it soon." Turner set the paint down and to the side where it would be less likely to be knocked over. "Christopher, while you're in Annapolis I want you to keep your eyes and ears open. I got the feeling the last time I talked to Thomas that he might be involved in more than just his tobacco business. I don't like to worry your mother needlessly, that's why I wanted to talk to you here."

"Is Thomas in some kinda trouble?" Christopher asked, wondering if this had anything to do with what Ol' Put had been talking about.

"I don't think so. Least wise, not yet. Maybe it's nothing, but there's some folks about who're thinking of organizing against the Crown." Turner placed his right hand upon Christopher's shoulder. "Whether it's right or whether it's wrong, I don't know. I don't have it straight in my own mind yet. I do know such things can lead to trouble. I'm worried what it might mean to Matty and the baby, so stay the week if you feel a need to. Benjamin and I can manage. Now get along with you before you miss the mail boat and have to swim all the way to Annapolis." Turner gave his son a fatherly hug and said, "Be careful, Christopher."

"I'll be careful. See you next week." He picked up his duffel and the package containing the quilt, said good-bye to Ol' Put and briskly went off to the other side of the small harbor where the mail boat was moored to the public landing.

The forty-foot sloop *Nancy* was tied up to the small wooden wharf that was built along the end of the quay. The *Nancy* had been making the trip between St. Michaels and Annapolis for nearly nine years now. Before that she ran passengers between Cambridge down on the Choptank River and Cove Point on the western shore of Chesapeake Bay for almost as many years. She showed her years but was still a stout vessel and strong enough for the service she was doing now. That was limited to carrying mail, light cargo, passengers or anything else that would fit into her that had to travel between the eastern shore of the Chesapeake and Annapolis on the western shore. She was certainly a sounder craft than the one she replaced. That one had met its end in one of those peculiar summer thunderstorms that can suddenly turn the Chesapeake into a witch's brew.

As Christopher approached the *Nancy* he was met with the loud friendly voice of Captain Cobbs. "Come along, Christopher. We're about ready. This hogshead's all we have left to load."

"Hello, Captain Cobbs."

"Goin' to see yer sister Matty I understand." There was little that went on in St. Michaels that wasn't known by all.

"Just for a few days, Pa's keepin' the boat in to do some work on it 'cause things are so slow."

"There's truth in that, Lad. There's truth indeed. Come on board. Stow yer bag for'd under the foc's'le."

Big George Scheper, Captain Cobbs' combination first mate, deck hand and friend, had just finished rolling the hogshead on board. One might say Big George was part of the *Nancy*. He came with it when Captain Cobbs brought it up from down the bay. He had no relatives that anyone knew about and no home for that matter. He slept aboard the *Nancy*. The small sloop was his workplace, his home and his family. This arrangement was all right with Captain Cobbs. It was good to have someone to watch over the boat. Big George was, as his name implies, a big man, taller than any other in St. Michaels. From his massive shoulders hung arms that could lift about as much as any two men in town. But Big George also had a big heart. He was liked by everyone and loved by the children with whom he spent most of his free time, telling wild stories or showing them how to carve model boats or tie knots many of them had never seen before.

"All's secure, Cap'n," boomed Big George's voice.

"Good, we'll get under way as soon as our other passenger arrives."

Christopher gave Captain Cobbs a puzzled look. "I didn't know anyone else was going to Annapolis today. Who is it?"

"You wouldn't know him. He's not from St. Michaels. Came over from Annapolis three days ago, headed for Oxford in a big hurry. Made sure he could go back today, even paid me in advance. Strange fellow, didn't say much, kept to himself most of the way over."

Captain Cobbs had hardly finished when they both turned toward the sound of a carriage approaching through the narrow streets. With the increasing sound an unusually fine carriage suddenly appeared from around a corner and came to a stop at the end of the quay. It was finer than any carriage Christopher had ever seen. There wasn't anyone in St. Michaels he knew who had such a carriage or could afford one like this. The driver secured the reins then climbed down to open the door for his passenger. Out stepped a man dressed inconspicuously in black except for his white knee stockings and a white jabot that formed the ruffles on the front of his shirt. He carried a silver tipped walking stick in his left hand with his cape over that arm. In his right hand he firmly held a small leather valise. He gave a quick glance about him and without a word to the coachman proceeded down the quay toward the *Nancy*.

As the stranger approached, Captain Cobbs reached out to take the man's valise and help him aboard. "Good morning, sir. I trust your visit to Oxford went well."

Without acknowledging the Captain's greeting and without relinquishing his valise the stranger stepped aboard. "How soon will we be leaving?"

The Captain, not very pleased with the stranger's lack of cordiality, simply replied, "Immediately. You can take a place forward, if you please." Turning to Big George, "Let's get going before the wind changes. Back the jib and cast off for'd."

The wind against the backed jib slowly swung the bow around away from the quay. As the sloop became perpendicular to the quay Big George brought the jib sheet around to the larboard side while Captain Cobbs let the stern line slip around the bollard then pulled it on board. The wind was light but steady and soon the *Nancy* was away from the wharf where the main sail could be hoisted on the opposite side. As the *Nancy* slipped smoothly out of the small harbor Christopher looked back to see his father wave then turn back to his work.

Once out of the harbor Captain Cobbs brought the *Nancy* over onto a larboard tack for the trip out of the Miles River. At the same time, Big George began clearing his lines in readiness for the numerous maneuvers that would be required to get them out of the river, first into Eastern Bay, then into the main part of Chesapeake Bay. As they rounded the first point of land Christopher watched St. Michaels slip slowly out of sight. The stranger sat alone in the forward part of the boat. He did not speak and it was obvious he did not want to be spoken to. He just sat there, looking ahead, tightly holding his valise under his left arm and his silver tipped cane in his right hand. Christopher noticed the handle was unusual in that it was shaped like a wolf's head, not like the numerous canes he'd seen with the more common duck's head. It seemed to Christopher a duck's head would be much more comfortable to hold than a wolf's head, even though this wolf's ears were laid back somewhat. "Well, that was his business," thought Christopher, "strange things for strange people." All the while, the stranger just sat there. An occasional bit of spray seemed not to bother him. His thoughts were somewhere else.

    The sun was already high overhead when the *Nancy* cleared Bloody Point Bar off the southernmost tip of Kent Island. Kent Island came down like a long arm embracing Eastern Bay, the small bay into which the Miles and Wye Rivers flowed before continuing into the Chesapeake. Boats coming out of Eastern Bay had to sail a south easterly course, which required much tacking back and forth against the prevailing winds. Once clear of the point and out into the main part of Chesapeake Bay Captain Cobbs brought the *Nancy* around to a larboard tack to catch a fair wind that would take them all the way up to Annapolis. There was little to do now except steer a straight course. In just a few hours they should be entering the Severn River.

    Big George had taken the tiller and Captain Cobbs was sitting in the stern watching a coastal schooner, under full sail, beating down the bay. Christopher came over and sat down next to him.

    Aware of Christopher's presence but not turning away from the sight of the schooner, Captain Cobbs said, "It's a beautiful sight, no matter how many time you see it. It's a beautiful thing to see—a ship under full sail with somewhere to go."

    "Where do you think she's headed, Captain Cobbs?"

"No idea. Maybe down to Charleston. Maybe up to New York or up Boston way, or maybe to some new adventure we've never dreamed of, and perhaps they haven't either."

After that, they both silently watched the schooner disappear down the bay. Their other passenger remained where he was and looked only ahead as though that would somehow speed their progress.

Rounding Horn Point to larboard they entered the mouth of the Severn River. Numerous small boats were plying back and forth from one side to the other or in and out of the many estuaries that line the banks of the Severn. Between two of these estuaries, just a short distance on the left, lay the town of Annapolis. Captain Cobbs and Big George were mow being kept busy tacking and maneuvering among the many boats. Christopher watched intently as they turned into Carrol's Creek (to be known in later years as Spa Creek). As on previous visits, Christopher felt a bit of excitement passing Windmill Point and seeing the town dock come into view. There was always so much activity there, tobacco being loaded aboard ships, tea being unloaded. There were fewer ships this time but nonetheless, Christopher was fascinated with all that was going on.

Captain Cobbs threw the tiller over and the *Nancy* luffed up into the wind. Big George dropped the sails and the craft slowly and gently drifted up to the wharf kept available for the mail boats. Bow and stern lines were quickly made fast and the *Nancy* forfeited her freedom as she was again tied to the shore.

Without waiting for the gangplank to be put into place the strange passenger, valise still in hand, stepped over onto the wharf and quickly walked toward the square. He was soon met by another man, somewhat shorter and heavier, who simply shook his hand and gestured toward the Middleton Tavern. Without a word they both proceeded in that direction.

Big George had already started to off load the few pieces of cargo they had onto the wharf. "Can I give you a hand?" offered Christopher.

Captain Cobbs smiled at Christopher and said, "No need, my friend. But thank you. There's no hurry. We're not sailing back until tomorrow. Will you be going back with us then?"

"No, I want to stay a few days. I'll probably be going back on your next trip."

"Well then, give my regards to your sister and her family. Does she live far from here?"

"No, just a few squares over on the west side," replied Christopher as he picked up his duffel and package then stepped ashore. As he walked across the square he glanced here and there at all the activity. Even though Annapolis too had felt the oppressive effects of Great Britain's trade laws there was still much more going on here than in St. Michaels. There were barrels and crates, bales and bundles, and a myriad of other objects sitting about waiting to go on board the ships or to be loaded onto waiting wagons for their journey inland or just to the numerous warehouses in Annapolis. There were also the smaller crafts that carried on the commerce around the shores of Chesapeake Bay. There were the stalls where local farmers sold their various products. All this would be nothing without the many sounds that went with it. The voices of men working, the whinnying of impatient horses mixed with the clatter of wagon wheels on cobble stones and the occasional thud of cargo being dropped on wooden decks all created a scene that kept Christopher looking about not wanting to miss anything. A visit to Annapolis was always exciting.

Although he stopped several times to watch the goings on, it did not take him long to reach his sister's street. The houses were small, one room wide but neat, some brick, some framed, all close together. Few had yards about them and those were just vestiges of such. Christopher could not remember a visit in which Thomas had not boasted that the day would come when he would give Matty a fine home like those over on Prince George Street.

Soon he was at her house, a white framed one with flower boxes at the windows. He remembered Matty had always been fond of flowers. As he knocked on the door he could hear little

Michael crying. After receiving no response he knocked again, and harder. In a few moments he could hear the sound of light footsteps, and he felt the excitement of knowing that within seconds he would see his sister. The creaking door slowly opened, revealing a young, slender woman in her middle twenties. She was wearing an apron around her waist and an infant over her left shoulder. Her black hair was done up into a bun with a few stray wisps framing a beaming smile.

"Christopher! What are you doing here? Come in. Come on in." Matty stepped back opening the door farther, all the while gently rocking from one foot to the other and rubbing the baby's back.

Christopher stepped inside and set his bag and package on the wooden bench by the door. It was a good sized room, not as large as those in the more well to-do homes, but somewhat larger than most of those in St. Michaels. In the center of the rear wall was a door leading into a small dining room. To the right of this was a double fireplace that serviced both the front sitting room and the dining room.

There was a mixture of styles depicting the fact that Thomas and Matty Owings were in that intermediate stage of "getting someplace", as some would say. They both had good taste and appreciated fine things for their home but they both realized that the style and quality of their furnishings would have to develop at the same pace as Thomas' tobacco brokerage. This was evident by the contrast between the Spartan wooden bench by the door and the brocaded settee in front of the fireplace or by the imported mahogany, round table at the front window and the old and somewhat crudely made pine wood bookcase that stood against the left wall. A fine, blue and white deft vase, imported from Holland, looked down from the mantel upon crude wrought iron fire place tools. Such was this home, clean, comfortable and reflecting the transitory social status of its occupants.

Christopher gave his sister a hug then explained his presence, "Just came over to visit a few days. Pa's keepin' the boat in to do some work on it. You know how slow things are."

Matty softly closed the door, as the baby was beginning to quiet down. "How well I know," she replied. "Is everything all right at home?" Her smile had turned to an expression of concern.

Christopher leaned around Matty to get a look at his tiny nephew's face. "Sure, everything's all right. It's like I said, Pa's workin' on the boat and I just came for visit."

Having heard it for the second time Matty's face relaxed into a special loving smile she seemed to reserve for her brother. "Oh, it's so good to see you, Christopher. Come on in here and sit down. You must be hungry." She led him back through the small dining room into the kitchen. These three rooms made up the first floor. There were two sleeping rooms upstairs, one over the front room and one over the dining room. There was nothing over the kitchen, it having been added on later so the former kitchen could now serve as the dining room. Matty motioned for him to sit down at the bare, oak table that filled the center of the room. "I just made a pot of fish chowder a while ago. Let me put little Michael down. He seems to have settled for the time being."

Christopher sat down at the end of the rectangular table so he could watch Matty as she gently placed little Michael into the cradle. After making sure the baby was comfortable she went over to the large, red brick fireplace and swung the kettle out where she could ladle out the steaming chowder into two bowls. "Think I'll have a bit of it myself," she said, smiling over her shoulder at Christopher.

"Smells good, Matty. It's worth a trip to Annapolis just to taste your chowder."

"You mean this is all you came for? I oughtn't to give you any, little brother."

"Naw, I miss you, Sis. I have to admit it. We all do, even Benjamin."

Matty smiled at his reluctant admission of affection and set the two bowls on the table, took out two spoons from a nearby drawer, gave Christopher one and sat down opposite him. As if by some silent signal they both bowed their heads as Matty recited a brief thanks to the Lord as they had done countless times before while growing up.

"Good as ever, maybe even better," said Christopher between his third and fourth spoonful.

"Thank you." Nothing else was said until both bowls were empty.

As Christopher pushed his bowl away he remembered the package. "Oh, Ma sent something for you. I'll get it." He quickly went back into the front room and retrieved the package. He returned ceremoniously holding the package at arm's length and placed it before Matty as though it were tribute being presented to some royal personage. "A gift from her loyal subjects on the eastern shore to her royal highness, the Princess Matilda of Annapolis."

"What's this, you clown?"

"Something Ma made for Michael. Open it."

Matty carefully untied the string so it could be saved. Without looking up and with a smile of anticipation on her face as she continued to unwrap the package. "I wouldn't be using words like 'royalty' and 'highness' too freely around here," she admonished. "Some folks in these parts have mighty strong feelings about such things and might take you for a Tory."

"Are things getting that bad?"

"I'm afraid so. There's a lot of discontent and things going on that I can only guess about. Oh, my! What a beautiful quilt!" Matty held up the quilt, turning it one way and then the other, examining the expert stitching.

"Ma said she wanted to make sure the baby would be warm next winter. I think she's a little early but you know how Ma is about little Michael."

"I think I recognize some of the fabrics she used in it. Here, look here, there's a piece of that favorite dress of mine when I was about ten years old." Matty began to reminisce as she fondly stroked a sky blue patch of cotton percale. "Ma saved every scrap we ever wore. How are things at home, really?"

"All right. Kinda slow, you know, like everywhere else I guess."

But Ma and Pa are fine. I can tell Pa would be happier if the demand for fish was better. If he's worried he doesn't let on much about it. You know him."

"And Benjamin?"

"He's good. Seems to grow an inch a day. He can do 'bout everything I can do helpin' Pa. I expect before long he can take my place on the *Elizabeth* so I can go out and become a rich and famous tobacco broker like Mr. Thomas Owings. Where is Thomas, down at the warehouse?"

"No, he went up to Philadelphia over two weeks ago, to find 'new inland business', he called it. Should be back today or tomorrow."

"Good. I'll get to see him then before I go back. Oh, I almost forgot. Ma sent you a letter." Christopher went back to the front room again, this time to fetch his duffel bag. When he returned to the kitchen he extracted the letter from the bag and handed it to Matty without sitting back down. "Goin' out to the jakes. Be right back."

As Christopher made his way out to the privy, Matty anxiously opened the letter. Concern began to show on her face again but slowly dissolved into a smile as hers eyes swept across the lines of her mother's delicate handwriting. She had just finished reading it for the second time when Christopher came back in. She stood up holding the letter in her right hand down against her apron in an expression of wonder and exasperation. "I'll swear to goodness!" she said with half a laugh. "Ma either thinks I'm losing my memory or she's surely losing hers."

Christopher only answered with a puzzled look.

Holding the letter up she said, "Everything in here she told me in her last letter."

"What's that?"

"How to bathe the baby, what to do for colic, how to dress him, how to put him to sleep when he's fussy, and so on and so on. My how she frets so. I wonder if she was that way with us."

"Maybe so. It' hard, your bein' so far from her. I guess she feels helpless. I know she thinks about you a lot, and Thomas too, as well as Michael."

"I suppose," sighed Matty. "Now, enough of serious talk. Let's get you settled in. Take your bag up to the back room. I have to tend to little Michael I think he's in need of a change. Or would you rather do that and I'll take your bag up?"

"No thanks, I'll take my own bag up. I'm not ready for baby changin' just yet." With that he started up the narrow stairway and to the back room. It was a small room with a bare, broad planked wooden floor and a single window that looked out to the rear giving only a view of the back yard with its privy and wood shed. To the right of the door, against the front wall, there was a single bed with feather ticking. Except for a lone, willow cane chair by the window and two large storage trunks in the corner opposite the door, there were no other furnishings. Clothes were to be hung on six wooden pegs that formed a row along the wall over the trunks. Christopher was familiar with this room. He'd stayed here before and always enjoyed its comfortable atmosphere. Yet, this time something was disturbing that comfort. Was it his father's concern over Thomas's activities? Was it Thomas's absence? Or more likely, the combination of the two?

CHAPTER II

It was Tuesday morning and three days since Christopher had arrived in Annapolis. He was enjoying his visit with his sister, but he had a growing and alarming feeling that something, he didn't know what, was very wrong.

As he sat by the window in the front room watching the events on the street his mind slowly drifted back to Sunday. At Church he had got to see some of the people he had met on previous trips, and more than one showed some degree of surprise that Thomas had not yet returned. Of course nothing was said to alarm Matty. They all seemed so fond of her; but then, Thomas and Matty were well thought of throughout the whole community as well as in church.

Christopher liked going to St. Anne's; it was so much larger and prettier than the church back home. It smelled the same though, and he wondered why all churches smelled that way. Of course he hadn't been to very many, three to be exact, including the one at Oxford down on the Tred Avon River.

It had been a long sermon, that is, by Christopher's standards. He couldn't understand why they couldn't make the pews softer and the sermons shorter, at least one or the other. It could have been worse he thought, the summer heat had not yet begun to bear down on them and the foot ovens under the pews had not needed coals in them for many weeks. It was a rather pleasant day actually. As soon as the service was over, the congregation poured out onto the circular church yard to enjoy the spring air. A few people went on about their way, but most gathered in small groups to exchange greetings and news, or to make social arrangements for the following days. It was here that Matty and Christopher were invited to the Wickham's for dinner the next evening. Ellis Wickham, one of the town's most successful and respected merchants, and his wife Martha had no children and, they being the same age as Matty and Christopher's parents, had little prospect of any. To fill this void they had unofficially adopted Matty as the daughter they never had, and Martha doted over Matty as if she were her very own. Matty in turn had grown extremely fond of them both. Because of the Wickhams, Matty's adjustment to life in Annapolis as a new wife in a strange town had been made much easier.

Christopher was still gazing out the window, thinking about the visit to the Wickhams, when the clatter of a passing produce wagon, on its way to Market Street, broke his spell. But, as soon as it had passed, his thoughts returned to the Wickham's and the dinner the evening before. The Wickhams had extended their affections to include Christopher and the dinner had been like a homecoming. Unlike most people, the Wickhams preferred their main meal in the evening, and Christopher could easily recall what an exceptional dinner it had been. It was said Martha Wickham sat one of the finest tables in Maryland. Christopher could still picture the long, dark mahogany table, so polished it reflected the oil painting on the wall opposite him. He could almost make out the individual red clad figures and their horses that were gathering for a hunt. Martha had put out her best china and each place had been set on a delicate, white lace mat. In the center was a charger piled with fresh fruits and nuts of different kinds. Christopher was not used to such finery and found comfort in the fact his mother had always insisted on good table manners. Many times he had heard her say, "Not everybody can afford fine things but there's no excuse for not having fine manners."

But as Christopher sat by the window reminiscing about the dinner his thoughts were not on what had been served, though good as it was, fried chicken, potatoes and gravy, green beans that Martha had put up herself, biscuits and finally, sweet potato pie. Instead, they were on the conversation he'd had with Mr. Wickham.

After they had finished the meal Ellis Wickham stood up, and patting himself on his somewhat too large stomach, smiled and said, "Martha, I'll swear to goodness, each meal you cook is better than the last. Didn't you say you wanted to show Matty that sampler you are working on? If you ladies will excuse us, Christopher and I will retire to the parlor to see if we can solve some of the world's problems." Then with a smile and turning to Christopher he gestured toward the other room, "Young man, if you please."

Ellis Wickham followed Christopher into the parlor, a room rich with fine poplar woodwork and several more oil paintings like the one in the dining room. They looked as though they might have been by the same artist. There were two leather settees facing each other in front of the fireplace. There was no fire, it being too warm a day; but there were ashes from the last fire, probably last week. There had been a couple of rather chilly nights early in the week.

Ellis went over to the mantle and took down a rather ornate box made of teak wood and inlaid with ivory. Holding it in his left hand he carefully opened it and took out a long dark cheroot. "Would you care for a cigar," he asked.

"No thank you, sir. I don't smoke," replied Christopher as he sat down on one of the settees. I tried it once when I was younger, me and Jake Simpson . . . I mean Jake and I, well, he's a friend of mine back in St. Michaels. We sneaked out one o' his pa's old pipes and went back in the woods to try it. Well, Jake, he turned green and I got so sick I fell in the creek. Jake's taken it up since then but I haven't had much care to."

"Well, you're just as well off. But don't tell your brother-in-law I said so. He is in the tobacco business you know." Ellis' expression became more serious as he continued, "I noticed Matty seemed to be worried this evening. Is anything wrong?"

"Nothing unless it has to do with Thomas not being back from Philadelphia yet."

Ellis's expression slowly changed from curiosity to concern as he sat down on the other settee. He did not sit back but remained on the edge of the seat facing Christopher. "When did he go up there?"

"Matty told me he's been gone over two weeks already. Is that unusual?"

"No, not really. There's been some rain up that way. The roads can get to be like a regular hog pen this time of year." Ellis leaned back, took a long draw on his cigar and hoped he'd not alarmed Christopher too much. For a moment neither of them spoke. Only the blue-gray smoke from Ellis's cigar, spiraling slowly upward, showed any movement. Then, forcing a complete change of both subject and mood, Ellis stood up and said, "Come here a minute, I want to show you something."

As Ellis walked over to the window Christopher rose and followed. As they both looked out over the Severn River, Ellis began to describe his vision of the commerce that would someday come if the Colonies could only get out from under the yoke of England. Nothing more was said of Thomas for the rest of the evening.

These things Christopher pondered as he continued to watch the activities out on the street.

That evening, after Christopher and Matty had finished their meal and things were cleaned up and put away, Matty took young Michael upstairs to put him to bed. Christopher, with little to do and looking about, had taken a curious interest in the bookcase in the front parlor. He'd not paid it much attention before, three of its four shelves contained nondescript piles of papers, probably something to do with Thomas's tobacco business. However, the top shelf was devoted to books, and a rare assortment it was, or so it seemed to Christopher. There was "Morrison's New Atlas and Gazetteer", "A Lexicon For Modern Use", a rather worn copy of "Leviathan" by Thomas Hobbes, and a very attractive edition with gold leaf lettering of John Locke's "Essay Concerning Human Understanding" and his "Two Treatises On Civil Government". There was a very old looking volume of "Nichomachean Ethics" by Aristotle, a faded blue copy of "Wendell's Guide to Social Conduct for The Gentleman", and another beautifully bound copy of "Du Contrat Social" by Jean-Jaques Rousseau. After leafing through the Atlas and Gazetteer for several minutes—he was fascinated by maps—he picked up and opened the last volume. He stared at it in brief bewilderment before he realized it was in French, or that's what he thought it was. He replaced it without further examination.

During Christopher's preoccupation with the books Matty had returned from putting Michael to sleep and was sitting at the table in the kitchen gazing into the few remaining coals from the cooking fire. As soon as Christopher became aware that she was back downstairs he returned to the kitchen to join her. He went over to the dry sink to pour himself a cup of water from the large porcelain pitcher, then sat down at the other side of the table, across from Matty. "Boy, Thomas sure has himself some strange books. I didn't know he could read French, I guess that's what it is. I reckon he learned that when he went to William and Mary." Christopher rambled on for another moment or so before he realized Matty was not listening. Sensing something was wrong he asked, "Matty?" She did not answer. Speaking more loudly he repeated, "Matty?"

With that she raised her head and turned to Christopher but said nothing.

"What's wrong, Matty?" With a voice filled with concern for his sister he continued, "Is it Thomas? Are you worried about him not being back yet?"

Matty looked down at her hands, nervously opening and closing them into tight fists. Without looking up and with a voice weakened by a gnawing anxiety she could no longer conceal she answered, "No . . . yes . . . there's really no need." Then turning to look directly at Christopher as if it were the problem itself she was confronting, she confessed, "Yes, I know I shouldn't but Oh, Christopher, I can't help it. I just feel something's wrong. I don't know what, I just feel it." Tilting her head slightly she continued to look straight at Christopher. Her moist eyes sought the reassurance she couldn't ask for in words.

"Mr. Wickham told me the roads up toward Philadelphia are bad from the weather. That's most likely slowed him, and besides, with business down he's probably ended up havin' to talk to more people than he expected to. Don't you think?"

Without answering and with sudden alarm showing on her face she asked, "Were you talking to Mr. Wickham about Thomas? Does he think there's something wrong? What else did he say? Christopher, tell me!"

"Wait a minute. Calm down. He just said that he noticed you looked worried and that he thought there was no need and told me about the roads. That's all, honest."

Neither spoke as Matty tried to convince herself nothing was wrong while at the same time Christopher began to have doubts and wonder if perhaps something was.

Matty forced a smile and said, "I guess I'm just being foolish. When you don't know what's happening you always imagine the worst."

"I've been thinking, with things the way they are Pa won't need me at home for a while. If it's all right with you I'll just stay until Thomas returns."

"Of course it's all right, you know that. But shouldn't they be expecting you back soon?"

"Pa said I could stay the week if I wanted to." Christopher did not say anything about the conversation with their father just before leaving. There was no use in aggravating her worries by relating his. "The mail boat doesn't go back until day after tomorrow anyway. I'll send a message back with Captain Cobbs just to let them know I'll be a little longer."

"Thank you, dear brother. I do feel better with you here." Matty began to relax and even show a hint of a smile. "I suppose if there was really anything to worry about I would have heard from Mr. Hampton."

"Who is Mr. Hampton? I don't remember that name. Have I met him?"

"You may have met him last year when you were here. It was

just a brief introduction. I think you and Thomas ran into him down at the Inn. I barely recall Thomas mentioning it."

"Well, who is he?"

"He just happens to be one of the most well to-do and influential men in Annapolis, or all of Maryland for all I know."

"What's that got to do with Thomas being gone?" asked Christopher with a hint of impatience in his voice.

"He's also Thomas's silent partner. I guess you didn't know that."

"No, I didn't know that. How could I if I don't even remember there was such a person. What is a silent partner anyway?"

"He helped Thomas get started in his tobacco business. Mr. Hampton provided much of the financial backing. Thomas carries on the business and in his name, 'Thomas Owings & Company'. Mr. Hampton is too busy with his own chandlery business, and who knows what else, to be active in tobacco too. That's why he's called a silent partner."

Christopher knew little about the business world, and would be the first to admit it, but at least he could now see why Matty had thought of this Mr. Hampton. After all, if he was Thomas's partner, even though a silent one, he might know of some plausible reason why Thomas had been detained. Whom else could they turn to?

"Maybe we should go see Mr. Hampton," offered Christopher. As soon as he said it he knew it was a mistake. Lines of worry began to creep back into Matty's face. Then trying to reassure her he added, "I'll wager he'll have a very simple reason why Thomas is not back yet. After all, he's in the business with Thomas. It stands to reason he'll know what Thomas is up against in trying to find some new markets."

"All right, if Thomas doesn't return tomorrow we'll go see him," replied Matty, still trying to force a smile.

Wednesday came and was a beautiful day, clear but somewhat cool for that time of year. The morning had been spent helping

Matty with the chores common to every household. That afternoon Christopher roamed around exploring the sights and sounds of Annapolis. The markets and shops were busy. Here and there a housewife could be seen sweeping her steps or talking to a neighbor. The familiar clangings of a blacksmith somewhere in the distance were occasionally mingled with the clattering of horse's hooves and wagon wheels. Down at the wharf a brig that arrived from the Indies the day before was being unloaded. He found Annapolis to be much like it was on his other visits, that is, except for two things. First, he'd heard many people excitedly talking about a meeting the night before. It had something to do with some resolutions and trade with Great Britain. "Annapolis Resolutions" he believed they called them (note 1). The other thing that was different that day, and was of far more concern to Christopher, was the fact his brother-in-law, Thomas Owings, had not returned.

That evening little was said during the meal. Matty had prepared salmagundi, one of Thomas's favorites, thinking for certain he would have returned that day. Christopher was not sure of this dish at first but when Matty told him what was in it, chopped meat, pickled herring, onions, oil, vinegar and pepper, he was ready to let the adventurer in him go forth and give it a try. He not only liked it but asked for seconds. This helped to raise Matty's spirits somewhat for as the day had worn on she had become increasingly depressed. To add to her problems little Michael had become colicky that afternoon and simply refused to nap no matter what she tried. She had even prepared a sugar-tit for him and that failed to calm him.

Christopher had finished his second plateful when Matty pushed hers dish away from her, the food only half consumed. Christopher was not sure what to say to her. He wanted desperately to reassure her but by this time his concern for Thomas was almost as great as hers. "Matty . . . ," he paused, "Matty, I think it's time we go see Mr. Hampton."

"Yes, I'm afraid so. I hope he doesn't think I'm silly. He's such a busy man." Matty was torn between anxiety and the probability of embarrassment but could wait no longer. She had to know something and there was no one in Annapolis, that she knew of, besides Mr. Hampton, that could help her.

"Well then, lets get things cleaned up and go see him," said Christopher as he got up from the table and started collecting the dirty plates. "Where does he live?"

"Over on the east side of town. But Christopher, I wonder if I should take the baby out. You know how fussy he's been all day and there's no one to leave him with. I'm afraid he might be coming down with something. Oh, drat! I don't know what to do."

"I can go by myself if you want me to. Just tell me how to get there."

"Could you . . . would you? Oh, Christopher, what a dear brother." The deliverance from just this one dilemma restored some of the cheerfulness that was so characteristically Matty's. "I'll clean up this mess if you go see Mr. Hampton. He lives on Hanover Street. I'm sure he's home by now. It's the street just the other side of King George Street."

The sun was still well above the horizon, but shadows were getting noticeably longer as Christopher turned from North East Street onto Hanover. It was apparent the people that lived on this street were successful at whatever they did. The houses were large and had good sized yards; some even had flower gardens. He had no difficulty in following the directions Matty had given him, there were not many streets in Annapolis and this one was not very long. "Ah, there it is on the other side," he said to himself.

It was a large house, a mansion actually, which appeared to get larger as Christopher approached it. The house was a two story red brick of the Georgian design with five large windows across on the second floor. Its tall roof had a gable in the front with a round window that suggested there might even be a third floor. The pediment over the front door matched the roof gable with its egg and dart frieze, and was supported on two small columns of simple

Doric design. This added a bit of classic flavor to the whole structure without making it too ornate.

For several minutes Christopher just stood there in front of the house taking in all the details. Then he carefully opened the wrought iron gate and proceeded up the three steps to the highly varnished, oak door. He was taken aback by a huge brass door knocker, shaped like a lion's head, that looked as if it were the guardian of the household. Mustering up his confidence he grasped the ominous looking knocker and gave three firm raps to announce his presence. Shortly, the heavy door swung open and he was greeted by a tall, neatly dressed black man with gray hair who, without smiling asked, "May Ah help you?"

"Yes, please. I'd . . . I'd like . . . I'd be very pleased if I could speak with Mr. Hampton if I may, please," answered Christopher somewhat annoyed with himself for saying please too many times and sounding nervous.

"An' who should Ah say is callin'?"

"Christopher Hall, sir," replied Christopher. Then realizing that wouldn't mean much to Mr. Hampton he added, "I'm Matty Owings' brother, Thomas Owings' brother-in-law."

The servant stepped back and motioned for Christopher to come in. "Please wait heah. Ah'll see if Mistah Hampton will receive you."

Christopher carefully stepped inside, and was so awed by the surroundings he did not even notice the servant close the door and disappear down the hall. The house was even more impressive on the inside. The hallway ran all the way to the rear of the house. The light blue walls were decorated with oil paintings, mostly of people, none of which Christopher knew. The narrow planked oak floor was uncarpeted but sanded smooth and immaculately clean. On the left side of the hall was an open set of double doors that displayed a large and elegant dining room. The rest of that wall was taken up by a straight stairway that lead to the second floor. On the right side of the hall was a partially open door that appeared to lead to a parlor. To the left of the door stood a half round table, flanked by two side chairs; to the right was a large mahogany coat rack and stand. The two cloaks hanging there were quite ordinary, but what caught Christopher's eye was the stand containing two walking sticks. One was of a common style, but the other had a large silver head shaped like that of a wolf's with its ears laid back. Christopher thought it very odd that he should see two such unusual walking sticks within a week. Or was it two?

Christopher was so engrossed with the walking sticks he was startled when the tall case clock behind him began to strike six in the evening. Regaining his composure he noticed the old servant had reappeared at the rear of the hall and was beckoning him to follow. "This way, Mistah Hall. Mistah Hampton will see you."

Christopher followed, glancing into the parlor on the right and the dining room on the left as he walked down the hall. He'd not seen such elegance before, not in Annapolis or St. Michael's, not even in Oxford. When they reached the end of the hall the servant opened a door on the right and motioned for Christopher to enter.

It was not a large room but it immediately gave the impression its occupant was a man of some importance. Its completely walnut paneled walls were broken only by a window on the left, which looked out to the rear of the house, the one door, and opposite that, a small fireplace flanked by two overflowing bookcases. To the right was a fold-down desk at which a rather heavy set man with balding hair was applying the sealing wax to a letter he had just written. When he finished that task he turned and handed the letter to the servant who had stepped forward anticipating his master's request. "Jason, please take this to our visitor upstairs."

"Yas Suh, Mistah Hampton." With that he disappeared, closing the door behind him.

After closing the desk Mr. Charles Hampton stood and turned to face Christopher. With a smile that failed to conceal his concern over more serious matters he offered his hand and said, "Well, young man. I understand you are the brother-in-law of Thomas Owings."

Stepping forward from where he had nervously remained standing Christopher shook hands with this impressive yet friendly man. "Yes, sir, I'm Matty's brother."

"Both very fine people, fine people, indeed" he extolled. "Here, please sit down." He motioned for Christopher to take the burgair that sat near the fireplace then turned the desk chair around for himself to sit on.

"Thank you, sir," said Christopher as he sat, or rather sank into the large upholstered chair, he guessed it was the most comfortable thing he'd ever sat on. By now he figured everything in this house must be comfortable. He was surprised at how much at ease he felt in such surroundings.

"Well, I've heard quite a bit about you young man. What brings you here, and what can I do for you?"

Looking up at Mr. Hampton he replied, "It's Thomas, sir. He's not back from Philadelphia yet. I guess he's overdue by the way Matty talks. I don't know about such things but Matty's awful' worried and is almost sure somethin's happened to him."

Mr. Hampton, who had been listening intently, began to frown and rub his chin. "I knew he was going to Philadelphia. Let's see, when was it he left?"

"Matty said it was two weeks ago last Saturday. She said he was looking for more tobacco business. She said you bein' his silent partner, I think that's what she called it, might know some reason for his bein' gone so long."

Mr. Hampton thought for a moment then said, "You know how bad things have been lately. Five years ago tobacco sold for twenty four shillings a hundredweight; today you're lucky to get thirteen for it."

"Yes, sir, things are pretty bad in St. Michaels too. Pa's fishin' business is real slow. He doesn't complain much but a body doesn't need to be very smart to know it worries him." Then remembering the things Ol' Put had told him the day he left St. Michaels, Christopher repeated the old timer's thoughts, "It's just plain stupid the way King George keeps on makin' things worse for everybody. I guess he doesn't care a fig about anyone over here."

"It's that way all over the colonies, Christopher. Parliament has even passed a law closing the port of Boston. I'm afraid it's not going to get any better until we make it better ourselves. I don't like to think about what that could lead to, but we can't just sit and let them squeeze us to death. In the meantime we have to do all we can to make up for the drop in prices. That's why Thomas had to go look for new markets, and believe me, they won't be easy to find."

"Is that the only reason Thomas went to Philadelphia?" asked Christopher, suprising himself with the boldness of the question. He hoped Mr. Hampton did not think he was questioning his truthfulness.

A knock on the door interrupted the answer to Christopher's question. "Yes, what is it?" asked Mr. Hampton.

The door opened revealing Jason. Mr. Hampton rose and went to the door to hear what the servant wanted. After a few hushed words they both stepped out into the hall to finish talking. All Christopher could catch from the conversation was something about a doctor. When Mr. Hampton came back into the room he was visibly upset. "Please excuse me for a few minutes, I have something I must attend to right away. Make yourself comfortable. If you want anything just ask Jason." He then went out closing the door behind him. Christopher could hear footsteps hurriedly ascending the stairs.

It was at least twenty minutes before Charles Hampton reentered the room to find Christopher standing before the fire place examining the map over the mantle. It was a map of the American Colonies showing the major cities, rivers and harbors.

"I'm sorry that took so long," apologized Mr. Hampton as he stepped up beside Christopher and also began studying the map.

Christopher could tell Mr. Hampton's interest in the map was more than just a matter of curiosity; he was a man deeply absorbed with a problem. A problem for which there were few if any solutions, a problem that somehow involved that very map, or to be more exact what it represented.

Although Christopher felt he should not pry into other people's business, the chance that whatever was wrong might involve Thomas prompted him to ask, "Is anything wrong?"

When Mr. Hampton turned to look at him his expression was grave and seemed to be studying Christopher very carefully. "Perhaps . . . yes, perhaps," was all he said. This was not an answer to the question Christopher had asked but an answer to one he had asked himself. "Yes, perhaps you can help."

Christopher only stared at the man, confused at what he had heard. He was certain it involved Thomas and had a growing feeling it was about to involve him.

"Christopher, please sit down. I think I can talk with you. I'm not sure where to begin but to get back to your question, the answer is 'no'. Tobacco business is not the only reason Thomas went to Philadelphia. Thomas went to find new business all right but there was another purpose for his going. Christopher, . . . ", he hesitated then continued, "You've got to swear that the things I am about to tell you, you won't repeat, not to anyone, not even to Matty."

"But . . . ," protested Christopher.

"There can be no 'buts', Christopher. What I have to say must be kept strictly confidential. There are things I think you need to know; you may even be able to help, but you must swear to secrecy. Trust me."

"Yes, sir, you can depend on me. Is Thomas in any danger?"

"No, I don't believe so, but the possibility exists. From our conversation earlier I gather you have some understanding of our situation here in the colonies. We simply cannot buckle under to the unreasonable demands of England, and we certainly cannot continue for very long the way things are now. What are our alternatives? I don't know, but one thing is certain, we, the colonies that is, must stand together. If we do not support each other we each will remain under British domination forever."

Christopher listened intently to what Mr. Hampton was telling him. It was new, yet it wasn't new. It all fit together with the things he had been hearing for some time and even with his own observations. Yet all he had ever heard was complaining, nothing that even came close to suggesting resistance. "But what about Thomas? What has this got to do with him?"

Mr. Hampton got up and moved to the map over the fireplace. Pointing to the New England states he said, "Whatever happens here," then pointing to the Carolinas, "has its effect here. The reverse is just as true. Whatever we let happen to any one will eventually happen to all." Sitting back down he continued, "We must know what is happening in all the colonies, up and down the coast. To do this some have established what are called Committees of Correspondence. We've been trying to do the same here. So while Thomas was in Philadelphia he was to meet with the committee there and establish a preliminary contact. On the way back he was to stop in New Castle in Delaware for the same purpose."

"Is this dangerous?" asked Christopher.

"No, I don't think so, not at this time. However, there are still many who are loyal to the crown and will remain so no matter what. If things get worse they could be a threat."

"Then why isn't Thomas back yet."

"Things have been happening at a faster pace lately. I'm sure some events in that area have made it necessary for him to delay his return for a few days. Just yesterday we here in Annapolis adopted resolutions of sympathy with Boston and finally appointed our own Committee of Correspondence."

"I thought something was going on but I didn't know what," said Christopher. "Isn't this what you wanted? You seemed kinda upset when you came back a awhile ago, if you'll pardon my sayin' so."

"Yes, of course. It's what many of us wanted. But you're right, there is a problem and perhaps this is where you can help."

"How is that?" asked Christopher. He was bursting with interest and curiosity. "What could I possibly do?"

"The courier who was suppose to carry the news of our actions to Philadelphia has taken on a very untimely illness. He was to leave tomorrow morning but we just found out he has a stone and cannot possibly travel. He's in terrible pain and the doctor insists he remains here until it passes." Mr. Hampton leaned forward in his chair and looked straight into Christopher's bewildered eyes. "I'd like for you to do it."

"Me! Why I . . . I'm not . . . I mean I've never . . . ."

"You could go by way of New Castle and that way you might run into Thomas or at least find out what is delaying him. You'd not only be helping us, you'd be helping Matty. I'm convinced we can trust you and that you can do it."

Christopher was overwhelmed by the possibility of going to search for Thomas. He'd do anything for his sister.

"Sir, I'd be willing and proud to help. I'm expected back home soon but I suppose my brother can help Pa in my place. But there's a problem, I don't have the money to travel."

"The money is no problem. I'll see that you have more than sufficient funds for your expenses."

By now Christopher was even more excited at the idea and was rapidly convincing himself Benjamin was old enough to help on the boat. "It is for a good cause. Certainly I'll go," he said with sudden confidence and determination.

"Good. You only need to tell Matty you're going to look for Thomas. If she seems alarmed at that, tell her I need to inform him of some recent changes in tobacco shipments and I've asked you to take the information to him. There's a boat leaving for the upper bay at six in the morning. It goes all the way up the Elk River to a town called Head of Elk. There you can find lodgings for the night. There's a coach that leaves there early in the morning for New Castle over on the Delaware River."

"Where should I look for him? I've never been to New Castle. I haven't been much of anyplace."

"He was to stay at the inn where the coach stops. It would be best if you took a room there, if you can. If Thomas is not there, go to the Blue Fox Tavern on Front Street. It's easy to find. You'll have no problem. When you get there, ask for the owner, a Mr. VanDrees. I'll have a letter for you to give to him explaining who you are and that I sent you. He can tell you if Thomas has been there or not. He can also instruct you on how to get to Philadelphia, if that is necessary. If you find Thomas in New Castle and Mr. VanDrees has someone else who can deliver the message to Philadelphia you can return." Mr. Hampton stood up and smiling offered Christopher his hand.

Christopher rose, and shaking Mr. Hampton's hand said, "You can count on me, sir. I'll do my best."

"I'm sure I can. Now be here at five o'clock tomorrow morning and I'll have everything ready for you. That will give you plenty of time to get to the boat." He then walked Christopher to the door himself and said good-bye.

As Christopher walked back to Matty's house the sun was beginning to set over low hills to the West, painting the high flying clouds with changing streaks of gold, crimson and violet. The panorama overhead seemed symbolic of the rapidly changing events that were taking place around him. He paid little attention to the other people on the street; his mind was busy trying to predict what things he might encounter on this new adventure. He could hardly believe all that was happening, and that he was to have a part in it! But most important, he was going to look for Thomas and he was going to find him!

CHAPTER III

The ketch *Manokin* was making good use of the fifteen knot wind out of the west-southwest. The vessel's speed created a foamy trail that pointed back to Sandy Point, the furthermost point on Cape St. Claire, behind which Annapolis had just disappeared. Christopher stood by the larboard rail watching the world with which he was so familiar fade away. He sensed it being slowly replaced by an unknown future. It would be a future unlike any he had ever imagined for himself.

Although he had sailed these waters, north of Annapolis, with his father in the *Elizabeth*, this was still new to him for never before had he been on a vessel of this size. The *Manokin*, just over sixty feet at the waterline, was half again the length of the mail boat *Nancy*, the largest Christopher had been on until this day. Its sixty-five tons were enough to command the slow rolling swells to give way and let it pass through with a minimum of pitching. Even this slow and easy motion was new to Christopher.

Looking down at the water rushing along side he could see jellyfish being rolled over and over in the swishing bow wave then finally right themselves as they passed out of sight. He wondered if his life, which too had just been turned upside down, would ever right itself and return to that familiar pattern in which he'd grown up. It was puzzling, all this talk of resisting the laws of England. Was he not English? He thought everyone in the colonies was considered English. Hadn't he always been taught to respect and obey authority? How many times had he heard his mother read from the Bible the passage: "Put them in mind to be subject to principalities and powers, to obey magistrates, to be ready to every good work." or "Render, therefore, unto Caesar the things that are Caesar's . . . "?

These things bothered Christopher for they were ingrained into his upbringing. Respect for authority was as much a part of him as his blue eyes or the crescent shaped scar on the inside of his left forearm. When he was only ten years old he fell overboard from his father's boat. He had made a grab for the rail, but something, he never knew what, caught him in the arm and made a gash. It hadn't seemed very bad and he had thought the scar would have disappeared long ago. It hadn't. Some things in life seem to persist, and like that scar, Christopher's respect for authority would not let itself be forgotten. Yet, he was asking himself, who's authority? All of the men of authority that he knew, his father, Mr. Hampton, Mr. Wickham, Captain Cobb, were speaking of being free from Great Britain. He knew in his heart he agreed.

His thoughts were suddenly broken by the shouting of the first mate, "Make ready to tighten sail! We're gettin' a header and I want to fetch Powel's Island on this tack. Stand by with the sheets! Main first!"

Christopher watched with fascination as the crew made ready by bending the main sheet to the windlass in preparation to tightening the large spread of canvas that loomed overhead. These maneuvers were quite familiar to Christopher for he'd performed them many times on his father's boat, the *Elizabeth*, but always by hand. On a vessel this size mechanical help was needed.

"Ready! Haul!" cried the first mate.

Christopher watched intently as the mainsail, then the mizzen and jib were trimmed in that order. He could feel the ship heel a bit more to starboard and pick up a knot in speed. The smooth white billows of canvas against the blue sky made a pretty sight. There were only a few wisps of very high cirrus clouds way up to the North. It was a beautiful day, indeed.

His thoughts went back to his sister Matty for she had said if it turned out to be a nice day today she would take little Michael out for some air. He supposed that was what she was doing now. He'd told her what Mr. Hampton had suggested he tell her, that he needed to forward some information to Thomas regarding the tobacco business. He thought he'd done well at not arousing any suspicions. Her response had taken him by complete surprise.

"A fine story, Christopher, but you needn't try to keep anything from me. I know more than you think I do." She had looked him straight in the eyes and said, "Thomas and Mr. Hampton both are involved with the Committee." Her voice revealed a mixture of scolding and annoyance.

"How . . . how did you know . . . "

"I'll never understand why you men think you are so smart and we women are all stupid," she had interrupted. "You sneak around with your secret goings on as if we were both blind and deaf. A woman doesn't live with a man day-in and day-out without knowing what's going on inside him."

Christopher looked at his sister with amazement and a new degree of respect. "You knew what this is all about? Why didn't you tell me?"

"And what would've been the gain of it if I had? Besides, you'd know sooner or later. It wasn't for me to explain it, anyway. After all, I'm not even supposed to know. Remember?"

In a way he was relieved. He didn't like deceiving anyone, especially his sister. He knew that now there was no way to keep her from worrying. "You're right, I do have a message for Thomas and it isn't about tobacco. Mr. Hampton told me where to look for him and whom to ask for to get help. I'll be going to Head of Elk then on to New Castle. I've never been to either place. Mr. Hampton said he'd cover the expense if I'd go."

"I'm glad you're going. It's about time you saw some of the world and I'm sure you will find Thomas for me."

"I'll find him , Sis. I promise I will. I won't stop "til I do, you can count on it. I need to send a message to Pa tellin' him what I'm doin'. I'll just say I'm delivering a message to Thomas from his partner. No need to say any more for now. That'll be the truth if I leave it at that."

"I think that's best," assured Matty.

"I figure Benjamin should be able to help him in my place. Don't you?"

"Of course he can," she replied with a smile. "He's already bigger than you were when you first started working the boat."

Christopher remembered that smile as he stood by the rail watching the western coastline of Chesapeake Bay slide by. The wind suddenly died then resumed with full vigor causing the sails to slacken momentarily then refill with a thunderous clap. As the ship shuddered in response, Christopher reached inside his doublet to feel the letter Mr. Hampton had entrusted to him. Having reassured himself it was still safely inside the pocket, he decided to sit down for a while and have a look at the book Matty had let him borrow.

It was one of Thomas's books, "Wendell's Guide To Social Conduct For The Gentleman". Christopher had been leafing through it the night before when Matty came into the room after putting Michael to bed. She told him if he was interested in it to take it along on the trip.

He found a place on a hatch cover where he could sit down and still be out of the way. He recovered the book from his duffel and began to examine its contents.

Leafing through the book just to get an idea of what was in it he soon realized much of it covered just plain good manners, the sort of things he'd been taught at home while growing up. But, there was also a lot that dealt with situations unfamiliar to him. He found it fascinating as he imagined himself being introduced to important dignitaries at affairs of state, or bowing before some beautiful lady as he asked her to join him in the next dance at the governor's ball. He laughed at himself; he didn't even know how to dance. "Imagine me all dolled up like some dandy, prancin' around some ballroom," he said to himself. He closed the book and returned it to his duffel bag. For the rest of the trip up the bay he was content just to watch the coastline as the ship worked its way closer to its destination of Head Of Elk.

After several hours the *Manokin* reached Turkey Point, and the mouth of the Elk River. It was a scene unlike any Christopher had ever seen—a silvery, slow flowing river separating mountains on the left from low rolling hills on the right. Sailing on up the river required more than an average degree of skill for the high bluffs on the left blocked the wind that had shifted until it was directly out of the West. The occasional shoals that jutted out from the low shoreline on the right made it even more difficult by limiting their freedom to maneuver. However, both captain and crew were familiar enough with the Elk River that they were making steady progress.

Christopher's attention was being drawn alternately between the changing shorelines and the activity of the crew as they worked the *Manokin* on toward Head of Elk. As the river became ever narrower he was surprised at the size of the vessels he saw there. Ordinarily it would have seemed to him an unlikely place for ships to venture into, but there was a good reason for their risking such restricting waters. Mr. Hampton had explained to Christopher the importance of the town of Head of Elk. From there it was a short trip by land, only ten or twelve miles, to New Castle on the Delaware River, where one could travel by either land or water up to Philadelphia. It was an important link in the commercial route between Philadelphia and the towns and cities on Chesapeake Bay.

After an hour or better of constant maneuvering they reached their destination. As soon as the *Manokin* was secured to the wharf Christopher stepped ashore. It was a strange land, at least strange to him, even though he was only sixty miles from home, that is, as the crow flies. Not only were the terrain and the town new to him, the people even seemed different. They were different, for they represented not just this town but those various places from which they had traveled. It was already proving to be an exciting adventure, but Christopher's main concerns were still locating Thomas and delivering the letter. He realized he must concentrate on that, for the day was getting on.

"Mr. Hampton was right," he reminded himself. "It's too late to go on to New Castle today. I'd best find a place to spend the night and then make arrangements for the coach in the morning. After that's taken care of I can ask around about Thomas." So, putting all other interests aside, he began looking for a place to sleep.

It did not take long to arrange for lodgings. The inn where most of the travelers stayed was full but the innkeeper had suggested a home not two blocks away where he could put up for the night. It was a modest home run by Mrs. Minton, a widow lady. She was the motherly sort and was known throughout the town for her good nature and kindness towards strangers. Yet, she harbored one element of bitterness, one from which she could not rid herself but did manage to conceal from most folks. Her husband had been killed during the French and Indian War when the British took Fort Duquesne from the French. She could never understand why men had to go so far from home to get themselves killed, or why they even had to go to war at all. In the sixteen years since his death she had struggled to support herself by letting out her three rooms to travelers and doing their wash when they felt the need for it, which was not too often.

Christopher took a liking to Mrs. Minton right away, and she to him, for he reminded her of her oldest son, who had moved away to Baltimore. He had established a rather successful bookbinding business there and was only able to come home for a visit once, maybe twice, a year. Of course he helped her out financially, as best he could, but it was his visits that mattered the most to her. Christopher's appearance gave her an opportunity to relieve at least some of her pent up motherly love. She had insisted that Christopher come into her kitchen, an otherwise jealously guarded domain, and sit down at the spotlessly clean table, still damp from a recent scrubbing. Setting a large piece of hot, fresh-baked apple pie before him, she said, "Here, a young man like you can't be traipsin' all over the countryside without gettin' hungry. It's over an hour before supper time. I'm sure this won't spoil the appetite of a big, strappin' fellow like you."

"Thank you, Ma'am," Christopher said smiling, "You're very kind."

"Nonsense, nothin' kind about it. But thanks. Now go ahead

and eat it before it gets cold." She then turned to busy herself on the other side of the kitchen.

As Christopher was finishing the last few bites of the pie he wondered where would be the best places here in Head Of Elk to inquire about Thomas. Perhaps Mrs. Minton could help him. He would ask her for suggestions but he would only mention the tobacco business of course.

Placing his fork on the empty wooden plate and pushing them away from him, he said, "That sure was delicious. Thanks again."

She picked up his plate and started to take it away but then turned back to Christopher. Holding the empty plate in front of her with both hands she looked at him and asked, "What brings you to these parts anyway?"

"I'm looking for my sister's husband. I have an important message for him from his business partner. I'm going on to New Castle tomorrow but I thought I might make some inquiries around here tonight. Where would I most likely find someone who might have seen him?"

"Back over at the Inn or at one of the taverns . . . maybe at the wharf?"

"I think I'll go ask around. You never know. Someone might know him or have seen him."

"What does your sister's husband look like?"

"Well, he's about as tall as I am and maybe a little bit thinner. He's got real dark hair and kind of a long nose but he doesn't like for you to notice it. It's not really so long, it just looks that way because it's so thin. He's really a nice looking man. I suppose you could say he's handsome. At least that's what my sister Matty calls him."

"Don't recall seein' anyone of that description 'round here lately. Go ask about, maybe someone's seen him. Remember, supper will be in about an hour."

"Don't worry. If it's as good as that pie I sure don't want to miss it."

"Enough of your flattery young man. Now off with you."

Christopher first arranged for a seat on the morning coach then went around town inquiring about Thomas. He asked at the places Mrs. Minton had suggested, but to no avail. Some people were suspicious and would not even respond to his questions, but most were friendly, even though they could be of no help. No one remembered seeing anyone resembling Thomas.

Things were quieting down in the town as Christopher returned to Mrs. Minton's place. It came as no surprise that her supper was as good as the pie he had sampled earlier. The other two guests, a man and wife on their way from Trenton to Baltimore, were less enthusiastic. They said little and retired to their room as soon as the meal was over. For Christopher, it was too early to turn in so he decided to just walk around and do a bit of sightseeing. After all, it was not likely Thomas had yet reached this point on his return within the last few days. If he had, he would have been back in Annapolis by now. The only thing that bothered him was the possibility they might pass each other without knowing it. The *Manokin* had passed only one other ship on the way up from Annapolis. They passed close enough, he thought, that if Thomas had been aboard he would have seen him, unless he had been below deck for some reason.

"I think I'll just go have a walk around and see what there is to see," said Christopher.

"Well, I don't expect that should take very long," replied Mrs. Minton, "There's not a whole lot to see in Head of Elk."

Christopher had a curiosity that compelled him to learn all he could about his surroundings, and this was all new to him. But Mrs. Minton had been right. It did not take long to satisfy that curiosity and soon he was back at her lodgings. It was just as well for he wanted to catch the first coach in the morning for New Castle.

Because travel by either water or land was slow and time consuming, early departures were the rule rather than the exception. Consequently, Mrs. Minton was used to having her guests well fed and on their way by sunrise. And so it was, that before the sun was above the treetops Christopher was on his way to New Castle and whatever lay ahead. He very quickly came to the conclusion that he preferred travel by water to that by land. A boat, even one as small as his father's *Elizabeth*, could accommodate waves and swells far better than this coach could manage the many ruts in the road. Spring rains and the many wagons and coaches traveling between the Delaware River and Chesapeake Bay had made the road almost impassable in places.

He'd thought he might be able to read Thomas's book on the way to New Castle. However, that was quite impossible. He contented himself just to observing the scenery, as did the only other passenger, a British army officer, a major he believed, but he wasn't sure. Christopher had greeted him cheerfully when they arrived almost simultaneously at the coach station. However, it didn't take long to realize the man was not happy with his circumstance, whatever that may be. He apparently had little desire to socialize with colonial riffraff, especially one so young and so obviously unimportant as Christopher. So it was for the trip to New Castle—uncomfortable and unsociable.

However, the journey was not uninteresting. The rugged coach road meandered through rolling hills covered with stately beech trees, hickories and oaks. In spite of the deplorable condition of the road they were making fairly good progress. Gradually the hills turned into low, undulating flatlands. Loblolly pines, black tupelos and willows began to appear where the land had not yet been cleared for farming. An occasional marshland was encountered as they got closer to the Delaware River. Christopher felt they must surely be getting close to their destination. They were.

As the coach crested a small rise Christopher leaned out the window and there, ahead in the distance, was the city of New Castle. It was an old city, that is, for that time and that part of the world. It was originally called Fort Casimir when settled by the Dutch in 1651. Peter Stuyvesant himself chose the spot for its strategic location on the river. Because of the importance of its location it was later taken by the Swedes, retaken by the Dutch and finally by the British. The influence of each could be seen in its inhabitants as well as in its architecture.

As they drew nearer, Christopher could make out more and more details. It was a pretty town of many fine brick homes, well laid out around a common green. Beyond the town the Delaware River flowed placidly by like a giant silvery ribbon under the bright sun that had just passed its zenith. Anchored a short distance out in the river was a British sloop of war. Its black and buff hull gleamed under a fresh coat of paint and even at this distance Christopher could catch flashes of sunlight reflecting off its brass work and well-kept guns.

It was past noon when the coach rattled into town and the driver reined his team of four to a stop in front of the inn that served also as a station. It wasn't until Christopher had alighted from the coach that he felt hungry. But he decided the first thing to do was get a room for the night. Perhaps it would not be too late to get something to eat here.

He thought his silent traveling companion might be staying here but he was wrong. The officer had suddenly disappeared. With some relief, he dismissed that from his mind, turned and went up the three stone steps to enter the inn.

Opening the heavy wooden door revealed a long narrow room almost like a hallway. On the right a door opened into a large eating room where to Christopher's relief several men were just being served food. The hall-like room ran all the way to the rear of the building and to an open door through which an old woman could be seen peeling what appeared to be potatoes. On the left, behind a counter where guests could register, a rather rotund man in his early fifties, with little hair and a face round enough to match his body, was busy writing in a ledger.

Christopher was still looking about when he was startled by the man's voice. "And what can we be doin' for ye, m' lad? Is it a room, or vittles, or both? If it's a doxy ye'r a lookin' to find ye'll not satisfy yer lust here. I run a fine respectable establishment and aim to keep it that way."

"Yes, sir. No, I mean no, sir." Christopher stopped, regained his composure and said, "What I mean is, all I want is a room for the night. I'm not interested in doxies, honest. I just want a room." Then he added, "And something to eat if it's not too late."

"Well now, I think we can take care of ye on both counts. How many nights?"

"Probably just one," answered Christopher. "I'm here looking for my brother-in-law, Mr. Thomas Owings. He's in the tobacco business. Would you happen to know him? Have you seen him?"

"As a matter of fact, yes," the man answered.

"You did? Where is he?" Christopher excitedly asked. "When did you see him?"

"Not for some time now. Let's see . . . um . . . maybe four or five months ago was the last time, maybe longer."

"You haven't see him since then?"

"Well now, If I had, that wouldn't have been the last time. Would it?"

"No," replied Christopher, somewhat embarrassed and realizing his search was still on. "I guess he's not come through here yet. How much is the room?"

"That'll be two and six, in advance. That's just for one night mind you. Just put yer name here in this book. If ye can't write yer name just make yer mark."

Christopher reached into his doublet and withdrew a small, brown leather purse from which he took two shilling pieces and six pence. After laying the coins on the counter he took the white quill from the ink well, shook off the excess ink and began to write his name carefully and as neatly as he could. "The very idea!" he thought. "I can probably write better than he can. I'll show him." Then he considered the fact that many people of different degrees of education must pass through here. It was probably quite common for someone not to be able to write his own name.

As Christopher wrote, the man picked up the coins, examined them, and put them into a drawer. Locking the drawer he turned and yelled up the stairs that ran behind the counter, "Essam, get down here!"

Almost immediately a small, red headed boy of about ten with dirty, tattered clothes and no shoes scampered down the stairs. "Yes, sir?" he said, appearing somewhat apprehensive, as if he had done something wrong and had just been found out.

"Show our new guest up to number three, the small room in the back."

The boy smiled a smile of relief and said, "Yes, sir," as he picked up Christopher's duffel bag and began to lead the way up the stairs.

Without another word the man returned to his ledger.

Christopher followed the boy up the narrow stairs to a room that overlooked a rather cluttered rear yard, some empty lowlands and the river beyond. It was a small, musty smelling room. The bed didn't look very comfortable; a fact that was confirmed as soon as Christopher sat on it. However, he did have the room to himself. It was quite common for travelers to have to share a room, sometimes three in a bed.

After availing himself of the necessary facilities he washed up a bit to remove some of the dust accumulated during the ride from Head of Elk. He checked to see if his purse and letter were still secure in his inside pocket then tied his duffel shut and pushed it under the bed. The next step was to get something to eat, then on to the Blue Fox Tavern and, perhaps, some word about Thomas.

After consuming a bowl of hot beef soup and some fresh brown bread, he left the inn.

It was a bright sunny day and Christopher was glad to be outside in the fresh air again. His senses told him that Front Street would be near the water so he headed in that direction. As he came closer to the river he could see the British warship he'd seen earlier from the coach. It was anchored just a short distance out in the river and lay with its bow to the current. Even at this closer range it still had that exceptionally neat appearance, fresh paint, sails triced up tightly to the yards, everything stowed properly. Perhaps it was this condition of order and readiness that gave warships such an ominous look. Yet one thing distracted from its immaculate appearance. As the ship rolled ever so slightly in the gentle current long tresses of green algae could be seen streaming from its sides below the waterline. Obviously, it had been a long time since this ship had last seen its home port.

Christopher suddenly realized he'd come to the last street before the river and that it was the one he sought. Front Street ran parallel to the river. It appeared much like the other streets, the narrow houses and shops, mostly of red brick, were so close together they seemed as though they were one continuous building.

Just past the first alley, on the right, there hung a wooden outline of a fox, very faded, but unmistakably blue. As Christopher walked toward the tavern he wondered if this is where his trip would end. If not, where would it end?

It was not a large place, or at least, not as large as Christopher had expected. There were several horses tied to the hitching post so he knew there must be customers inside. He went up the two granite steps, opened the door and stepped in.

He found it to be no more pretentious on the inside than it was on the outside. However, even a blind man would have known it was a tavern. It had that distinctive aroma created by years of too much spilled ale and not enough sunshine. A simple, undecorated bar filled up most of the wall on the left side of the room. A stone fireplace was against the rear, probably sharing a common chimney with another fireplace in the room behind it. The rest of the room contained only four, round, wooden tables, two of which were occupied. At the one in the corner there were two men who by their appearance were farmers; they probably had brought their products to town that morning. Neither paid any attention to Christopher as he entered. At a table near the unlit fireplace sat a very young British Naval officer, a midshipman to be exact, and no more than sixteen years of age. With him were three seamen. The oldest and most sea worn looking of these was nursing a large brown pipe from which emanated an aroma not unlike that of burning grape leaves. It seemed not to bother the others for their attention had immediately been diverted to Christopher when he entered the tavern. They said nothing but continued to eye Christopher as he walked across the room to the bar. There, a rather plumpish woman, perhaps in her fifties, was wiping the counter with a not so clean rag. As soon as Christopher approached her she stopped her pretense of cleaning.

Leaning on the bar with arms spread wide she smiled and asked, "What'll it be young man? You look a bit thirsty."

Christopher was not thirsty but he answered, "I'll have a pint of ale if you please, ma'am." He thought he would draw less attention to himself if he acted as though he were just another casual customer. As the woman filled a pewter mug from a large wooden cask behind the bar he managed to glance toward the four uniformed men. He was relieved to see their attention was no longer on him and that their conversation had resumed.

"Here you are, friend. This should fix you up all right." She set the mug down and slid it toward him. "I've not seen you around here before. New in town?"

"Just got here." He started to ask her if she had any knowledge of Thomas but suddenly instinct told him it would be better to first seek out Mr. VanDrees. "Would you happen to know a Mr. VanDrees?"

"I ought to. I've been married to him for the last thirty six years. What business would you have with him? What's he been getting in to now?"

"Oh, nothing, ma'am. A friend of his in Annapolis just said I should look him up when I got to New Castle." Christopher felt it would be better to leave it at that. Even though she was his wife he preferred to talk to Mr. VanDrees in person. "Is he about?"

"Sorry," she replied, "went up to Chester on business yesterday." When she saw the disappointment on Christopher's face she added, "He'll be back before nightfall, or so he said. Come back this evening."

"Thank you. Yes, tell him I'll be back."

"Now go ahead and finish your ale. I've got things to do in the back. If you want anything else just pull that cord." She pointed to a frayed green cord that obviously was connected to bell in the kitchen. She then took her leave in that direction.

Christopher finished the ale and, not wanting anything else, left the tavern and returned to the inn.

When he entered his room he had the feeling that something was different or had happened during his visit to the tavern. He looked around examining all that was there. Although the room was not familiar to him nothing seemed missing or out of place. Satisfied that all was well he decided to spend this opportunity reading some of Thomas's book. He pulled his duffel bag out from under the bed and was about to untie the cord when he suddenly stopped. He had always secured the bag by tying the two ends of the draw cord in a square knot. It was not tied with a square knot.

The feeling he'd had upon first entering the room was justified. He quickly checked the contents of the bag and was satisfied that everything was still there. However, one thing was certain, someone had been into it. But why? He had nothing of value in it. He kept his money with him. But, of course, who would know that. "Should I complain to the innkeeper?" he thought. "No, what good would that do? Besides, nothing was missing." The incident was disturbing, but a good reminder that he must be more alert and cautious in the future. He removed the book from his bag and lay down on the bed to read it.

Several hours later, when he opened his eyes, he was confused by his surroundings. Then he remembered where he was. He had fallen asleep shortly after opening the book. The sun had already set but the room was still dimly lit by what little twilight remained. It was time to return to the Blue Fox.

After washing up he gathered all his belongings and placed them in the duffel. He'd take no chances this time, he'd take the bag with him. After all, it wasn't heavy. He'd only packed enough clothes for a few day's trip to Annapolis. Little did he know his journey would lead all the way here to this town on the Delaware River and who knows where else.

By the time he stepped outside the last bit of twilight had disappeared and the moon had yet to make its appearance. All was dark except where an occasional window lamp would cast a dim patch of yellow light on the cobblestone street. This provided just enough light for someone familiar with the town to find his way around. Fortunately, Christopher had already visited the Blue Fox and though he knew very little about the town he did know his way back there. Christopher had always exhibited a remarkable sense of direction and ability to find his way. He'd not been to very many strange towns, but in fog, rain or sudden nightfall he'd shown he could navigate his father's boat through the many islands and inlets along the Chesapeake coast as well as most folks could in broad daylight.

As he walked down toward the river he thought about how different things looked at night. It was almost like two different worlds—one in daylight, the other engulfed in darkness. Houses that in daylight could be described in terms of colors were now only represented by different shades of gray. Even sounds were different at night. The singing of birds was replaced by the sound of crickets and an occasional flutter as a bat swooped down to capture another unsuspecting insect in flight. There were fewer scraping feet or clopping hooves on the street. The sounds of work were replaced by the sounds of leisure. Muffled sounds of laughter and sometimes even words of anger could be heard coming from behind the darkened doors of the houses he passed. As he neared Front Street and came closer to the river, sounds of singing came drifting across the still water of the river. The seamen on the British warship had their day's toil behind them and were now providing their own entertainment. Among the voices could be heard the sound of a pipe and occasionally the clomping of feet on a wooden deck as some sailor was moved to dancing.

Front Street was as easy to find at night as it had been in the daytime. As Christopher turned the corner he could see the large wooden figure of a blue fox hanging in front of the tavern. There was a lantern hanging on each side of the sign so it could easily be identified from either direction. It appeared to be busier than it had been when he was there earlier that day. Several people were entering while two more stood outside contemplating doing the same. Feeling new assurance that he was soon to find out something about Thomas he shifted his duffel bag to his other shoulder and increased his pace.

As he came closer he could hear loud voices coming from the tavern. They were not the sounds of men arguing but of men who were seriously engaged in revelry and were already several pints of ale into that activity.

Christopher crossed the opening to the alley and was thinking only of what lay ahead in the tavern. Suddenly a slight breeze came from out of the alleyway carrying with it an aroma he remembered smelling just recently—that of burning grape leaves. He started to turn toward its source but before he could do so a large, coarse bag came down over him. He started to struggle but was held firmly by a pair of massive arms from behind. He thrust his right elbow back into his assailant's midsection as hard as he could. There was a grunt and for a moment the grip loosened. He had no idea why he was being attacked but he did know that if he were to get away he'd have to get his arms free and the bag off his head. He tried to force his arms up and twist at the same time. Then he knew there were more than one to deal with as he heard a graveled voice proclaim, "Well lads, it looks like we've got ourselves a feisty one this time. If 'e can be tamed the Cap'n 'll be well pleased with this'n." Then another voice said, "Here, this'll tame 'im fer now."

There was a rushing sound followed by a heavy blow to the right side of his head. All his efforts immediately stopped as severe pain took control of his body and consciousness, a consciousness that was not to last long. As nausea and dizziness consumed him he felt as though he were falling down a long dark well. Sounds were becoming faint. The singing from the ship faded away, as did the shouting in the tavern. Then there was total silence and he was still.

When Christopher awoke he did so slowly, aware first of the awful pain in his head and neck. His wrists were sore where they obviously had been tied but now were free. He was lying in a foul smelling bunk in a small room with wooden walls and ceiling. Sharp rays of sunlight coming through an opening in the ceiling told him it was daylight. What time was it? How long had he been there? The lingering pain and the completely new surroundings coupled with his losing track of time held him in a state of confusion that was hard to shake off. He was trying very hard to regain his wits and as they slowly returned, he became aware of the fact the room seemed to be moving. Then he remembered Mr. Hampton's letter . . . Mr. Hampton's letter! In a panic he reached inside his doublet for the pocket that held his purse and letter. The purse was there; the letter was not! "Did I drop it?" he asked himself. "Did my captors find it? If they did . . . "

His thoughts were interrupted by footsteps. They were coming down a ladder at the other end of the room. As the figure emerged from the shadows Christopher heard him say, "Well, have you had a nice rest?" As he came into the light Christopher recognized him as the midshipman he'd seen in the Blue Fox the day before, or at least he thought it had been the day before. Right now he wasn't too sure.

Rubbing his head Christopher snapped, "Where am I?"

With a sardonic grin on his face the young midshipman bowed and ceremoniously announced, "You, my friend, have been granted the extreme privilege of becoming a member of His Most Britannic Majesty's Navy, aboard the sloop of war *H.M.S. Derby*."

CHAPTER IV

Boston Harbor—
Wednesday, April 19, 1775

As the sun began to seek its nightly refuge behind the low hills of Cambridge, to the west, the ships that lay at anchor between the city of Boston and Noddle's Island, to the north, swung lazily about their cables. Twilight is usually a peaceful and restful time aboard a ship at anchor, and so it would have been aboard the sixty-four gun frigate *H.M.S. Briareus*, but not this day. It was quiet all right, but there was an air of anxiety that ran throughout the ship. The minds of every man and boy on board were occupied with one set of events, events that caused each person on deck to repeatedly glance toward the shore.

The night before, over seven hundred of his Majesty's troops had been sent marching to Lexington and Concord. Word had it that they were sent to confiscate a cache of arms that had been stockpiled by the colonials. That such a large force was dispatched caused many aboard the *Briareus* to wonder what the troops expected to encounter. However, the night had passed with little discussion over the matter. But that morning, when word was received that over one thousand additional troops, the bulk of the Boston garrison, had to be sent inland as reinforcements, rumor replaced rumor about what was taking place. One thing was certain; it was a matter of no little consequence.

Christopher was sitting on the foredeck by the starboard cathead mending a torn awning. In the eleven months since he had been pressed into service at New Castle he had never forgiven himself for being so careless. He felt deep in his heart he had let Matty down. He had sworn he would look for Thomas until he found him and he had hardly begun the search when a British press gang ended it. Much to his dismay he had heard in a letter that Thomas was still lost. Being aboard a British naval vessel was probably the closest thing to being in prison.

This confinement greatly frustrated Christopher, especially with the *Briareus* anchored here in Boston Bay with his homeland in sight. His bitterness had almost erased any question of his allegiance. But what could he do about it? There had been only one consolation. For a long time he had worried about what could have happened to Mr. Hampton's letter, but finally realized it must have got lost in the scuffle or he would have been confronted about it shortly after being brought aboard. Convinced there was no escape and that it was in his best interest to do so, he early on decided to make the best of his situation and learn all he could about the ship and the navy. As a result, he'd made a number of friends among the crew and even among some of the officers. But his closest friend, and somewhat of a mentor, was an old Scotsman named Colin Dumfries, whom everyone simply called "Colie."

Colie was one of the best gun captains in the British Navy. Though he was continuously being kidded for his Scottish accent, he had the respect of every man on board, officers and crew alike. He had distinguished himself on several occasions. The most notable having been in the Battle of Quiberon Bay sixteen years earlier when the combined fleets of Admiral Lord Hawke and Vice Admiral Robert Duff put an end to France's plan to invade the British Isles. Colie had already been a part of the *Briareus*' crew when Christopher came on board from the sloop *Derby*.

When the *Derby* left New Castle, Delaware it had been ordered to return directly to Portsmouth, England for repairs and refitting. The crossing had been an easy and uneventful one with good weather and a fair and steady wind all the way. Thus, they reached the waters off the "Lizard", that southernmost point of

England, earlier than expected—a fact that was to have a profound effect on Christopher's life.

They had just passed the point and had gone over to a more northerly course to enter into the English Channel when they were spotted and hailed by the Frigate *Briareus*, outward bound for the Mediterranean Sea. Events in both Europe and the colonies had seriously strained the manpower of the British Navy. The *Briareus* had sailed with less than a full crew, but with instructions to make up this deficiency from any homeward bound ships they encountered.

Eighteen of the *Derby's* crew, including Christopher, were transferred over, along with two midshipmen and a young lieutenant. The *Briareus*, then having attained its full complement, proceeded to the Strait of Gibraltar and the warm waters of the Mediterranean, where it patrolled for the next eight months. Except for several small encounters with Barbary pirates it had been very boring duty. Thus, there was a certain degree of relief felt throughout the ship when orders were received that the *Briareus* was to be dispatched to join the fleet guarding the American coast. Almost everyone looked forward to a change, especially those who had never sailed the western Atlantic.

But once there, it did not take long to see that expectations had again exceeded reality. This was even less exciting, just sitting in Boston Harbor day in and day out, the scenery never changing. Only officers were allowed to go ashore. Too many seamen disappeared when given shore leave any place except on small islands, the only exceptions to this rule being boat crews and press gangs. Even then, there were never any colonials entrusted with the task.

Christopher had stopped sewing and was studying the shore. He knew the only way he would get to see this city would be from a distance.

"Ha' ye ever been in these parts afore, Christopher?"

Christopher turned, somewhat startled. He'd been so deep in thought he'd not heard Colie approach and sit down next to him. "No, Colie, never been this far north, on land, that is. Have you?"

"Nae, I've 'ad noo such luck. But I 'ear Boston's quite the toon, tha' is if ye'r lookin' fer a place t' kick up yer heels. And the lassies, I 'ear . . . ." They were interrupted by a stirring on the quarterdeck. The several officers that had been in quiet conversation had rushed to the starboard rail and were peering toward the town of Charlestown. Although it was well into dusk and darkness was starting to consume the scene around them, some activity on shore had been sufficient to catch their attention. At once, Christopher leaped to his feet and climbed part way up the foremast ratlines.

"Wha' is it, Lad?" yelled up Colie.

"There's much commotion on shore over Charlestown way—a lot of troops. It's hard to see. There's a lot of confusion. Looks like maybe there's wounded with them."

"I d'na like the looks o' this," Colie replied.

"They're loading up the boats to come back over to Boston. They've built some fires on shore and I can see by the light there are wounded men. Many are being carried, some might even be killed. Can't tell for sure about that though."

And so it went, on into the night. Troops continued to pour into Charlestown to be ferried back across the Charles River to Boston. Christopher returned to the deck when it became too dark to make out any details of what was happening. But he and Colie remained at the rail watching anyway, trying to analyze the events by the light of campfires and torches. It was a scene which told of a disaster that had taken place—what was more important, it was one which foretold of even graver events to come.

The scene on the shore was bad enough, but what made it seem so foreboding was the increasing number of campfires that were appearing on the hillsides around Charlestown and Cambridge. It seemed that not only had His Majesty's troops fared poorly but they had even been pursued by colonial militia that were now taking up a vigil on every hillside overlooking Boston. Before the night was over, the number of campfires looked like so many fireflies on a summer's evening and were beyond counting. One could only guess how many colonial militiamen stood around each of those fires warming his hands, hands which had that day fired upon His Majesty's troops, hands that had started an irreversible course of events that would either create a new nation or bring disaster to an already troubled colony.

Although several hours had passed and his work for that day had been completed, Christopher still remained topside. Except for those assigned to the deck watch he was alone—alone with only his thoughts. The noise and stench of the dark and crowded berthing deck below were not conducive to clear thinking and on this night Christopher had much to think about. It was a different scene that was set before him this night as he leaned on the rail peering out over the black water. The few dim lights of Boston and Charlestown seemed to be under siege by the multitude of flickering campfires on the hillsides above. He was oblivious to the sounds from below where his shipmates had, for the moment, set aside all thoughts of serious matters and were engaged in their evening games, singing and arguing. His thoughts were only interrupted by the creaking and splashing of an occasional guard boat passing by. The traffic between ships and between the ships and shore was much greater this night, adding also to the anxiety of the situation.

For the first time in many months Christopher felt like a stranger. As he stood there by the rail looking toward the scene on shore his thoughts traveled back and forth between the land of his countrymen and the *Briareus* that had been his home and workplace for almost a year. He had grown accustomed to being a part of the crew and had come to feel a certain loyalty to its captain and officers if not the nation it represented. Yet, he was still haunted by the events just prior to his being taken on board. He felt he had failed not only his sister, Thomas and Mr. Hampton, but also that nebulous cause to which he had begun to subscribe, if only out of faith in those people close to him.

He was confused and he was frustrated. He felt helpless to respond to the events that were unfolding around him. He was an

American and America would soon be at war with England. He shouldn't be where he was, not aboard a King's ship. What was going to happen? What should he do? What could he do? He hadn't realized his thoughts had subconsciously drifted into a prayer until he heard himself softly say, "Amen."

"And amen," repeated Colie who had quietly returned and was standing next to Christopher in the darkness. "I think I ken wot ye're a prayin' and if it'll help, ye can put my name t' the bottom o' it too."

"Oh . . . Colie. I didn't know you were there. I wasn't . . . well, yes, I guess I was . . . ."

"Ne'er ye mind. "'Tis the proper time fer it if there ever was. Looks t' me, lad, ye've found yerself on the wrong side o' the fence."

"You think it's going to get worse?"

"I d'na see it gettin' better, 'n things d'na usually stay the same fer vera long."

Their conversation was suddenly interrupted by the thumping sounds of a boat coming along side. They both leaned over the rail to watch silently as its crew made fast its bow and stern lines to the ship. Even before the last line was tied, a young officer with a canvas pouch secured to his side had scampered up the ladder. The next moment, he was standing by the gangway punctiliously saluting the Officer of the Deck. After a few hushed words a messenger appeared and escorted the visitor aft and below to the captain's cabin.

"I wonder who puts the starch in 'is britches," muttered Colie with half a grin on his face.

"What?"

"Wi' a' the pomp tha' 'e shows I'd say 'e's from the flagship or 'eadquarters ashore."

"It must be something very important, not to wait 'til daylight. I wonder if we'll be puttin' to sea again," commented Christopher.

"Wuld na surprise me a bit. Ye might be takin' yer last look o' Boston come mornin'," replied Colie.

Christopher said nothing and they both turned to look toward the shore.

After a while Colie leaned closer to Christopher and whispered, "Aire ye gonna do it, lad?"

"What," asked Christopher, "do what?"

"Shh," admonished Colie, "nae so loud." Colie turned so his back would be to the quarterdeck. "I mean, lad, ge' off the ship. That's wot ye want, aint it?"

"Yes, I guess so . . . yes," whispered Christopher with a chill running up his spine as he realized the consequences of being caught doing such a thing.

"T'night might be yer last opportunity. After t'night ye'll nae be able t' be booth Anglish 'n American. 'Tis one or t' other from 'ear out, like it or nae."

"How? I can swim but it's at least three cable's distance to shore. And how would I get off the ship without being seen?"

"S'pose ye 'ad 'elp," said Colie moving closer.

"But why? Why would you risk helping someone jump ship?"

"'Cause I'm a Scot, tha's why. If ye ken a thin' or twa aboot the Scots 'n the Anglish ye'd nae ha' t' ask." Suddenly Colie sensed someone approaching and quickly changed the subject. "'Cause the ball d'na always fit snug in the barrel, the explodin' gases escape aroond it causin' yer powder to ha' less o' a punch or a' times the ball might e'en chatter doon the barrel. In either case it shortens yer range 'n the shot falls short o' its mark. That's when ye needs a sabot, the wooden plug tha's attached t' the ball t' make a tighter fit."

Christopher was at first confused at Colie's sudden shift to this topic, especially this subject, for he already knew it. It was one of the first things he'd learned from Colie. Colie had himself boasted about Christopher's ability to pick things up and that he'd someday be as good a gunner as any he had ever taught. Then Christopher too heard the footsteps and understood Colie's caution. "I'll try to remember that, Colie. You must know all there is to know about gunnery," replied Christopher, hoping the newcomer had heard nothing more.

Christopher turned to see Pickett, the cook's helper, approaching. Pickett was a thin man, perhaps too thin, with an abrasive personality that was born of constant sarcasm. He had no close friends among the crew but this didn't seem to bother him. He was a young man with few skills and no apparent desire to improve on this lot. He certainly did not give the appearance of someone you could trust and Christopher hoped their conversation had not been overheard.

"Give the lad a break, old timer. You'll wear out his brain." Pickett said no more as he passed on to the leeward side to toss over a pail of slop. Without another word he returned below to the galley.

As soon as Pickett was out of earshot, Colie whispered, "He d'na hear. If 'e 'ad 'e'd a said somethin', ye can be sartain o' that. Now listen." Colie lowered his voice even further as he continued. "If ye swim fer it ye'd best wait 'til just afore high tide. 'Tis better it be comin' in so ye wull nae be carried oot t' sea, and ya d'na want t' be in the rush or ye might be carried a way o'er t' Charlestown where a' the troops are."

"But I'm not sure I can swim all that far, Colie," whispered Christopher.

"Ye d'na have t', Lad, I'll fetch an empty powder keg. Wi' a barrel hitch aroond it ye can use it fer a float t' hang on ta. Swim 'n rest, swim 'n rest."

Christopher felt his body fill with excitement as he finally began to realize the possibility of succeeding. "But how can I get off the ship?" he asked.

"Quietly, vera quietly. Ye ge' yerself ready fer it and when the tide is richt, check t' be sure there's nae a soul up on the foc'sle, then make like ye're goin' up t' the head. When ye're on t' other side o' the breakwater bulkhead look t' the larboard side past the Seat o' Easement. I'll ha' the keg 'n a length o' line there fer ye."

Christopher listened intently to every word, hardly able to believe Colie was risking so much when he had nothing personal to gain.

Colie looked around to make certain they were still alone, then continued, "Wait 'til there's something t' distract the attention o' the watch. If naught 'appens, I'll ha' t' distract 'em some way m'self. When tha' 'appens lower yerself into the water easy like." Colie looked straight at Christopher and squeezed his arm to emphasize the point. "D'na jump 'r make a splash! Yer success depends on gettin' away unnoticed. Yer best bet's t' make fer Boston itself. Try t' go in oonder a pier, ye'll be less likely t' be seen tha' way. Stay clear o' any guard boats or 'tis o'er fer the both o' us."

"Don't worry, Colie, even if I do get caught I'll never tell you helped me."

"Ye won't ha' t', they're nae stupid. They'll ken who was on deck when ye went o'er. He paused, then, placing his hand on Christopher's shoulder, he admonished, "Just be careful, Christopher, very careful."

"Colie, I don't know what to say or how to thank you. I hope we meet again."

"Ye'd better hope we doon't. If that 'appens I'll probably be a lookin' at ye through a gun port. I'd 'ate to think I'd gin t' a' this trouble just t' blow your 'ead off later. Now do wot ye need t' do but d'na try t' take anything wi' ye. Ye'll be lucky enough t' ge' away wi' yer skin. The tide should be richt in aboot an hour. Be on the gun deck. I'll gi' ye a sign when all's ready." With that, Colie turned and left the foc'sle to go below.

Christopher remained at the rail looking at the string of dim lights that represented the shore he would soon be swimming toward, a shore that represented home even though home was actually over three hundred miles to the south. The thought of being caught frightened him. He knew that the punishment for desertion from an English warship was severe and might even be hanging if "it so pleased the crown". But, he could not stay aboard with events turning out the way they were. He could never bring himself to assist in firing upon his own people. If he refused, then what would be the punishment? That thought made it easier to risk what he was about to do. Having reassured himself he was doing the right thing he began to go over in his mind what he had to do to get ready. Actually, there was very little, if anything. Colie was right. He should not be encumbered with anything except the clothes on his body. The only thing he regretted was having to leave Thomas' book behind. But it would be ruined by the water anyway if he tried to take it.

When the time approached, Christopher casually made his way down to the gun deck that also served as the crew's sleeping quarters. Most of the crew had already slung their hammocks in preparation for the night. Some were already asleep and making their contribution to what would soon be a loud and continuous drone of snoring. There was nothing Christopher needed to get but he felt there would be less chance of suspicion if he went about a normal routine. He unfolded his hammock and slung it between the appropriate cast iron hooks on the overhead beams that supported the main deck above. He continued to busy himself with his things to make it look as though he would soon be going to sleep.

He was beginning to get nervous and wonder if he was spending too much time working with his bedding, after all, there's really not much to do in putting up a hammock. Just then he saw Colie appear from the shadows of the aft part of the deck and walk casually toward the ladder leading to the upper deck. As he passed, a subtle nod of his head told Christopher it was time and all was ready.

After a brief but discreet wait Christopher too ascended the ladder to the upper deck. There was a light breeze starting to blow and the fresh air that hit him in the face seemed like a portent of the freedom he was about to seek. As he turned and started to walk forward toward the breakwater bulkhead he glanced up to see if the foc'sle was clear. It was not. It was Pickett again and this time there was someone with him. Christopher had to delay. Anyone on the foc'sle could look over the breakwater bulkhead and have a full view of the head, for privacy aboard a navy vessel held a rather low priority. Instead, he walked over to the rail and pretended to look at something in the water and then at the shore. His actions appeared normal enough but after a while he felt he was becoming conspicuous so returned to the lower deck.

Fortunately, Colie was able to observe all this and understood the problem. He had been near the quarterdeck engaging a young midshipman in conversion about the good and bad points of swivel guns. Colie, it was said, could talk about guns from dawn to dusk without repeating himself. So, he continued at that, hoping Christopher would be ready when an opportunity finally presented itself.

Meanwhile, Christopher, afraid his anxiety would soon show if he continued to mill about, climbed into his hammock and listened for any sounds that could be heard from above. He was directly under the foc'sle and thought he might be able to hear Pickett and the other person when they walked off. He waited. He waited and prayed Colie could still be able to help him when the time came—if the time came.

Finally, after more than half an hour, he heard the longed-for sound of footsteps overhead and hoped they were leaving the foc'sle. After waiting a few minutes, he rolled out of his hammock and returned topside. By now there was no one on deck except the deck watch, which consisted of one officer and two crewmen. To his relief, the foc'sle was clear but Colie was nowhere to be seen. What should he do? With no distraction and Colie not here to cause one, the slightest sound might be heard and he would be detected. He had to act. He'd already lost the biggest part of an hour and the tide would soon be turning. "I've got to go ahead with it," he thought to himself.

Mustering all the courage he could; he continued his charade of answering nature's call. He proceeded toward the head. He'd just have to be extra careful and not even make the slightest sound. The deck was darker now, only the anchor light and the dim lantern on the quarterdeck provided any illumination at all. Every shadow suggested the presence of someone who could suddenly appear and spoil everything.

Filled with a mixture of resolve and terror he reached for the handle that would open the door leading to the head, and he hoped—freedom. The cold of the brass handle in his hand sent a chill up his spine. He squeezed it as if to seek some semblance of security from the act. Slowly he pushed open the door to reveal what appeared to be only a black void. But he knew what was there and where everything was. If only he could be certain he was alone.

Suddenly a hand grabbed his right arm. His heart seemed to leap in his chest and he became frozen with fright. He started to cry out but fortunately he couldn't make a sound. Then relief swept over him as he heard Colie's familiar voice in a whisper.

"Easy, Lad. There's nae a body here but the twae o' us."

"Colie, you near scared me to my death," whispered Christopher.

"Ye've lost some time, but yer luck d'na leave ye altogither. There's a boat approachin'. Wait'll the watch is busy seein' whoever it is then make yer move."

"Is the keg here?" asked Christopher.

"Aye, 'n the line too. Ye're almost standin' on it. I'll go ward off anyboody who migh' be 'eadin' this way. Good luck to ye, lad." With that, Colie disappeared into the darkness.

After several agonizing minutes Christopher heard the familiar sounds of a boat coming along side. He immediately felt around the deck at his feet and found the line and the keg. Because the boat was along the starboard side of the ship he moved to the larboard side. He tied one end of the line to the keg then passed the line around one of the stanchions. Quietly he lowered the keg into the water. Moving quickly, he climbed over the side and carefully began to lower himself into the darkness below. He did not make a sound until he was in the water. He gasped at what seemed like the coldest water he'd ever been in; for the moment, he lost his equilibrium. Regaining his composure and his breath he hesitated a moment to listen for sounds from above. Hearing only the normal sounds and voices of the watch and boat crew he let go of the line. With one hand holding the small keg by the barrel hitch Colie had tied to it, he began to swim away from the ship and toward the shore.

It was slow going, very slow. It was difficult to swim while holding on to the keg but he knew he needed the extra flotation if only for periodic resting. Christopher was a strong swimmer and had good endurance but he had never attempted to swim such a distance and under such conditions. He could swim with only his free arm and kick with his feet but he soon could tell he was making progress for the black outline of the ship was beginning to gradually diminish. Because of the delay in getting off the ship the tide had already reached the flood. There was certainly no danger now of being carried to the beach at Charlestown and he didn't have to compensate for any cross drift but he knew he must reach his goal before the tide began to ebb.

After swimming about a cable's length, he was startled by the sounds of oars and muffled voices. He stopped to listened. It sounded as though the boat was a safe distance from him but he could not tell in which direction it was traveling. He resumed his swimming but paused every few minutes to monitor the sounds of the boat. Suddenly he realized it was getting louder and must be approaching him. If he tried to swim faster, in which case he'd have to jettison the keg, he might make too much noise. If he didn't, they might run right into him. It was difficult to think clearly, being half exhausted and shivering from the cold. He must remain still and hope the boat did not pass too close. He had only one advantage, darkness.

Holding on to the keg with both hands and staying as low in the water as possible he tilted his head back and allowed only his face to break the surface. He remained as still as he could keeping the keg between him and the source of the sounds. How glad he was he'd not taken off his shoes. He'd been tempted to do so earlier because they seemed to slow him down but now their weight kept his legs and body from floating up and breaking the surface.

The sounds continued to become louder. It seemed like an

eternity waiting, not knowing if he was directly in the boat's path or not. Then he realized the direction of the sounds had changed, indicating the boat was passing to the side of him. Relief swept over him but he was shivering now, half from the cold, half from the close call he'd just had. Still, he had to wait until the boat had traveled far enough away from him before he dared risk moving again.

He kept his body motionless, biding his time, but his mind was more active than ever. Suppose his absence had been discovered. They might even now be sending a boat out to search for him. Had Colie been seen helping him? When he realized what he was doing he rebuked himself for dwelling on everything that could go wrong. Hadn't he already overcome the greatest obstacles? He looked toward the shore and tried to think about what lay ahead.

When the sounds from the boat had at last become barely audible he decided it was safe to move on. Feeling some small degree of increased vigor due to the unplanned rest, he resumed his swimming with renewed enthusiasm. He picked out two lights in the city by which to guide himself. They were slightly higher than the rest and would be easy to identify when he had to periodically check his course.

After a while he noticed the two lights seemed a bit farther apart, indicating he was getting closer. This spurred him on to even greater effort. He'd swim awhile then check the lights, swim awhile then check. Each time he looked the lights seemed to be a little farther apart. He was going to make it. He knew it. But the next time he looked, the two lights appeared no different than before. "Maybe I looked too soon," he said to himself, trying to push aside a tinge of alarm. "I must wait longer before checking."

He allowed at least ten minutes to pass before looking at the two lights again. Meanwhile, he just swam toward the general array of dim lights that outlined Boston's waterfront. When he did check again, feeling certain that progress would be quite evident this time, his reaction was not relief but horror. He was suddenly overcome with that feeling of numbness that most often precedes panic. Not only had the two lights failed to appear farther apart, they seemed closer to each other. This could mean only one thing. The tide had changed and in spite of all his efforts he was moving farther away from the city. Worse yet, he was moving toward the open sea.

Instinctively Christopher turned around to view what lay behind him and where the tide would take him if he was not able to overcome it. All he saw was a great, ominous void. He could not even discern sky from sea for each was as black as the other. He was tired, more tired than he had ever been in his life—and he was cold, incredibly cold. But the dread of what might befall him if he rested gave him the strength to swim even harder. He wanted to get rid of the keg for it slowed him so much. However, he knew that if he couldn't make landfall the keg would be his last hope for survival, slight as it was. He'd just have to do the best he could even with keeping the keg. "I've got to get rid of my shoes," he said to himself, pausing just long enough to remove them. As he let each one drop he could picture in his mind its slow descent into the dark depths of the bay as though it foreshadowed his own fate. Shaking the morbid thought from his mind he began to swim harder than ever. There could be no stopping to rest now. Every pause would take away some of the precious progress already gained.

He tried to swim without stopping and he did so for minutes that seemed like hours. Sheer determination was now his driving force, mostly because he had never given up hope of finding Thomas, in spite of all the time that had passed. But exhaustion and loss of body heat had taken their toll on his coordination. It was a Sisyphean effort and no amount of effort could overcome the force of the tide. Christopher realized this and stopped swimming. Holding on to the keg with both arms he just drifted, trying to rest, catch his breath and think. He had to think; he couldn't give up now. But slowly the tide was carrying him toward the vast and dark open ocean.

After a while Christopher realized that if he just continued to drift he would probably remain in the main channel with the maximum tide flow, but if he swam perpendicular to the tide he could possibly get to where the flow was slower. Perhaps he could make it to one of the many islands in the harbor. With this in mind, he arbitrarily decided to swim toward the south, keeping the diminishing lights of Boston on his right.

He was now in a state of exhaustion. His movements were merely mechanical but because he was no longer trying to swim directly into the tide his efforts were beginning to produce some results. He'd been able to divert his course sufficiently that he was passing between Castle Island and Dorchester Point where the depths were shallow enough to be measured in feet instead of fathoms. Several times his feet dragged the bottom and stirred him to a momentary excitement but each time he tried to stand the bottom seemed to disappear again. It had been several hours since Christopher left the *Briareus* and after this length of time in the water under such cold and exhausting conditions he was barely conscious. He could swim no longer. It required what little energy he had left just to keep afloat by holding on to the keg with both arms. He just drifted with no further effort to control his course.

When his feet began to drag along the stones and sharp clam shells on the south end of Spectacle Island he didn't even react, his senses had become so numbed. The gentle waves slowly moved him closer to the beach and when his knees touched the bottom he instinctively began to crawl up the gradual slope and out of the water. He made only one feeble attempt to stand. When that failed, he collapsed on the beach and at last surrendered to unconsciousness.

CHAPTER V

It was perhaps the sound of rustling fabric that began to awaken Christopher. He usually experienced some degree of confusion when waking up in a strange place but this time the contrast between what his senses were telling him and what he last remembered was bewildering. He was dry, not wet; warm, not cold; and certainly not lying on the sharp stones and shells of Spectacle Island. He slowly opened his eyes, only to see blurred images, but after blinking several times things gradually became clearer. The white, lace canopy above him told him he was in a bed. But whose bed? Where? As his eyes began to examine his surroundings he could tell it was a well-appointed room. Then he heard the sound again; it came from the left. Turning his head toward the source he saw a woman doing something at a wash stand. He could only see her back but he could tell that she was young, tall, slender and moved with an unusual grace. He tried to sit up, but the energy to do so just wasn't there and the expenditure of what little he had caused him to fall back to sleep.

It was several hours later when Christopher was again awakened, this time to the sound of voices, male voices. Opening his eyes he saw two men standing beside the bed. It was at first difficult to make out their features but as his vision began to clear he quickly noticed the contrast in their appearances. One was heavy featured and tanned, with a weathered look. His heavy, black hair had receded considerably, except for a singular tuft that remained on the front of his head. Below dark, heavy brows were a pair of eyes that appeared to be set in a permanent squint, brought about by years of searching the horizons of an open sea.

The other man's appearance was the antithesis of that of the first. His was a thin face and clean shaven. Its lacking of much color suggested a profession that required his presence indoors much, if not most, of the time. He had removed his spectacles and was cleaning them with his handkerchief when the other man spoke.

"Well Doctor, looks like our catch from the sea has finally had enough sleep."

"I'm afraid not, Captain. He'll need a good bit more rest before he'll be up and about again. He's had a very close brush with the grim reaper. One is fortunate enough just to recover from lung fever. Don't expect two miracles in a row. He'll need much more care before he regains his full strength."

"Yes, yes, you're quite right," answered the one called captain. Then turning to Christopher, he asked, "Can you talk now?"

"I . . . I don't know, sir." Even in his weakened state Christopher knew to be careful. If he was in the presence of Tories he certainly didn't want them to know he had deserted from a King's ship. He had to be cautious.

"You don't know!" remarked the captain. "You seem to be able to speak well enough."

"This is one on you, Captain Pierce," injected the doctor with a chuckle. "In all your blockade running you've never brought us anything without knowing its complete manifest. This time, all you bring in is one half drowned soul and you can't even determine what you've caught."

The words "blockade running" was all the reassurance Christopher needed. He'd heard of the blockade runners, those men who risked everything, even their lives, to bring supplies to the city of Boston. Knowing he was in friendly hands he relaxed, and smiling said, "My name is Christopher Hall. I'm from the town of St. Michaels in the colony of Maryland."

Captain Pierce looked at the doctor with a puzzled expression and then back to Christopher. "You didn't swim all the way from the Chesapeake Bay to Spectacle Island."

"Oh no, sir," answered Christopher, taking the captain's comment seriously. "I was aboard the frigate *Briareus* anchored off Boston."

The doctor, much surprised, asked, "You were on board a British war ship?"

"Yes, I was caught by a press gang in New Castle down in Delaware almost a year ago." He went on to relate the story of his brother-in-law's disappearance, his search for him, and how he, himself, had been caught and taken aboard the *H.M.S. Derby* and later transferred to the *Briareus*. He went on to say, "I jumped ship last night after the fighting at Lexington and . . . that other town."

"Concord," said Captain Pierce.

"Yes, that's it. After I heard about the fighting there I figured I'd better get away. I tried to swim ashore at Boston but the tide carried me further away. Try as I might I just couldn't overcome the current." Christopher paused and momentarily closed his eyes to rid himself of a sudden wave of dizziness and weakness. Then, opening them again he asked, "Where am I? How did I get here?"

"You're in Squansett Cove, about ten miles south of Boston. We found you washed up on the beach on Spectacle Island," answered the Captain. "And it wasn't last night, young man. It was four days ago. You've had quite a sleep. We weren't too certain you were going to make it; you probably wouldn't have had it not been for Doctor Peter Finlay here and his bag of tricks."

"Tricks you say!" exclaimed Doctor Finlay with a look of feigned indignation, "Since when have we come to refer to the latest in medical science and skill as 'tricks'?"

"Call it what you will," said Captain Pierce smiling. Then turning to Christopher he added, "I'll have to admit he has the best set of tricks . . . I mean . . . medical skills in all of New England. That makes you very lucky, Mr. Hall."

At first, Christopher was puzzled by this raillery between the captain and the doctor. But he soon recognized it as two very dear friends bantering each other in a manner that only close friends can do. Christopher felt even more secure now. The men who had saved his life were not only a colonial blockade runner and a doctor but they were men with a sense of humor. There always seems to be less to fear from such men. Perhaps it was because those who find more enjoyment in life are less apt to bring strife to it.

Both the doctor and the captain must have been reading the concerns on Christopher's face. The Captain placed his hand on Christopher's shoulder with the gentleness of a father and said, "I assure you, you are safe here. You must relax. Save your strength. The good doctor's right, you are going to be all right but you've a good ways to go before you can shake out your mains'l and set a steady course again. Now rest, we'll talk more later." Then turning toward the door the captain simply said, "Peter."

The doctor turned and followed the captain out of the room. Before the door was closed behind them Christopher was again asleep.

It wasn't until the next day that Christopher awoke again and it was to that first sound he had heard in this room, the rustling of fabric. Remembering its source from the first experience, he turned to look toward the wash stand to his left. Just as he did so, the same slender figure of a woman he'd seen before, but only from behind, turned and moved toward him. It was perhaps his own reaction that surprised him the most for never before had he experienced this feeling. There was sort of a light headidness, but he knew it wasn't caused by his illness. He said nothing, just watched as she approached the side of his bed.

She was a young woman, not quite twenty years old, with hair the color of fine mahogany and sparkling dark brown eyes to match. Her dress was of an expensive looking gray and white, striped satin with a close fitting bodice and half sleeves ending in fine lace. The decolletage was accented by a fairly large salmon colored bow which Christopher forced himself to ignore to avoid any embarrassment. Never before had he seen a dress cut this low.

She was a beautiful girl and moved with an unusual grace. Her most striking feature, the one that seemed to hold Christopher in a momentary trance, was her smile. It was one of those not too common smiles that instantly and sincerely convey the feeling of friendship.

"Good morning," she said as she placed her hand on his forehead. Her touch was soft and gentle.

Christopher underwent a confusion of feelings as he simultaneously felt relaxed by her tenderness and excited by her beauty. "Good morning," he replied, too caught off guard to say more.

"How are you feeling this morning?"

"Much better, thank you," he answered, wondering who she was and whether he was adequately covered. He'd never had a woman see him in bed before, that is, except his mother and sister Matty. He felt somewhat embarrassed.

"Well, your fever is almost gone and that's a blessing," she said as she removed her hand from his head and began to straighten the covers around him. As she leaned over him he could not help noticing the graceful curvature of her body, from the narrowness of her waist to the fullness of her youthful and firm breasts. As she moved about, her perfume filled the air around him with the faint scent of lilacs. Everything about her was pleasant.

He had to say something; he couldn't just keep staring at her. But, "Thank you," was all he could manage.

"You're quite welcome," was her only reply.

He didn't want her to leave, not yet. Who was she? He'd have to start a conversation but he felt so awkward. Then he finally managed to ask, "Where is Captain Pierce?"

"Father? Oh, he left early this morning. He sailed for Connecticut—he and Jacob."

"So, Captain Pierce is your father. And Jacob?"

"He's my brother. He's the oldest. Molly is the youngest and I'm Marion. And you, I understand, are Christopher Hall from St. Michaels in Maryland."

"Yes. I guess I owe my life to your father. He told me I've been here four days. I don't remember anything except being in the water."

"It's been five days now. It was yesterday he talked with you."

"Whew! I've never been in bed this long before. I've got to get up."

"Not yet you don't! Not a minute before Doctor Finlay says you can," she scolded him, with a smile that betrayed her attempt at sternness. "Besides, you probably couldn't even stand by yourself yet, much less walk. You're going to stay put until we nurse you back to health."

The thought that she would be around to help him recover put his mind to rest. He liked the idea he would see more of her. "All right Ma'am, I'll do as you say. I'll not get up until you say so but I . . . I . . . "

"Yes, of course, I understand. You have human needs just like anyone else. Our man, Joseph, will help you when you need him. Just ring this bell here on the table. I'll move it closer so you can reach it." Then placing her hand on his she said, "It's about time you started taking some nourishment. I'll go see that something is prepared for you. In the meantime, just rest." With that she turned and left the room.

His eyes followed her as she left and for a while remained fixed upon the door she had closed behind her. He could still feel the touch of her hand on his, its softness, its tenderness, its warmth . . . its . . . its . . . and slowly he drifted into the most pleasant of sleeps.

It was less than an hour later when Christopher was awakened by a girl's voice. "Hey! Wake up. Do you want to starve to death?"

Christopher didn't know how long he'd been asleep this time but it wasn't long enough. He knew, or at least was almost certain, it was not the voice of Marion and opening his eyes confirmed this. Standing beside him, holding a tray with a bowl of steaming beef broth, was a younger girl. Although she bore some features similar to those of Marion, in most ways she was quite different, if not in appearance then most certainly in countenance. Her hair and eyes were the same as Marion's but her face was broader and slightly square jawed. Her broad smile revealed gleaming white teeth that were in contrast to her darker complexion. It appeared a good bit of her time must be spent outdoors.

"Well, Mr. Hall?" She stood there akimbo, one hand holding the tray, the other on her hip.

"Molly! Don't be so rude." It was the voice of an older woman.

Turning his head toward the door he saw Captain Pierce's wife, Rena, enter the room.

"That's no way to treat our guest," she scolded. "Do you expect him to take broth lying down? Set the tray down and help me prop him up." Turning to Christopher she apologized, "Please excuse my daughter's manners, or should I say lack of them. She's a bit too saucy for her own good some times."

"That's all right, Ma'am," Christopher assured her. Then, not wanting to get involved in a disagreement between Molly and her mother, he turned his attention to the tray. "That sure smells good."

Molly set the tray on a nearby table, then helped her mother get Christopher into a sitting position, propped up with extra pillows.

Mrs. Pierce retrieved the tray and placed it on Christopher's lap. "Eat what you can but don't force too much. It will take a while before you can handle a regular meal." With that she motioned for Molly to follow and they both left the room.

During the weeks that followed, Christopher slowly regained much of his strength. Fortunately for him Doctor Finlay was one of the few doctors who did not completely adhere to the accepted medical practices of that day. He had serious doubts about the benefits of bloodletting in cases like this. He had observed wounded patients die from loss of blood and could not understand how intentionally letting blood could do anything but make a bad situation worse. However, he did not deviate from common practices completely and one of the accepted treatments for reducing fever had been employed. He had prepared plasters by dipping flannel in a caustic made from Spanish fly or green blister beetles. These had been placed on Christopher's chest where they produced the expected blisters and the "counter irritation" that was believed necessary for restoring the body's equilibrium. If this provided any benefit at all it was by means not understood to this day. Fortunately, the blisters soon healed. If anything helped him it was the prescribed rest and the low diet of thin diluted liquids Mrs. Pierce provided until he could handle heavier foods.

The Pierces could not have been more hospitable and they treated Christopher as though he were a member of their own family. And so it was, that under such loving care his recovery progressed at a rate that even amazed the good Doctor Finlay, who came by each day to pay his respects to the family of his good friend and to see how his patient was faring.

When it had become time for Christopher to get out of bed Mrs. Pierce selected a few items of clothing for him from her son's wardrobe. Fortunately, Jacob was nearly the same size as Christopher except Jacob's feet were a bit larger, but better that than smaller. Christopher felt a little awkward wearing someone else's clothes but Mrs. Pierce assured him that Jacob would have offered them himself if he were there.

At first he was able only to walk about the room, and even that required holding on to something. However, by the end of the second week he was able to go outside where he found the perfect place to recuperate. The Pierce's home, one of the finest in the little town of Squansett Cove, had, like so many others of that time, a formal garden behind it. It was here Christopher spent much of the day walking, exercising his legs. He would walk until tired then rest on one of the several benches along the path. Of course a good bit of this time was shared with Marion who seemed to have claimed him as her personal ward and patient. As it was, they spent many hours together and thus became good friends, but for Christopher it was something more than just good friends. There was a certain feeling he experienced when he was in her presence, a feeling he'd not had toward anyone else, ever. He hoped she felt the same toward him.

Of course Molly, as blithesome and carefree as she was, was not unaware of this developing relationship between her sister and Christopher; and, she was not the least bit hesitant at providing some occasional teasing. Although Marion properly displayed her annoyance at such behavior she could not conceal at least a certain degree of enjoyment in it. Christopher also feigned annoyance at Molly's antics but, by them, gained some reassurance that there was something there between Marion and him. He also began to feel toward Molly as though she were a little sister.

Although he was becoming more and more attached to the Pierce family, Christopher knew he must make his way home to St. Michaels as soon as he was able and could find the means to do so. He had written a letter to his parents as soon as he had been well enough to hold a quill, explaining all that had happened. He'd only had one other opportunity to get a letter to them since he was pressed into service and that was over seven months ago. As far as they knew, he was alive but still in the British Navy. He knew they would be happy to hear he was now safe and no longer aboard the *Briareus*, especially in light of recent events that would most certainly lead to war. He longed to hear how things were at home and was especially concerned about what might have happened to Thomas, but he knew it was much too soon to expect a reply. He still felt guilty for having not delivered Mr. Hampton's letter, even though he knew it had not been his fault. Nevertheless, he felt he had failed. He hoped that failure had not brought harm to Thomas, or to anybody else for that matter.

In spite of these anxieties, Christopher was enjoying his stay with the Pierce family, particularly the time spent with Marion. On Wednesday afternoon of the third week, he and Marion were sitting in the garden discussing one of the many volumes from Captain Pierce's library. It was a book of poetry. Christopher had never cared much for poetry, but this afternoon he appreciated it. It was giving them a reason to be together and that was enough.

It was a beautiful sunny day with only a few isolated clouds drifting slowly along in the blue sky. Assurances that spring had come to stay were everywhere. The daffodils that had been in their glory the week before were beginning to give way to the irises and peonies. Other, late spring flowers were starting to take their turn as days became longer and the breezes warmer. But Christopher's attention was not so much on the signs of spring as they were on Marion. She was wearing a simple yellow taffeta dress with few frills. It was attractive but not distractive. His thoughts were focused on her.

At Marion's suggestion they were taking turns reading aloud from the book. They had just finished discussing the last poem Marion had read and it was again Christopher's turn. He opened the book to Richard Lovelace's "To Lucasta, on Going to the Wars" and began to read:

> "Tell me not, sweet, I am unkind,
> That from the nunnery
> Of thy chaste breast and quite mind
> To war and arms I fly.
>
> True, a new mistress now I chase,
> The first foe in the field;
> And with a stronger faith embrace
> A sword, a horse, a shield.
>
> Yet this inconstancy is such
> As you, too, shall adore;
> I could not love thee, dear, so much,
> Loved I not honour more."

"Oh Christopher, that's so beautiful." She turned and looked directly into his eyes. She appeared deeply concerned. "But it's so sad."

He'd not seen her express such feeling before, but even in such seriousness she was all the more beautiful. He started to speak but before he could do so she placed her hand on his.

"Christopher, which would you love the more? You wouldn't prefer to go off to some nasty, old war than to be with me would you?"

He was speechless; such words, such thoughts. He felt so very light, completely oblivious to everything else around them. For that moment all that counted in the world was just the two of them. She did care about him. She must. Why else would she have said such a thing? He gathered new courage and began to speak. "Marion, I . . . "

Suddenly, a commotion within the house attracted their attention. As they turned to see what was going on, Molly appeared at the rear door and yelled, "Papa's home! Papa and Jacob are home!"

"Come on," said Marion as she jumped up, took Christopher's arm and started toward the door.

Christopher's emotions were mixed and left dangling. He didn't want the conversation to end but neither did he know how to keep it going. At least he knew she cared for him. He consoled himself, "Another time will come. I'll be better prepared."

He felt a little apprehensive as they rushed to the house. He'd come to know Mrs. Pierce and her daughters fairly well but his only contact with Captain Pierce had been the one, rather limited conversation when he first awoke after his rescue. He'd never met Marion's brother Jacob. It felt especially strange meeting someone for the first time while wearing that person's clothes.

Christopher and Marion entered the house to find Captain Pierce, Mrs. Pierce, Molly and Jacob all embracing and talking at the same time. Marion immediately joined in. It was obvious, that here was a family in which the members cared for each other and were not afraid to show it. This made Christopher even more ill at ease for he was being completely ignored, although he certainly understood the situation.

However, the commotion did not last long and as the noise died down Captain Pierce turned toward Christopher and asked, "And how is our visitor from Maryland?"

"Very well. Thank you, sir. I . . . "

"He's doing just fine, Father," injected Marion. "Dr. Finlay says that in one more week he'll be fit as a fiddle."

Looking at the others, then back to Captain Pierce, Christopher spoke. "I don't know how to thank you all. You've done so much for me."

"My goodness," said Mrs. Pierce, "whatever happened to our manners? Christopher, this is our son, Jacob. I almost forgot, you two haven't met."

Jacob smiled and held out a well-calloused hand to Christopher. He was about the same age as Christopher, a bit taller, and had the same dark brown hair and eyes as his sisters. "We've sort of met, but you weren't in too good a shape when I saw you last. Anyway, I'm pleased to meet you, now that you're up and about. So, you really jumped off one of the English ships in Boston Harbor?"

"Yes, I'd been pressed into service almost a year ago. I guess what I did was rather foolish. If it hadn't been for you and your father I'd most certainly be dead right now."

"Foolish or not," said Captain Pierce, "I'm glad you had the courage to do it. We're going to need all the good seamen we can get."

"That's a fact," added Jacob. "The English have the greater numbers but they'll soon discover we Colonials can out sail and out fight them any day."

"Now that's enough of that," declared Mrs. Pierce. "This is no time for talking politics or of fighting. Let's just praise God you and your father have returned safely."

With the subject changed, Christopher said to Jacob, "I feel a little awkward standing here in your clothes. I hope you don't mind my borrowing some of them."

"Of course not," replied Jacob with a sincere smile. "We can't have you running around here in front of my sisters in your birthday suit. Can we?"

"Jacob!" scolded Mrs. Pierce. "You'll embarrass everyone."

"Yes, Mother," said Jacob with a smile. Then to Christopher, "I'm sure there are some other things you can have. I'm pleased to share."

In the week following their return, Captain Pierce and his son proved to be just as gracious and hospitable as Mrs. Pierce and her daughters. Christopher and Jacob very quickly became good friends.

By the middle of the next week Dr. Finlay's prognosis proved to be accurate. Christopher was again fit as a fiddle. And feeling fit, he was becoming more anxious to return home to St. Michaels and his search for Thomas. Although he had become very fond of the Pierce family and would miss them, especially Marion, he felt he shouldn't impose on them any more than was necessary. But what about Marion? In their days together he'd felt himself drawn closer and closer to her. It was a new experience for him and he felt so awkward at expressing himself he simply didn't. He just could not get up the courage to tell her how much he was attracted to her. Somehow, he was certain she felt the same toward him, or was it wishful thinking? If only he had more time. But time was growing short, for as soon as he was able, he had to return home. Nevertheless, one thing was certain, and although he did not know how or when, he would return to Squansett Cove.

The next morning, as they were having their breakfast, the conversation between Captain Pierce and Jacob turned to the ship. Jacob asked, "Did you noticed the shrouds lately? I think they're starting to look a bit worn."

"I noticed that too," replied Captain Pierce. "They should be replaced. It'd be mighty poor economy to lose a mast overboard just trying to make your lines last a little longer. I already asked Doyle to get some tar on board."

"I'll go down and give him a hand," Jacob answered.

"Mind if I go along?" asked Christopher. "I'm starting to feel as useless as . . . ."

"Don't mind at all. I can use the company as well as the help. Are you sure you're up to it?"

"Quite sure."

It was a short walk, less than a quarter mile, down to the small, protected harbor. The houses they passed were neatly kept but seemed to be rather close together, somewhat like those at Annapolis. Christopher surmised it was because of the low, pine covered, rocky hills that rimmed the harbor, a natural barrier to a growing town. As they rounded a corner onto a street that led directly down to the water Jacob stopped and, pointing out toward the middle of the harbor, proudly announced, "There she is, the *Otter*. Isn't she a beauty?"

Christopher had to agree. Out in the middle of the harbor, swinging lazily about her anchor was, a sixty foot topsail schooner, freshly painted dark green with black railings. Her trim lines told Christopher that here was a ship that would not dawdle along even in the slightest breeze. "Looks fast," said Christopher.

"She has to be to out run the British patrols."

"Is anyone aboard?"

"Oh, yes. We've a regular crew of three. Sometimes we take on an extra hand or two. Doyle should be on board; he's probably below. Renck lives here in Squansett Cove; Juan's off on some personal business somewhere."

When they reached the waterfront Christopher saw why the *Otter* had to be anchored out. There was but one pier and there were boats tied up to it on both sides. All were being loaded or unloaded. There was more activity here than he had expected.

As it was, Doyle was not on board but had come ashore to pick up the tar for the standing rigging. He was just lowering the small keg into the dinghy when Jacob spotted him.

"Ahoy! Doyle, wait up," shouted Jacob.

Doyle turned and waved to acknowledge seeing Jacob. Doyle was not an exceptionally large man but gave that appearance because of his muscular build. With his youthful face and smile one would take him to be in his late twenties if it were not for the fact his hair was well on its way to becoming completely gray, and a midsection that seemed more prominent with each passing year. The truth was, Doyle was already in his mid to late forties.

Jacob and Christopher hurried on down to the end of the pier, Jacob exchanging greetings with several acquaintances along the way. By the time they arrived at the dinghy, Doyle had the keg secured in the small boat and was waiting to cast off. As they approached, Doyle eyed Christopher with an expression of polite inquisitiveness.

Jacob spoke, "Well Doyle, does he look any better than when we hauled him on board at Spectacle Island?"

Doyle looked Christopher up and down with a warm smile and extending his hand replied, "A bit haler I'd say, and a whole lot drier. Glad t' see ya up an' about, lad."

Jacob smiled and said, "Christopher, meet Percival Doyle. Doyle meet our new friend Christopher Hall from St. Michaels in Maryland."

"Pleased to meet you, Percival," replied Christopher as he shook Doyle's hand.

"Just call me Doyle," he answered with a smile.

"Well, let's get going," said Jacob as he motioned them to step down into the dinghy. Doyle took up the oars while Christopher sat in the bow. Jacob sat in the stern with the tar keg.

Even with the three of them and the keg loading it down, the small boat seemed to glide across the water as Doyle's muscular arms worked the oars in a steady rhythm. In a very short time they were bumping along side the *Otter*. Christopher made fast the painter to the ladder and steadied the dinghy while Doyle climbed on board to swing out the sling he'd already arranged for hoisting the tar keg onto the deck.

As soon as the keg was on board, Jacob and Christopher followed up the ladder. Stepping foot aboard the schooner reminded Christopher how much he'd missed being on a vessel. There was something good about having a deck under one's feet, with that subtle feel of the water below it. Jacob gave Christopher a quick tour of the ship, then they turned to the task at hand. The three of them worked until late that afternoon replacing worn shrouds and tarring them for protection against the weather.

It was at dinner that evening that Captain Pierce announced he would be making another trip within a few days. "Oh, Abraham, not so soon!" bemoaned Mrs. Pierce.

"I'm afraid so, Rena. Boston's lifeline was the sea and the blockade has made that more apparent than ever. They just can't get enough supplies overland to support them. You know what our roads look like."

"Especially in wet weather," added Jacob.

"Christopher looked puzzled. "How can you help if the ports are closed?"

Captain Pierce laid down his fork and smiled. "They're not all closed. Oh, don't be mistaken, they'd like to seal off the entire coast. But there's even a limit to what the almighty King George and his precious navy can do."

Jacob, apparently enthusiastic over their adventures, spoke up. "There's many a small cove and inlet where a vessel with a shallow draft can off load cargo close enough that wagons can take it the rest of the way. They can't patrol it all, and it's a good thing too for if anyone got caught it would be the gibbet on Nix's Mate or Bird Island for sure."

"That will do," admonished Captain Pierce. "You'll have the women worried half to death."

Christopher sat wondering a bit then asked, "Where will you be going this time?"

"Down to the Delaware."

I was just thinking, sir. You've done so much for me. I wouldn't be alive today but for your finding me on Spectacle Island and for the wonderful care I've received here in your home."

Captain Pierce interrupted, "Now don't concern yourself with that. It's nothing more than any good Christian family would do. Besides, it was a pleasure to snatch one the lion's victims from his clutches."

"I know, sir, and I'll be eternally grateful. But now that I'm back on my feet I don't want to impose upon your hospitality any more than I have to. I was wondering if I could go with you. It would get me very close to home and I could be of help on the way. I'm no stranger to the sea, you know."

Captain Pierce smiled and said, "Of course you can come along.

I was going to suggest the very same thing, though you are welcome to stay here if you wish. We're not chasing you out."

"I'm sure you're not. You've been most gracious." Christopher began to feel the excitement of going home then added, "I will certainly miss all of you. I feel almost like you are family to me."

"We're glad you feel that way, Christopher," added Mrs. Pierce. "You know you will always be welcome here."

"Yes, we'd be most upset if you didn't come see us," said Marion with a tone in her voice that implied more.

Molly, feeling the moment too serious for her usual levity, simply said, "We'll miss you."

Little was said during the remainder of the meal.

CHAPTER VI

It was eerie, gliding along in complete darkness with the only lights being a few dim specks on faraway shores. There was no moon in the sky; it was planned that way. To avoid the British patrols they had to leave in darkness and sail as far as they could before daybreak. They would be vulnerable sailing down the east side of Cape Cod but if they could reach the tip of the cape before dawn they could lay over in Provincetown until nightfall and make the run around the cape under the cloak of darkness.

It was almost midnight and it had been little over an hour since they had cleared the small harbor of Squansett Cove. Although Christopher could see nothing he was enjoying the familiar smell of the sea and the gentle breeze that brushed against his face. They were running before the wind with the mainsail far out on the larboard side. The effective wind across the deck was slight and belied the progress they were making across the bay. Only the sound of the black water rushing along the *Otter*'s sides gave any indication of speed through this dark void.

As he stood there in the darkness leaning against the starboard rail, he could not help wondering what might lie just ahead, rocks . . . a sand bar . . . another ship? He could see nothing, but neither Captain Pierce nor the others seemed overly concerned. He placed his confidence in Captain Pierce's experience and began to think about what lay even further ahead. What will it be like, coming home after all this time? Was everyone well? Was there any news of Thomas? How did the people in St. Michaels feel about the recent events in New England?

Suddenly Captain Pierce's voice cut through the darkness. "Make ready to change course. We've just about cleared Nantasket."

Christopher looked around but all he could see were shadows moving about in preparation for the change. Doyle was at the wheel, Jacob and the other two crewmen, Elias Renck and Juan Tortosa, were getting the appropriate lines ready so they could quickly reset the sails when Captain Pierce gave the order.

Christopher had not met these other two crewmen until that very night when he came on board, and only then, when they were below decks in the light of the cabin lantern, did he see them. Elias Renck was a young man of twenty-eight. He was a little over five feet tall, not heavy but he possessed what one could call a full body. His broad face was usually fixed in a friendly smile that portrayed his jovial nature. He had lived in Squansett Cove all his life and married his childhood sweetheart, Hannah Lester, just three years ago. They had since been blessed with a baby girl who was now sixteen months old and the prettiest baby ever born, to hear Elias tell it.

The other crewman, Juan Felipe' Maria Alverado de Tortosa, was tall and lean with black hair, a mustache and small beard that gave him an unusual air of Castilian dignity. No one knew much about his background except that as a young Spanish adventurer he had arrived in Cuba just a few weeks before the British took Havana in 1762. He had made the mistake of venturing too close to the waterfront one night and was caught by a press gang. In the following ten years he was forced to serve aboard three different British warships and was finally aboard the armed revenue schooner Gaspee in June of 1772 when it was chasing a smuggler into Narragansett Bay. The Gaspee went too far, ran aground in the dark and was unable to get free. It fell easy prey to Rhode Island patriots who burned it to the waterline. The Sons of Liberty were jubilant, Parliament was outraged and Juan Tortosa was free.

Captain Pierce peered into the darkness, first to the right and then to the left. After a minute he repeated the act then said in a confident voice, "All right, ease off the topsail braces. Take in the lee braces." Turning to Doyle at the wheel, he said, "Steer sou'east by east."

As Doyle slowly turned the wheel the *Otter* began to point its bow more toward the south. To the accompanying sounds of lines running through squeaking blocks, the square topsail began pivoting to the left, seeking its proper position for the new course.

Without any further orders being given, Christopher followed Jacob's lead and the two began winching in the main sheet to give the large mainsail the best angle to catch the wind. Juan and Elias, having finished setting the topsail, turned to trimming the foresail and jib. Fortunately, the *Otter* had already been sailing with all canvas set and the changes required for the new course were neither great nor difficult.

In a very short time the *Otter* settled in on her new course. With the wind now coming in on the starboard beam the schooner was heeling well to larboard and slicing through the black night considerably faster than before. An occasional bit of spray breaking over the lee rail heralded their new rate of progress.

Shortly after they had secured from changing course Jacob replaced Doyle at the wheel so he and the other two could go below and get some sleep. Captain Pierce had lit his pipe and as he stood there, next to Jacob, the orange glow dimly revealed a pleased and smiling face. "Well, Christopher," said the captain, "let's you and I go forward and keep an eye out for trouble. We'll let the others rest for now. They'll relieve us in two hours. Stay away from the binnacle light so it doesn't spoil your vision. You watch to starboard I'll take the other side."

After they were settled in their places as lookouts Christopher said to the Captain, "I was wondering how you can tell where you are out here in such complete darkness. Isn't it dangerous among all these islands and shoals? And how did you know we'd passed, what did you call it, Nantasket?"

The Captain chuckled and answered, "You're right it would be very dangerous if we didn't have help."

"What help? I don't understand."

"What did you see as we were crossing the bay?"

"Nothing, nothing but a few lights on the shore very far away."

"That, my friend from Maryland, is the help I speak of. They might look like innocent lights from the homes of ignorant rebels, but we've arranged to have certain patterns of light serve as range markers."

"So that's how you do it."

"Yes, and the British don't know about it and wouldn't know the meaning of the patterns if they did."

For the next six hours the *Otter* plowed on toward the tip of Cape Cod through the darkness and ever increasing swells. She was a well-built schooner and met the onrushing mounds of water without spilling a bit of air from her sails. At three o'clock they had changed the watch and Christopher and Jacob went below for their turn to rest. Captain Pierce remained on deck.

With all the excitement Christopher found it quite difficult to get to sleep. It seemed he'd just dozed off when a stomping on the deck overhead was followed by Captain Pierce announcing they were nearing Provincetown Harbor. Christopher and Jacob quickly donned their shoes and joined the others on deck. As Christopher emerged on deck he could see a few lights off the larboard beam. They seemed to be not far away but passing rather slowly. The wind had died down considerably and the water was much calmer than before.

"'Tis a good thing we got here when we did," said Captain Pierce. The wind's almost gone. We'd not want to be caught bobbin' about in open water in broad daylight. The inquisitive British would like nothin' better than to poke their nose into our business and give us a difficult time."

"Will we be safe in Provincetown?" asked Christopher.

"We'll not be safe anywhere from those rascals, just safer than out in the open," replied the Captain. "There's usually a few fishing boats here. Enough to keep us from being conspicuous, I hope."

"How long will we stay?" asked Christopher.

"Just until nightfall. We'll need all the darkness we can get to cover our run down the outer side of the cape. Unfortunately, this time of year the nights are short." Then raising his voice so all could hear he said, "Now, stand by to come about so we can enter the harbor."

Soon all the necessary maneuvering was completed and they were inside the harbor anchored among half a dozen other boats and enjoying a breakfast of beef and cold potatoes that Mrs. Pierce had packed for them.

The sun rose quickly over the strip of land that lay between them and the open sea. When it had adequately detached itself from the horizon it assumed a more languid pace and proceeded to creep across the sky. Its intense rays beat down upon the bare deck of the *Otter* making it too uncomfortable to sleep below so Juan rigged an awning on the foc'sle under which they could try to get some rest. The night that lay ahead could be a trying one so rest it must be.

By the middle of the afternoon it had become too hot to sleep anywhere and because they had only been out for less than a day there was nothing that had to be done on the *Otter*. With Renck remaining on board, the rest went ashore. Captain Pierce took his glass with him and as soon as they were on land he went off in the direction of a rise of land from which he could view the sea to the east. Although they had already sailed nearly fifty nautical miles, they would not be clear of the British blockade until they were past the long outer stretch of Cape Cod. Doyle led the rest into a nearby tavern for some refreshment and to obtain whatever information he could about recent British ship sightings. Later, when they all met to return to the schooner the Captain announced the only things he saw were a few sails moving north, nothing in the south or headed that way.

Doyle's report was not as encouraging. The people in the tavern had told him a British revenue cutter had been stopping at Provincetown every four or five days and was expected to be there tomorrow.

"That leaves us no choice," said Captain Pierce. "We have to continue on tonight. Just pray that the Lord and the weather are both with us. Now, let's get back aboard and make ready to sail."

When the sun approached the western horizon and started to sink behind the strip of land that curved south and then east to form the harbor, the *Otter* weighed anchor. The small anchorage was becoming a little more crowded because of the local fishing boats returning from their days work, but there was still sufficient light and room to allow the schooner to maneuver its way out with ease. As they were working their way northward around Long Point, Christopher could see the remainder of the sun being reflected in some of the windows on the shore. The orange-red brilliance made it appear the houses were aflame. But this was beginning to grow dimmer and soon the only light remaining was a dull glow in the west where the sun had finally disappeared. By the time they had sailed back around the outermost point of the cape and were again on a southerly course it was again completely dark.

It had seemed a long night, working their way down the coast of Cape Cod, knowing that if they were spotted by a British patrol from the east they would be trapped between it and a long, straight coast that allowed only a few places in which to seek refuge. Instead of sailing nearer the shore they had steered a course south by east, in order to clear the Monomoy Shoals. The area south of the Cape and around Martha's Vineyard abounded in shoals and reefs, which Captain Pierce had pointed out to Christopher on his charts. When Christopher had asked how dangerous they were the captain said, "They can be your worst enemy if you're not careful, but if the Brits are chasing you and you know your way through 'em they can be your salvation."

As Christopher stood by the rail watching the eastern sky begin to grow a warm yellow it reminded him of the yellow dress Marion had been wearing that day in the garden when she placed her hand on his and expressed her fears concerning love and war. He remembered the feeling that had swept over him and could even now experience some of that feeling every time he thought of her. As with most people, the center of his universe was home and the people he loved there. But now, even though he didn't think of it in so many words, there was a feeling his universe now had two centers. He was surprised to admit to himself that his thoughts, and perhaps even his heart, was being drawn back to Squansett Cove as much as it was toward home in St. Michaels.

"You like her, don't you?"

Christopher was startled, he'd not seen Jacob come up beside him. "Huh, what? What do you mean?"

"I mean Marion, my sister. You like her, don't you? I mean more than just as a friend."

"Why . . . why yes I like her," stammered Christopher, taken aback by Jacob's straight forward question. He looked back to where the sun was about to appear and then down at the railing, not wanting to look Jacob in the eye over such a delicate matter as his feelings for his sister.

"Hey, it's all right. I've seen you two together. Some things you can't hide, even when you think you can. You're all right, Christopher; I like you. If you and Marion want to make eyes at each other it's fine with me. But, I ought to warn you, she can be a tease."

"I don't think she's a tease," retorted Christopher instantly, somewhat surprised at his own boldness.

"Whoa, don't get me wrong," said Jacob, a little surprised at Christopher's defensiveness. "Marion and I have always been very close. I'd never say anything against her. It's just that at times she appears to be more serious than she really is."

"I do like her. Yes, as a matter of fact, I'm quite fond of her and I hope she feels something for me," confessed Christopher. He felt he may as well be honest about it. Besides, it was a relief to have someone with whom he could share his feelings. He pushed himself back from the railing while still holding on, then leaned forward again and peered down into the water. The bow wave was beginning to glitter in the bright rays from the sun just peaking over the horizon. Christopher studied the helter-skelter movement in the wave and felt his chances with Marion were about as long lived as the confused bits of foam and droplets that skittered about momentarily before disappearing into the sea again. "The problem is, I don't have much to offer a girl like Marion."

"Like what?" asked Jacob.

"You know, a home and security. The things a woman has a right to expect from whomever she marries. I've no money and no trade to speak of. All I've ever done is fish on my father's boat back in Maryland. I know a little about the sea, thanks to a British press gang. I think she's used to a great deal more than I can ever offer."

"Well, my advice to you is to let her be the judge of that. Christopher, great things are happening around us. The colonies have always been a place of great opportunities and now a new nation is starting to rise from it, a great nation, if I can have my guess. There oughtn't to be any limit on what a young fellow can make of himself."

"Things are happening all right," agreed Christopher. "I'm afraid I've not been able to grasp it all."

"There's one thing you can be sure of, we're never goin' back to bein' King George's stepchild again. Father says that with independence from England the American colonies can grow into one of the greatest nations on earth. I know that's a pretty hard thing to swallow when you look around but father says we have three of the greatest assets a new nation could ask for—land, good harbors and a willingness to work. We have plenty of the first two. People like us can provide the third."

"That we can," agreed Christopher.

Captain Pierce, having approached and hearing the last of the conversation, added, "It's like that sun over there. A minute ago all you could see was a tiny bit of it, and for the most part, the world was still dark. Now look at it."

They all three turned to see that the sun had completely risen and was casting its brilliance across both sea and sky.

"Land Ho. Two points off t' starboard," cried Juan from where he had perched himself half way up the ratlines on the mainmast.

"That'll be Nantucket Island," said Captain Pierce.

"Will we be changing course?" asked Christopher, straining to see the low island just visible on the horizon to the right.

"Not just yet. Even though this course is still taking us further east, we need to hold this course a while to clear the Monomoy Shoals and then the Nantucket Shoals. There's some pretty treacherous water just east of Nantucket. I'd just as soon stay out of it."

It was late in the morning when the *Otter* had sailed far enough past the shoal waters of Nantucket that a course change could safely be made. The new course, southwest, was taking them back toward the coast and their destination but also closer to the wind which was directly out of the west. They were now beating to windward on a starboard tack and throwing water as the sleek schooner knifed through the challenging swells. Juan had been relieved as lookout by Elias who was now positioned above the topsail yardarm. Not a sail had been sighted since sun up; they were lucky. But, as they were drawing closer to the approaches to New York, extreme caution was required for it was in this area they had the greatest chance of being spotted by a British ship.

It came all too soon, just a little more than an hour after the course change. The dreaded cry was heard. "Sail to starboard," yelled Elias from his perch.

"Where away?" yelled the Captain.

"Two points off the starboard bow," answered Elias. "Believe she's comin' this way. Can't be sure without a glass."

Captain Pierce took his telescope from the box by the wheel where it is stored for ready use. Grim faced and without a word he climbed up the ratlines to join Elias.

After several long minutes he returned to the deck, leaving the telescope aloft with Elias. Without a word he walked to the binnacle, studied the compass, then after taking another look toward the strange sail he announced, "She's too far away to tell what she is, but she's on an easterly course."

Jacob expressed everyone's thoughts when he asked, "What should we do?"

"If we hold our course she'll pass astern on our starboard quarter." The captain thought for a moment then added, "But I'm afraid that'll be too close for comfort. With luck they may not have seen us yet. Let's put some distance between us." Raising his voice he announced, "Get ready to come about." To Doyle, who was manning the helm, he said, "We'll change course to sou'east. We'll be on the same tack with the wind more aft." Looking up and with his hands cupped around his mouth he yelled for Elias to return to the deck.

When everyone was at his appointed station Captain Pierce began to give the necessary orders for the *Otter* to turn ninety degrees to the left. First, the fore and mainsails were eased off to where they began to luff. Then the same was done to the jib and fore staysail. With that done it was safe to begin swinging the bow over to the new course. "Bring o'er your helm," ordered the captain in a loud and crisp voice in order to be heard above the fluttering sails. To the others, "Ease off the lee braces, haul in the windward."

The large topsail was kept at the same angle to the wind while the *Otter* was allowed to slowly turn beneath it to the new course. With that accomplished, attention was turned to a final trimming of the other sails. All in all it took surprisingly little time for such a small crew. The schooner was now heeling over more but moving well on her new course. Even before all sheets and braces were secured, Captain Pierce turned to Jacob and said, "Take the glass and go aloft. Keep a sharp eye on them. Let me know the second there's any change."

Jacob had hardly settled in his perch above the tops'l yard when the white speck on the horizon began to change appearance. After a minute's scrutiny with the telescope he yelled down, "She's changin' course to starboard. Looks like a small brig . . . might be a sloop-o-war. Got all sails set and movin' fast." He studied the strange vessel some more and came to the conclusion they had feared. "She's tryin' to cut us off," he added.

Down on the deck everyone turned to the captain. They said nothing, the expressions of their faces spoke for them. "We'll hold this course for a while. They might just be trying to steer clear of the Nantucket Shoals. Those not real familiar with 'em generally give 'em a wide berth."

Christopher asked, "Do you really think that's the case?"

Captain Pierce looked first at the distant set of white sails that was slowly appearing larger and then at Christopher. "No, I don't think so. I'm just hoping it is." After a moment's contemplation he spoke again, "Trouble is they've got the wind gauge. With our fore 'n aft rig we could out run 'em on a beat to windward but with the wind behind 'em their square sails give 'em the advantage."

For more than an hour the two vessels continued on converging courses. As they watched the stranger off their starboard quarter gradually appear larger it became apparent to everyone on board the *Otter* that the other ship was not avoiding the shoals but clearly trying to intercept them, and that she was a sloop-of-war. The converging courses had brought them to within six miles of each other with the sloop gaining on them all the time. The wind, which was shifting more to the northwest, was still pushing the sloop along at an alarming rate. It was pressing on and on under a full set of sails with its bow down, throwing spray high over its foc'sle. It was a beautiful although threatening sight.

Several times Captain Pierce had to give the order to ease out the main and fore sheets out to accommodate the shifting wind. They were now running before the wind with the sails far out, the slowest situation they could be in, other than being becalmed. Even the swells were beginning to pass them up.

For a long time they all watched the approaching sloop in silence. Then Christopher asked, "What do you suppose they'll do if they catch us?"

Captain Pierce answered, "At best, they'll come aboard to inspect us and finding nothing let us go. Fortunately, we've only ballast, no cargo for them to seize."

"The chances o' that are slim," added Doyle.

"I have to agree," said the captain. "They'll most likely confiscate the ship and press us into service."

Almost at once, both Christopher and Juan, realized their fate if the *Otter* were captured. Both, having been in the British Navy, albeit involuntarily, would likely find themselves hanging from a yardarm as examples for would-be deserters.

Captain Pierce had already thought of what would lie ahead for the two if they were caught. "Don't worry lads, we're not going to let 'em catch us." Suddenly he raised his voice and ordered, "Ready to furl the tops'l."

They all stared at the captain incredulously. Jacob expressed their disbelief, "What? Shorten sail?"

"Don't fret. We're not givin' up," assured the captain with a smile on his face that did not completely erase the worry that had been there. "By trying to cut us off they must have got a good three miles south of us. With the wind now out of the northwest we can quickly turn west on a beat, close hauled. The *Otter* can sail to forty five degrees of the wind. But not with the topsail out."

"And our friend over there?" asked Elias, pointing to the sloop still racing on far out on their starboard beam. "What'll he be doin'?"

"He'll have to change course immediately to northeast and come directly at us to have any chance of catching us. That's as close as he can get to the wind. I don't think he can maneuver that fast with all those sails set," explained the captain. "The good Lord willin', he'll pass to the stern of us and after that we'll have the wind gauge and its goodbye."

Simultaneously, smiles broke out on their faces. Where a few moments ago depression reigned, enthusiasm now ruled.

"Now get ready. This has to be done quickly to give our 'friend' over there as little time possible to respond." With that, the captain began the series of commands that would execute the maneuver he had just outlined.

As soon as the square topsail had been secured, all hands turned to making ready the other sails for the anticipated course change. When the order was given, Doyle, with his large hands on the wheel, pulled hard and quickly on its spokes to initiate the one hundred thirty-five degree turn to the right. The *Otter* turned and heeled far on its larboard side. The others did well to maintain their footing while handling the sails, but the job was done in an amazingly short time. The *Otter* was now in its element, racing along on a close hauled beat to the west and aimed at the spot the sloop had passed over only a short time before.

It did not take the captain of the sloop long to realize what Captain Pierce was trying to do. Men were clamoring aloft in response to threatening shouts from the sailing master and bos'n mate on deck below them. With a screeching of blocks and sheaves and the thunderous sound of masses of canvas being repositioned in the wind the sloop-of-war ponderously turned to the left and pointed directly at the *Otter*. Although it had taken the sloop much longer to alter course than it did the *Otter*, Captain Pierce was surprised at the efficiency and speed with which its crew performed.

The two ships were now racing toward a common point. The *Otter* must pass that point well ahead of the warship to avoid the reach of its guns. Once past that point escape would almost be a certainty, for the fore-n-aft rigged schooner could easily outrun the square rigged sloop on a windward course.

Until now, the situation had been one of slow suspense, but now things were happening at a breathtaking pace. There would be little time for mistakes. The two ships were closing fast. Minutes flew by and the approaching warship grew larger and larger. Through the telescope Captain Pierce could see their gun ports being opened.

The *Otter* seemed to throw herself forward, plunging and slicing through each oncoming swell. She was on a starboard tack and heeled well to larboard which caused her large sails to sometimes obscure the approaching menace.

"Think we'll make it?" asked Juan, knowing quite well what his fate would be if they didn't.

"It's gonna be close," said Jacob, looking at his father for confirmation.

SET A COURSE FOR FREEDOM

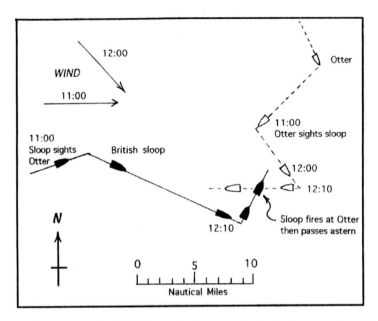

"Very close," added Captain Pierce as he looked up at the sails and pennant to see if the wind was still from the northwest and had not forsaken them. "They might even get close enough to get off a shot or two at us."

The distance between the two ships was getting smaller and smaller but there was nothing more they could do except pray the wind would hold. Suddenly there was a puff of smoke emitted from the bow of the charging warship.

"Stand by, Lads," cried the captain, "they've fired a shot. Seems a bow shot is all they can bring to bear at this angle."

Almost immediately there was a series of splashes in the water in front of them. The warning shot skimmed over the wave tops and finally disappeared into the sea off to the right.

"That was just their invitation to heave-to," said the captain. "The next one's the one that'll count."

The ships sped on with the *Otter* giving no indication of recognizing the enemy's signal. The enemy sloop was sailing as close to the wind as it possibly could but would still only be able to pass behind the *Otter*. Yet, the moment was fast approaching when the distance between the two ships would be at a minimum.

Within a few minutes the *Otter* passed the critical point where the two courses intersected. They were now upwind of the enemy and speeding away westward. Doyle remained at the helm, while the others stood by the stern rail, their eyes transfixed on the approaching attacker. A rustling of canvas drew their attention forward. The jib sail had began to luff and needed to be sheeted in a bit. Without a word being spoken Jacob and Juan went forward to perform the task.

The British sloop-of-war raced on and was less than a cable's length away as it crossed behind the *Otter*. It was a trim ship and appeared to be well maintained, as it was the custom of the British Royal Navy. Its shining black hull was accentuated by a wide, yellow stripe, above which, were six dark squares. Its gun ports were all open. It was a handsome ship in spite of the threat it posed. Suddenly its whole left side was engulfed in a cloud of smoke pierced by bright orange shafts of flame.

"Here it comes," said Captain Pierce in a calm voice, typical of those announcing the inevitable.

Instantly, geysers of water rose all around them. For a moment they thought they would remain unscathed. Then there was a sharp cracking sound overhead, followed by the sound of splintering wood and parting rigging. As they turned, they saw the tops'l yardarm come crashing to the deck.

With Renck manning the helm the rest raced forward to free the wreckage. Juan, with a horrified expression on his face, was trying to lift the broken spar by himself. When they reached the spot, they saw the cause of his horror. Beneath the heavy yardarm was the motionless body of Jacob, his face a pale white in contrast to the trickle of blood coming from his mouth.

"Mother of God!" cried Elias.

"Hurry!" said Juan, "I think he's still alive."

They went to work instantly cutting away the tangled rigging so they could lift the wreckage out of the way. It was a task that could receive their complete attention for now the *Otter* was speeding to windward with the enemy falling farther and farther behind.

With the pile of canvas and cordage out of the way they lifted the spar from Jacob. At once, the captain was at his side holding his son's head in his arms. The shock of what they saw numbed Christopher. Jacob's body had been crushed by the falling timber.

The captain, gently held his son's broken body, knowing there was no hope. "Jacob, my boy," he pleaded, praying for a response.

Jacob slowly opened his eyes and looked up at his father. His eyes revealed the depth of his pain and confusion.

Drawing upon year's of fatherly love, the distraught captain managed to force an encouraging smile as he spoke to his only and dying son. "Jacob, my boy, it's all right."

Jacob closed his eyes then opened them again for the last time and whispered, "Did we make it, Father?"

"Yes, my son, we made it."

CHAPTER VII

As the sun rose over a glassy sea revealing the low, rolling coastline of Rhode Island, the *Otter* lay motionless on the still waters outside Narragansett Bay. Her formless sails hung waiting for the breeze that would give them life while the crew completed preparations for getting underway. It had taken the crippled schooner fourteen hours, beating to windward, to reach the mouth of the bay. Because they had arrived shortly after midnight Captain Pierce decided to stand off shore and wait for daylight before going in to seek refuge at Newport.

They went about their tasks silently, each feeling and sharing in the captain's grief. Jacob's body had been taken down to the after cabin right after they had escaped the British sloop. Captain Pierce stayed below with his son for almost an hour before coming back on deck where he remained until now. His only words since the tragedy where those just necessary to manage his vessel. But the expression on his face spoke for him. It gave the appearance of being cut from stone, except for the eyes. They revealed something more than the grief that was now tormenting his soul. Deep down inside there was a seething mixture of anger and resolve, building a force that would not soon disappear and would most assuredly affect the lives of many others.

During the quiet of the night Christopher had reflected on the events that had occurred. Had he been responsible for Jacob's death? Was it because he and Juan were aboard and faced a hangman's noose for desertion that the Captain chose to run rather than heave-to and be boarded for inspection? Would Jacob still be alive if he'd not been with them? He wondered if Juan was asking himself the same question. But Juan had been in the crew for years and was probably forgotten by the British by now. No, Juan had not put them in jeopardy. It had only been he, Christopher himself, that had endangered them all, for only he had recently escaped and his description most likely had been spread throughout the fleet. He had brought this upon the family that had saved his life and nursed him back to health.

These are questions he asked himself again and again until he had finally convinced himself this was the case. As he stood leaning against the starboard rail, looking at nothing, but lost in thought, he remembered the familiar words from the Bible: "For God so loved the world, that he gave his only begotten Son, that whosoever believeth in Him should not perish . . . " A chill swept over him as he considered the parallel; and suddenly, both situations took on greater meaning.

The sun was now clear of the horizon and the morning calm was finally and suddenly ending. Ripples began to race across the smooth water, replacing the inverted image of the shoreline with millions of sparkling reflections of sunlight. The sails began to stir as gentle puffs of air reached them. Gradually the wind increased, reluctantly, at first, but then with increasing vigor. The masses of canvas filled then collapsed, filled then collapsed, as though they were awakening from a long sleep. Suddenly, and with a loud snap, they billowed out and maintained their shape. The *Otter* began to move.

With the wind from the southwest they were able to enter the harbor without having to tack. Doyle was at the helm, Captain Pierce was checking various range marks, and Juan was pointing out certain landmarks to Christopher. They had already passed Castle Hill on the starboard and were almost abreast of Dumplin Point on Conanicut Island to larboard. Juan pointed to the shore ahead and slightly to starboard, "Brenton Point over there . . . forms a hook that makes Newport Harbor."

Christopher peered in that direction and holding his hand up to shade his eyes from the glistening morning sun said, "Doesn't look like a point." Then as he could see the more distant shoreline passing behind it he said, "Oh yes, I can see it now." He then began to scan the shoreline from right to left and up toward the head of the bay. "How far up does the bay go?" he asked.

"All the way to Providence I'm told but I don't know how far that is," replied Juan.

"About twenty miles," injected Captain Pierce who had come up behind them.

They turned to see the captain gesturing toward the north with his pipe as though he were an artist painting a picture. "The Blackstone River comes down from the north and becomes the Seekonk River for a short piece until it reaches the town of Providence. It then becomes the Providence River for a few more miles before widening into Narragansett Bay. Not as big as your Chesapeake, Chris, but it's a mighty fine protected bay and probably the busiest for many a mile, north or south."

"We'll need to be tightening sail as we come around the point, Captain," reminded Juan. "Best we be ready."

Without another word Juan and Christopher joined Elias who was already preparing the lines for the maneuver that would take them toward the town of Newport. The task would be easier without having to change the tops'l; its damaged spar having been securely lashed to the deck. They were no sooner ready than the captain gave the word for Doyle to change course. As the crippled schooner's bow swung slowly to the right the sails were brought in closer for the new course, where the wind would be coming in over their starboard quarter. In response, the *Otter* heeled over more to larboard and the increased sound of the water running along the lee told them they had picked up a little speed.

With the lines now secured and the *Otter* moving sprightly toward what should be their destination, Christopher searched for the town but could see nothing of it.

Perceiving Christopher's bewilderment, the captain said, "It's there. What you're looking at now is Goat Island. It lies in front of the town providing extra protection from the sea. That's why this is such a good harbor."

"I see," said Christopher.

"Christopher . . . " Captain Pierce turned to look straight at Christopher. There was sorrow in the man's eyes as he tried to form the words he wanted to say.

Christopher's heart ached for this man. In the short time that he had known the captain he had come to recognize many of the traits he admired in his own father. He had even begun to feel a certain kinship towards this man and his grief touched Christopher deeply.

"Christopher, I . . . I have something to ask of you."

Christopher's puzzled expression could not hide his surprise at the captain's groping for words. This was a captain who was used to making instant decisions and knowing what orders and commands must be given in any situation. "Yes, sir. Of course, sir. What is it?"

"Christopher, I want Jacob buried at home, at Squansett Cove. But I want to ride on ahead to prepare his mother and the girls. If I arrange for his body . . . " he paused and turned to wipe a tear from his eye. It hurt to talk of his only son as a body. It was all he could do to maintain his composure, reminding himself he was supposed to be a man of strength, but knowing all the while he was on the edge of breaking down. He took a deep breath and summoning a strength from deep down within himself he continued. "Christopher, if I arrange for Jacob to be transported back to Squansett Cove will you be kind enough to accompany him? I know it's a lot . . . "

Christopher placed his hand on the captain's arm and said, "Of course, Captain. I consider it an honor."

The Captain put his arms around Christopher and sobbing softly, whispered, "Thank you, Christopher, thank you."

Two more small maneuvers and they were around the southern end of Goat Island with the Newport's waterfront lying directly ahead. The town lay in a low area between the hilly neck that went out to Castle Hill and Brenton Point on the right and a stretch of lower hills on the left. The long waterfront was lined with a multitude of small buildings typical of those necessary to maintain shipping. Numerous wharves jutted out into the water like fingers grasping the many vessels tied up along side them. Through the forest of masts and spars could be seen some of the larger and more prominent buildings, especially Trinity Church with its impressive, tall, white spire. Higher and farther away on the right stood a stone windmill with arms slowly circling in response to the same breeze that was pushing the *Otter* closer to its anchorage.

The *Otter* slowly and carefully plied its way through the boats and ships already anchored in the harbor until it reached an open area off the far right end of the town. Captain Pierce turned to Elias at the helm and said, "This will do. Starboard, into the wind!" The *Otter* turned sharply around and pointed directly into the wind as the rest of the crew hauled in the sheets. The air spilled from the sails and they began to flutter like large heavy flags, accompanied by the lashing about and clatter of loose lines and blocks. At the instant the vessel coasted to a stop, Captain Pierce gave the command, "Let go the anchor!" There was a loud splash forward followed by the slap and whine of the line running rapidly through the hawse pipe. Suddenly it stopped and went slack, then, as the *Otter* drifted back with the wind, the line drew tight and a slight shudder was felt throughout the ship. "She's holdin'," cried the captain. "Drop the sails. Heads'ls and fores'ls first."

As the dinghy moved closer to the shore, lurching with each pull on the oars by Doyle's strong arms, the Captain sat solemnly in the stern while Christopher, perched in the bow, earnestly studied every detail of the approaching waterfront. First came the aromas of shore life: wood smoke, food being cooked, decaying sea life at the water's edge, and of course, the ever present odors of animal life for almost everywhere Christopher looked he could see horse drawn wagons delivering or picking up goods from the ships. This was soon followed by a cacophony of sounds: the squeaking of block and tackle and the thud on wooden decks as cargoes were moved back and forth, the clatter of wagon wheels on cobble stones, the pounding of hammers and the chorus of voices that directed these activities.

Every pier appeared to have its capacity of ships or boats down each side. After some searching, Captain Pierce spotted a place to tie up at the end of one pier. He directed Doyle toward it and soon the small craft was deftly brought alongside the spot. The pier towered above them and the exposed barnacles on the pilings told them the tide was out. Christopher grabbed the slippery wooden ladder and tied the bowline to a rung high enough to allow for the rising tide. He then climbed up and awaited the others.

When the three where together, Captain Pierce said to Doyle, "Christopher and I are going to make arrangements to take Jacob back to Squansett Cove. I also want to catch up on the latest news. You go ahead to McKean's boat works. It's just a few blocks to the right. Tell Mr. McKean what has happened. He knows me. We'll join you as soon as we can. Tell him I want the *Otter* repaired as soon as humanly possible."

As Doyle went off to the right toward McKean's boat works, Captain Pierce led Christopher in the other direction toward the center of town. Walking along Thames Street Christopher soon came to the conclusion there was even more activity in Newport than he had ever seen in Annapolis. Often they had to step into the street to continue their progress and twice Christopher had to jump out of the way of a wagon hurrying off with goods just unloaded from one of the many ships and boats.

"Watch yourself, lad," admonished Captain Pierce. "Too much gawking will get you run down."

"Yes, sir. This is most certainly a busy place," replied Christopher. But he continued to take in all that was around him. His attention was torn between the forest of masts and spars on his left and the numerous and interesting shops and business establishments on his right.

After they had walked about a half mile, with Christopher wondering why they had gone so far, Captain Pierce motioned to his right and said, "This way. If there's any information to be had we'll most likely find it at the 'White Horse'."

Christopher saw they were turning on to Marlborough Street. And after two blocks, at the corner of Farewell Street, they were standing in front of a tavern from which hung the large outline sign of a white horse.

"Come," said the captain as he led the way into the tavern.

The tavern was crowded and noisy with pipe smoke drifting in layers across the room. Every table was occupied. They went directly to the bar where a rather short man was mechanically wiping the bar with large circular motions. "Good Day, Gentlemen. What be your pleasure?"

"Two pints, if you please," replied the captain who then turned to scrutinize the occupants of the tavern. With the exception of two nicely dressed women accompanied by two gentlemen whose apparel indicated they were men of some substance, the room was occupied solely by men. Many of these had the appearance of sea farers.

As the barkeep set the mugs in front of them, he asked, "Will there be anything else, Gov'nor?"

"Yes, two things. First, bring us something to eat, some beef perhaps and some bread. The other, can you tell me where I can hire a wagon and driver to go to Squansett Cove?"

"I might, if I knew where Squansett Cove was. I'm afraid I've not heard of it, sir."

"It's in Massachusetts, south of Boston town," answered Captain Pierce.

"In that case I might be able to help you on both counts." He pointed across the room to where three men were getting up to leave. "Just rest yourselves at yon table and I'll be about your needs."

It was not long after Christopher and the captain had seated themselves at the table that a young girl arrived with a platter containing not only cold beef and bread but also some cheese and apples. "Will there be anything else, sir?" she asked the captain, all the while keeping her eyes on Christopher.

"No, that will be all, thank you," said the captain while smiling at Christopher who was showing some discomfort at the girl's undue attention to him.

As she walked away, the captain said, "I believe she takes a shines to you, Christopher."

Christopher did not reply but felt his face grow hot. He was sure he was blushing. He tore off a piece of bread and began to eat, feeling it was worth a little bit of embarrassment on his part to see the smile it evoked on the captain's face, short lived though it was.

Suddenly a loud voice behind them boomed, "Abraham! Abraham Pierce, you old weasel." They both turned to see a monster of a man standing behind them. He was well over six feet tall and heavy built but not fat. His clean shaven, ruddy face matched his flaming red hair and bore a smile from ear to ear. "What are you doin' here? Did you give up blockade runnin' for something more lucrative?"

Captain Pierce rose to greet him. "Caleb . . . Caleb Stone, How are you?" They shook hands in the manner of old friends who seldom meet. "Sit down. Join us."

When they were seated Captain Pierce turned to Christopher and said, "Christopher, I want you to meet one of the orneriest but most capable captains that ever squeezed a quid's worth of profit out of a shilling's worth of cargo."

Christopher, quite bemused by such an introduction, cautiously offered his hand and said, "I'm pleased to meet you, sir."

The stranger grasped it with a hearty shake. "I hope you don't believe everything he tells you, young man. Abraham tends to exaggerate a bit at times."

Captain Pierce continued, "Caleb, I want you to meet Christopher Hall from Maryland."

"My pleasure," replied Caleb. Turning to Captain Pierce, he said, "When I first saw you over here I thought he was Jacob. Isn't he with you?"

There was a moment of silence, then Captain Pierce answered him in a somber voice, "Caleb, Jacob is dead."

As the shock of the news registered on Caleb's face Captain Pierce continued, relating the events that led up to Jacob's being killed.

When Captain Pierce finished the story Caleb brought his massive fist down on the table with a loud thud and in a booming voice cried out, "The bloody bastards!"

Every eye in the room turned toward the source of the outburst. Then in a sudden change of mood Caleb gently laid his hand on Captain Pierce's arm and in a soft voice said, "I'm sorry, Abraham. I'm very sorry."

"Thanks, Caleb. You know, sometimes I forget it really happened and . . . and that he's just somewhere else, maybe on the ship . . . and that he's all right. But then . . . then it hits me." The knuckles of his folded hands turned white as he tried to control his emotions. "He's gone, Caleb, he's gone!" He bowed his head in an attempt to hide the tears swelling up in his eyes.

Caleb laid his giant hands on Abraham's, and through those hands, strong, callused hands that had worked hard and fought hard, flowed a stream of compassion, understanding and love.

Abraham struggled to speak clearly. "I'm all right. I guess it's going to take some getting used to."

"You'll never get used to a loved one bein' gone," said Caleb. "There's always a part of them we carry around with us in our lives." He gave Abraham's hands a last, sympathetic squeeze then let go.

"You're right, Caleb, and thanks. The thing we must do right now is find the means to take Jacob's body back to Squansett Cove. I've asked the barkeeper if he knows of a driver and wagon that's available."

"What then?" asked Caleb in a low and serious voice.

"What do you mean?" Captain Pierce searched his friend's face as if the answer could be found there.

"I mean, what do you plan to do after you take Jacob's body home for burial."

"We'll return here, of course. Doyle's gone to McKean's to see about repairs to the *Otter*." Captain Pierce looked at Caleb as though he really did not understand the meaning of his question. He continued, "There's plenty has to be done. The people in Boston still need supplies. The blockade hasn't been lifted, has it?"

"No, and I don't expect it to be. And there's plenty to be done all right, more than you think. Or have you heard?"

"Heard what?" Captain Pierce leaned forward, eager to hear what Caleb had to relate.

"There's been a second Continental Congress called at Philadelphia. I hear all thirteen colonies are bein' represented. They've drafted new appeals to both the king and Parliament hoping they will consent to a redress of grievances. But there's damned few who believe it will do any good."

"Then what's the purpose? Looks like a lot of wasted time to me."

"Aye, you'd be dead right there, Abraham, if that's all they're doin'. Most know there's damned little chance for a change of heart in London so they're talkin' of creatin' our own army and navy."

"Abraham's eyes widened as he sat up straight in his chair. "Our own army? Navy? Have things gone that far?"

"Aye, that they have, and more. A British fort's been captured by a group from Vermont. They call themselves 'The Green Mountain Boys'."

"Where?" asked Abraham.

"A place on Lake Champlain called Fort Ticonderoga. Understand they took it without a fight."

"I've heard of it. What about Boston?"

"Still surrounded by a hodgepodge of militia trying to turn itself into an army. Gotta hand it to 'em though. They've really got the British boxed in and worried."

Captain Pierce sat back in his chair, obviously deep in thought. For a moment no one spoke, letting him digest all that he had just heard. Finally he broke the silence, "An army and a navy — from what, pray tell?"

Caleb leaned forward to speak. "Don't think the militia around Boston is all there is. There's folks all up and down the coast that's had enough of King George and his Parliament o' Dandies. Don't forget the burning of the Gaspee right here in Narragansett Bay. And it seems New Englanders aren't the only ones who know how to throw a tea party. I guess you didn't hear, last October down at Annapolis the owner of the brig *Peggy Stewart* was forced to burn his own ship for tryin' to bring in tea for which he'd made the mistake of payin' the tax."

Christopher was both surprised and shocked. He'd not heard of the *Peggy Stewart*. But of course, he'd not heard much of anything about home since he left there just a little more than a year ago. He was trying to visualize such an event in the busy but peaceful town he remembered as Caleb motioned for the girl to bring him another pint of ale.

Captain Pierce, his expression revealing a deep concern for the events being related to him, said, "I knew things were going pretty far, but I guess it's worse than I thought."

"Worse, better; better, worse," replied Caleb, "depends on your point of view."

Both Captain Pierce and Christopher gave Caleb a puzzled look as the serving girl arrived with his fresh mug of ale for Caleb and another smile for Christopher. After taking a long drink and smacking his lips in obvious approval of its contents Caleb continued, "There's some, like Sam Adams, fer instance, that welcome every little bit of trouble. They figure an all out revolution is the only way to solve our problems, so the sooner the better."

"How do you feel?" asked Captain Pierce.

"My guess is the fat's in the fire," replied Caleb, "and the way it's going it won't be long before there'll be no question about it. May be there already, for all I know. Sure doesn't look like diplomacy's goin' to work."

"I've just had a taste of their diplomacy," said Captain Pierce sarcastically.

"Guess you have at that, Abraham, guess you have at that."

Caleb paused and no one else spoke. As he pondered the significance of the events he'd just related he idly played with the mug in front of him, sliding it around in the wet rings on the table. Suddenly he realized from the silence that Abraham was thinking of his lost son Jacob.

"There's a lot more been happening," continued Caleb, trying to get his dear friend's mind off his grief. "Last December right here in Newport patriots seized some of the King's ordnance. Same thing happened up in Portsmouth a few days later."

"I heard about that," said Captain Pierce. Then turning to Christopher asked, "Did you?"

"No, sir. They didn't tell us much about anything on the *Briareus*."

Caleb gave them a puzzled look so Captain Pierce explained to him how Christopher had been pressed into service, served aboard the *Briareus* and later escaped.

"Well, young man, I doubt if you harbor many fond sentiments toward our glorious King George."

"No, sir. That's a fact for sure."

"Did you hear," continued Caleb with the fervor not unlike that of someone blowing on hot coals to make them flare up, "that Virginia's Lord Dunmore seized the provincial powder supply at Williamsburg. Open fighting was barely averted. Things went better in Charleston down in South Carolina; the patriots got to the powder first. Perhaps our southern friends were a little more wary because a secret committee had earlier seized the mail from the British packet *Swallow*. They discovered the British government's intention of coercin' the colonies into submission."

Christopher just watched and listened, trying to comprehend the significance of all Caleb said.

Caleb emptied his mug and setting it down as though mashing an insect said, "There's a growing number everywhere, New York, Pennsylvania, all over, willing to make a stand against British tyranny. I'm afraid, Abraham and my new friend," nodding to Christopher, "we've long passed the point of turning back. Sam

Adams may be right after all. But right or wrong, it looks like the die is cast and we've got a long, tough road ahead of us, all of us. We'll all have a role to play in this one."

"And what is yours, Caleb?" asked Captain Pierce.

Caleb paused and with a broad smile, proudly and simply declared, "Privateering, That's what! And you'd do yourself well to do the same, Abraham Pierce."

"But we've been blockade running—many of us have—and risking our necks doing it," objected Captain Pierce. Then with a lower voice, "It's even cost me my son."

"Aye, you're right on that account, Abe. And it's considerable credit you deserve for doing it—I'll not take that away from ye." "But 'til now all we've done is react to what Parliament has done. That's just surviving." Caleb's voice rose with excitement as he continued. "That course is no longer good enough. It's got us nowhere and it'll get us nowhere. It's time to set a new course—a course for freedom."

CHAPTER VIII

"Squansett Cove 5 miles". The small, white, weather-beaten sign by the road brought a silent sigh of relief from Christopher. Here the road forked and the arrow on the sign told them to take the road to the right. The driver, a short man in his late fifties, in need of a shave and an even greater need of a bath, was a pleasant enough companion for the trip. He talked neither too little nor too much, which pleased Christopher under the circumstances.

"Here's where the road gets a bit rougher," said the driver. "Not traveled as much as the one we've been on." He gave a momentary tug on the appropriate reins and the two horses obediently responded turning them onto the road to Squansett Cove. Christopher knew the dreadful trip would soon be over.

The trip from Newport had been slow, painfully slow. The road was dry but what had been a sea of mud the week before had been sun-baked into rock hard grooves. These not only bounced the wagon up and down but caused it to be thrown first right then left. Jacob was beyond harm now, but Christopher's respect for the dead required his constant admonishing the driver to be careful. There was only Christopher and the driver, no passenger to urge them to hurry, so for almost seventy miles they plodded and maneuvered to keep the coffin from bouncing around too much. Sometimes, even riding off the road was smoother.

In spite of the constant jostling, Christopher had spent much of the time in deep thought. It had been just a little more than a year since he'd left home to spend the weekend with his sister. The question of Thomas haunted him constantly. Had he failed him? Had he failed Matty? He could hardly believe all that had happened. But he was not only looking back. He was also looking forward, forward to seeing Marion again although it was with mixed emotions. Of course he wanted to see her, but Oh, if it could have been under any other set of circumstances. He realized that by now, she would already know of her brother's death, Captain Pierce having arrived the day before with the dreadful news.

As Christopher visualized seeing Marion again it occurred to him he was not sure how he should act. "What should I do when I see her?" he asked himself. He would like to take her in his arms to comfort her, hold her and let her cry on his shoulder and at the same time tell her how much he cared for her. But, if she didn't feel the same toward him such a display would be considered quite inappropriate and presumptuous. He would embarrass them both, terribly, and at such bad time. On the other hand, if she did have similar feelings toward him and he showed too much restraint she might wrongly conclude he held no strong feelings for her. "Oh rats! What a mess! I never thought caring for a girl could be so complicated," he muttered under his breath.

On they rode with Christopher turning these thoughts over and over in his mind. Finally, they crested a small hill, and there, before them, lay the town of Squansett Cove and its small harbor. The road leading down into the town was moderately steep and the driver had to rein the horses and occasionally apply the brakes to maintain control of the wagon. As this slowed their progress it gave Christopher an opportunity to study the town from a new vantage point. Low, pine covered, granite hills seemed to reach out from the land like two arms forming the small cove and embracing the several vessels lying at anchor there. The air was clear under the high afternoon sun and the well-kept houses looked like those in a painting Christopher had seen in the Wickham's home back in Annapolis. Two other roads could be seen coming into the town, one from the north, which Christopher correctly surmised came from Boston, the other from the south. He could not guess where that one led. At this elevation the town appeared even more picturesque than it had earlier. Beyond the protecting arms of the cove and far out at sea was a ship, under full sail, plying its way northward.

As they drove into the town it became apparent the word of Jacob's death had spread. Everyone they passed along the way paused and watched in silent reverence as the wagon went by. The men removed their hats; the women held their handkerchiefs to their mouths as their gesture of sympathy.

As they approached the Pierce's home Christopher's dread of the impending encounter mounted. His head had started aching before they reached town; now it felt as if it would burst. If only he could be anywhere else, doing anything else. What should he say? How should he act? If only he'd known the Pierces longer. He already felt very close to them but realized how short a time it had been since he'd first been brought here, wet, unconscious and near dying.

As the driver pulled back on the reins the two horses reared their heads, stomped the gravel beneath their hooves several times then came to a stop, snorting and shaking their heads sideways. Someone must have been watching, for as soon as the wagon stopped, the front door opened. Captain Pierce and Joseph, their servant, came solemnly down the five steps to the drive.

It was a relief to see Captain Pierce first and not the whole family at once. Christopher respected the Captain so much he seemed to draw a certain amount of strength from him.

"You made good time," remarked the captain as he and Joseph walked around to the rear of the wagon. "I certainly appreciate your help, Christopher."

Christopher found it difficult to find words for a reply. How does one accept thanks from someone to whom he already owes so much?

As he climbed down from the wagon he nodded and said "I was glad to do it." But as soon as he said it he felt very stupid. 'Glad' was certainly not an appropriate word under such grievous circumstances. "I mean . . . ."

"I know," interrupted the captain with an understanding but forced smile. "I think the four of us can manage to get the coffin inside."

While the driver tied the reins to the hitching post Joseph propped open the front door of the house then rejoined the others. The four men carefully lifted the coffin containing Jacob's body and carried it inside.

"In the parlor, on the left by the bay window," directed the captain.

The room had already been prepared. The bay window area had been cleared of its usual furnishings and two wooden horses stood ready to receive the coffin. Black cloth was draped over each and on each side stood a single mahogany flower stand with an arrangement supplied from the garden Christopher so fondly remembered.

Christopher had yet to see Mrs. Pierce or the girls. His curiosity must have shown for Captain Pierce said, "Mrs. Pierce and the girls are upstairs. They wanted to wait until we had brought Jacob in before they came down."

"Beg pardon, sir," interrupted the driver, "will there be anything else?"

"No," replied Captain Pierce as he handed the driver a farthing. He'd already paid the man in advance at Newport but felt he should express his appreciation for the extra care the driver had shown in bringing Jacob back home.

"Will the young man be going back to Newport with me?" asked the driver.

"No," answered the captain, "he'll be staying."

With that the driver expressed his condolences once more then departed.

Until then, Christopher did not know what the captain's plans for him were. For a moment he feared he might not get to see Marion at all. He felt relief in knowing he was to remain but the apprehension that had been plaguing him returned. He wondered, "Did Mrs. Pierce, did Marion, realize yet that Jacob was killed because of him?" He was still convinced that if he'd not been aboard the *Otter* Captain Pierce would not have run from the British sloop and Jacob would still be alive.

All the while Christopher had been lost in thought, the captain had been standing, staring down at the coffin. He slowly turned and said to Christopher. "It's time for them to come down."

Feeling the family should be left alone, Christopher said, "I'll go wait in the garden, if that's all right."

"Certainly," replied Captain Pierce, appreciating Christopher's show of sensitivity.

As Christopher stepped out into the garden his thoughts went back to that certain day when Marion dropped the hint that she cared for him. He noticed the garden had changed. The flowers, which had been in bloom that day, were gone; other varieties were now taking their turn. "Change . . . I guess there's always change," he said to himself, "sometimes worse, sometimes better." He sat down on the bench he and Marion had shared.

It seemed like an eternity, waiting and wondering what sorrow and pain was being experienced inside the house. Gradually his eyes and thoughts drifted, first back to St. Michaels, then to Thomas. "What had happened to him?" he asked himself as he had done so many times before.

Suddenly he heard the rear door of the house open and close. He turned to see Marion coming toward him. Her movement was slow and without expression. Her eyes seemed to look right through him. They were red and moist from crying, yet unblinking. She neither spoke nor showed any sign of recognition. She just continued to move, solemnly and slowly toward him.

"She holds me responsible," he thought. "I can't blame her. I know how she must feel. What can I say? She'll never care for me now." He stood there like a confessed criminal ready to receive whatever condemnation she wished to pour out upon him. His heart was heavy.

When she was but a few steps from him she began to move more quickly, the suddenly, she threw herself into his arms. With her head buried in his shoulder she began sobbing and grasping for words. "Oh, Christopher, Christopher, dear, dear Christopher. Hold me tight."

For a moment his emotions were in complete disarray then as he felt her body so close to his and her moist cheek pressed against his, it was like a great weight had been lifted off of him. She didn't hate him. She came to him in her deepest moment of sorrow and need. He wanted to do everything in his power to ease her pain but all he could offer was to hold her close and let her cry. But to Marion, that seemed to be all that was needed. The important thing was that she had come to him.

After a while she lifted her head and looked up at him. He could feel the tears she had left on his cheek. They were her tears, precious tears, a part of her, and she had shared them with him. He was all warm inside with the love and compassion he felt for her. He softly brushed back a tear soaked strand of her hair, fondly stroking the side of her face as he did so. "Marion . . . Marion, I'm so sorry."

"It's all right, Christopher. I'll be all right." She backed away, then taking her lace handkerchief and lightly dabbing her eyes she said, "Let's go inside."

Because so much time had already elapsed, Jacob was buried the next day. Christopher, had long before, come to the conclusion the Pierce family was well thought of in the community. But he was still amazed to see that in the week following the funeral there was almost a steady stream of people coming by to pay their respects and express their condolences, not just citizens of Squansett Cove but many from neighboring towns, some as far away as ten miles.

Christopher had heard the expression 'Time heals'. As the week went by he was beginning to see this happen in the Pierce family. Of course it would be a long time before the grieving really ended, but as the ever present, everyday necessities of life continued to impose themselves on each member of the family there was less and less time left to dwell on their loss. Of course, with each visitor there was the reliving of their tragedy, but even then, the responsibilities of graciously receiving guests provided some diversion from their sorrow.

During that week, when not receiving visitors, Captain Pierce spent most of his time alone in his study or meeting with other prominent men in the community. His wife, Rena, was doing well, finding more tasks around the home to occupy her mind. The effects of Jacob's death appeared to be most telling on young Molly. Perhaps her sadness showed more because it was a greater contrast to her usual vivacity. Marion felt the loss of her brother very deeply but seemed to be taking it better. Perhaps being a little older helped. It also helped having Christopher there. She began to admit to herself that her feelings toward him were growing stronger.

The time Marion and Christopher spent together that week drew them more closely together. In one way they were sharing a loss, for in the short time Christopher had know Jacob he'd come to like him very much. And in this short time Christopher had learned an important lesson in love. When someone you care for very much is hurting, that person's hurt is also your hurt. That is why Christopher was reluctant to relate the events that led to Jacob's death. But Marion insisted and although it was painful to them both, Christopher told her in great detail all that had happened.

As he was telling of all that had occurred he could see she was holding back a flood of tears while listening intently. He admired such strength and considered it to be a part of her beauty. When he had finished, she turned to him. The sadness that showed in her moist eyes was crying out for help and comfort. He wished he could take away her pain but knowing that was impossible he took her into his arms and held her tightly yet tenderly. He could hardly believe the degree of intimacy that had developed between them in such a short time. He regretted the fact it had been brought about by so dreadful a tragedy but it felt so wonderful holding her so close to him.

For some unexplainable reason he suddenly felt the need to tell how he felt about his being responsible for her brother's death. "Marion," said Christopher, with a seriousness in his voice that alarmed her, "there's more." He released her and she looked up, puzzled by this sudden change in mood.

"What more can there be? What's the matter, Christopher? Are you all right?" She was concerned for he was having difficulty looking directly at her.

"Marion . . . " He paused, groping for the right words for he felt certain what he was about to tell her would end their relationship. But something deep within him was compelling him to go on. "Marion, you know that because I escaped from an English warship the British consider me a deserter?"

"Yes," she answered, still wondering what he was getting at.

"Well, even though I had been forcibly pressed into service against my will they would still consider it desertion. Do you know what the punishment for desertion is in the British Navy?"

"No, not really, but I suppose it is rather severe."

"Severe, yes. Most of the time it is death by hanging from a yardarm."

"But what has that got to do with you? You are an American, and besides, you're here safe and sound."

"Marion, I'm here, safe and sound, because your father refused to stop and be boarded by that British sloop. He ran from them because he knew what they would do to me if they found me on board and discovered I was a deserter."

"So?"

"Don't you see? Don't you understand? If I had not been on board the *Otter* your father would not have had to run. I am the cause of your brother's death." Each word tore at his heart as he spoke it. "Can you ever forgive me?"

"Oh, Christopher, Christopher, dear Christopher. That's not so. You must never think that!" She placed her hand against his cheek and caressed it tenderly as though trying to erase whatever hurtful thoughts were in his head. "If you only knew Father better you'd know he'd never be boarded under any circumstances. You had nothing to do with it. Please don't ever think that again." She pulled him closer. "Oh how you must have been hurting. We can't go through life with such wrong thoughts hanging over us."

He not only felt as though a tremendous weight had been

lifted from him but that a great barrier had been eliminated from between them. Her words had his head spinning with sudden joy 'We can't go through life . . . ' What did she mean?

He looked into her eyes with gratitude and adoration. She lifted her face to his and he instinctively responded. Their lips drew closer.

Since the conversation with Caleb Stone in Newport, Captain Pierce had not mentioned the subject of privateering to Christopher or to anyone in the household. Christopher had thought of the possibility, but considered that to be a subject for the captain to bring up at a time of his own choosing and had thought nothing more of it in the last few days. That is why he had no idea what Captain Pierce wanted when he asked him to come out into the garden where they could talk privately.

"Christopher," said the captain going straight to the point, "I would like for you to join me."

Christopher looked puzzled, not knowing how to answer for he did not know what the captain meant. "What do you mean, sir?"

"I mean, I'm asking you to come along on the *Otter* when it's ready to put to sea. It's going to take a while to refit her but when she's ready I want a crew that knows a thing or two about privateering."

"Privateering!" exclaimed Christopher. "But, sir, I know nothing about privateering."

"Not so loud," admonished the captain. "I've said nothing to Mrs. Pierce or the girls yet. I wanted to be able to tell them you're going too. And as for not knowing anything about privateering, it's what you learned aboard a King's warship that makes you so valuable. I've many year's experience at sea but when it comes to fighting at sea I'll be the first to admit I know next to nothing."

Christopher said nothing. So many thoughts were racing through his mind; his leaving home to visit Matty, his going off in search of Thomas, being pressed into the British Navy, risking death to escape from the *Briareus*, being rescued by Captain Pierce, the encounter with the British sloop, Jacob's death, and his feelings toward the captain and his family, especially his feelings toward Marion. So many thoughts, so many thoughts!

Captain Pierce continued, "I know it's a big decision, Christopher. There'll be dangers, that much is certain. A short time ago none of us ever dreamed of such ventures but the die has been cast now. You told us yourself you watched the troops march off to attack Lexington and Concord. And you know what news we received at Newport. I'm afraid the fat's in the fire now with no turning back. The days of isolated protests are over. I've just received news that the troops around Boston have been adopted as the 'Continental Army'."

Christopher watched the expression on the captain's face become increasingly obdurate. He knew this man's words were not just coming from his thoughts but from somewhere deeper within him for they were a mixture of conviction, determination and bitterness. He listened intently for he not only had great respect for the captain, he also realized that what he was hearing could tremendously affect him.

Captain Pierce went on, "Christopher, there'll be many a good man taking up arms for what we in the colonies believe in — the things your brother-in-law believed in. I know you promised to find him, but this way you'll be fighting for the same cause as Thomas. Who knows where he is? You just might have a better chance of finding him if you're in the same fight. As privateers we can cut off essential supplies to the British and at the same time provide them to our own men." For a brief time neither of them spoke. Then the captain added, "We stand up and fight or buckle under for good." Then with a lower, more understanding tone, "However, I appreciate your dedication to your sister. Whatever you choose to do will receive my sincere respect."

Christopher was stunned. Such decisions . . . they came down on him like a heavy weight. What would Mattey think? Perhaps he might find Thomas this way. He did not know where else to resume the search after all this time. He soberly considered the aspects of going to sea to attack British shipping. After all, he knew as well as anyone what a formidable force the British Navy was. As he pictured in his mind the *Otter* up against something like the *Briareus* a shudder went up his spine. But he also recalled how well Captain Pierce outmaneuvered and outran the sloop that had chased them, and he did owe this man his life. The possible consequences were so grave that as Christopher answered, it was like hearing someone else's voice. "Yes, I'll go." Then, with a better command of his thoughts, he continued, "You greatly honor me, sir. I would be most pleased to serve with you."

The captain smiled and, placing a hand on Christopher's shoulder, said, "Thank you, Christopher. You don't know how much it pleases me to know you'll be aboard."

"Thank you, sir," said Christopher, feeling some of the relief that goes with having made a momentous decision, even though, in this case, it was not a very difficult one.

"Let's not delay any longer," said Captain Pierce. "Come. We'll tell Rena and the girls." With that he led Christopher back into the house. Christopher was apprehensive about how Mrs. Pierce would receive the news for he knew no woman relishes the idea of her husband intentionally flying off into the face of danger. However, when the captain gathered his family in the parlor for his announcement it was very likely Mrs. Pierce already knew the nature of the gathering for she received the news with composure and understanding. Here was a woman with a strength of character rivaling that of her husband's. Of course, she was concerned for she was well aware of the dangers he would have to face and the thought of maybe losing him so soon after giving up her son tore mercilessly at her heart. But being the woman she was, she was careful not to add to his stress by reacting with useless and hysterical objections as some would do. Her response was simply, "If you must, Abraham. I'll pray to God every day for your safe keeping."

Both girls had remained silent, but now Marion, her face revealing her distress at the news, said, "Oh, Father, do you have to?" Molly rushed to him, hugged him and repeated the question, "Do you, Father?"

"Yes, my dears. It's been made very clear to me England will never let go of its grip unless we make it do so. If we're ever to be free we must act now." Then using Caleb's words he said, "It's time to set a new course—a course for freedom." He gently lifted his daughter's chin and looked into her eyes. The worried expression he saw distressed him and he felt it was time to lighten the mood. He smiled, and looking around at the others, said, "You needn't anyone worry. Christopher here has consented to go along and look after me. Haven't you, Christopher?"

"Yes, sir," replied Christopher, having nothing to add.

This did relax Rena and Molly somewhat but its effect upon Marion was the opposite. However, she was speechless for she could not voice any objection to Christopher's going while she knew her father must. Christopher could see she was upset but felt they should discuss it privately later.

Captain Pierce broke the silence. "We'll need to be going back to Newport soon but because tomorrow is Sunday we'll wait and start early Monday morning. Now everyone get smiles back on your faces and be about your business. It's not the end of the world, you know."

The captain kept Christopher occupied the rest of the day discussing the refitting of the *Otter*, naval weaponry and anything else he may have learned during his time aboard the *Briareus*. There had not been a moment of time available to spend with Marion the rest of that day.

The following day Christopher and the family walked the quarter mile to church where they endured several hours of the Reverend Mr. Peckham's preaching on the virtues of tolerance and the obedience to those placed in authority over you. It was an exceptionally hot day for this early in June and soon there was a fluttering of fans throughout the congregation to distract Christopher and keep him from listening too intently. This was probably fortunate for he had not yet reached the degree of patriotic fervor he had witnessed in those not restricted to the pulpit. True, he harbored a bitterness for having been pressed into service and he agreed with all the things he'd heard, everything from Ol' Put back in St. Michaels to Captain Pierce here in Squansett Cove, but the politics of the situation had not yet caught up with him. There was still a twinge of conscience, for all his life he, like most other colonials, had considered himself English. However, this feeling, like the events around him, was rapidly changing, very rapidly.

Christopher was not the only one having difficulty paying attention to the seemingly endless sermon. Captain Pierce's thoughts were on the *Otter* and all that had to be done to refit her. Rena could not help thinking about the dangers her husband would be facing and how she could ever face life without him. Molly's imagination had her aboard the *Otter* giving the British an awful licking while Marion's thoughts were directed toward Christopher. And Christopher wondered, in turn, what each member of this family was going through.

Later that afternoon Christopher and Marion finally managed some time together in the Pierce's garden. The day had grown progressively hotter and because the bench they had shared so often was in the sunlight they chose to sit on the grass in the shade of a mulberry tree in the far corner of the garden. Marion had on the same gray and white striped satin dress she wore the day she first came to his bedside when he lay recuperating after his rescue. As she gracefully sat down in the shade, carefully spreading her dress out around her, she seemed even more beautiful than when he first saw her.

Christopher sat down next to her with his his legs pulled up and his arms resting on his knees. The sky was clear and bright blue from horizon to horizon except for one small, lonely cloud drifting lazily along. As Marion sat watching it, Christopher looked only at her. He'd never seen such beauty and she was more beautiful now than any day before.

Finally, he spoke, "Marion, there's so much . . . so much I want to say but . . . "

She placed her soft, white hand on his and spoke in a voice that was almost like a whisper, "I know, Christopher, but words aren't really necessary when two people care."

He moved closer to her. She turned to him and lifted her head. There, in her eyes, eyes that sparkled with the love she felt for him, he saw everything in the world that mattered. He took her into his arms and she responded passionately holding him as tightly as she could. Their lips touched and it seemed as though nothing else existed, not even the earth beneath them.

For a long time they sat there, saying nothing. Then Marion asked in a voice that was almost a whisper, "You will come back to me won't you, Christopher, Dear?"

"Yes, Marion. I'll come back. That I promise."

CHAPTER IX

As the *Otter* slipped out of Narragansett Bay, under the cover of darkness, it was met by a freshening summer breeze and gradually increasing ground swells coming in from seaward. As the sleek schooner rose and fell to meet the challenging mounds of dark and foaming water, it carried the countenance, if a ship can have a countenance, of a large creature seeking revenge for some deep and unforgotten hurt.

The *Otter's* appearance had, indeed, changed. Both her starboard and larboard bulwarks now showed three square doors, hinged to swing upward. Behind each of these was a freshly painted red carriage supporting a cannon capable of hurling a four pound ball one hundred fifty yards with reasonable accuracy. These heavy instruments of death were held securely in place by block and tackle running to eye bolts in the deck and bulwarks. Not noticeable, but very necessary because of this extra weight, was the additional layer of deck planking and the extra beams, knees and chocks that had been added below. In addition to these heavy guns there were two swivel guns, twenty-eight inches in length, which could be mounted on the rail or taken aloft to fire down upon an enemy's deck.

Extra stays and shrouds had been added to make up for those that might get shot away by enemy fire. On deck there were built-in shot racks, sand tubs with wick holders, and water buckets in gimbaled racks. Below decks, in part of what had been the cargo hold, there was now a powder magazine, lined with copper sheathing to make it spark-proof and illuminated only through a thick glass window by a lamp on the outside.

But noticeable to the ear as well as to the eye was the number of persons on board. No longer could the *Otter* be manned with just five or six men. Each of the six guns required a crew of four and there had to be a sufficient number of men to handle the sails during action and to man any vessels captured and taken as prizes.

Captain Pierce had appointed Doyle and Juan Tortosa as his First and Second Lieutenants, Elias as Master at Arms, and Christopher as his Gunner because of his experience on board the *Briareus*. There were also four "Gentlemen Volunteers" serving as marines. They came from rather prominent families in Framingham, Massachusetts; two were brothers. All four claimed to be expert marksmen and to have taken part in routing the British troops from Lexington and Concord. These would be stationed aloft during a fight so they could have a clear view of the enemy's deck.

There was a ship's carpenter named Moses Wilson from Pawtucket who had served in that capacity aboard a privateer in the French and Indian War. Jeremy Best, a young man of twenty-four, signed on as ship's surgeon. He'd just completed one year as apprentice to old Doctor Draper in Newport. Although Doctor Draper would not sign a certificate unless an apprentice completed at least two years with him, he consented to a leave of absence for Jeremy so he could fulfill his 'patriotic duty', as 'Doc' put it. Besides, he'd already become proficient in amputations and the few ailments most common to shipboard life.

There was Otis Banks, a big strapping black man who signed on as cook, and William Abbott, a slight fellow with a permanently serious expression and a fondness for details who served as storekeeper. One of the most difficult positions to fill was that of sail maker. With the increase in ships being outfitted for privateering and the repairing of sails for those that had already seen action, sail makers were in much demand but short supply. It was by luck that Captain Pierce found Peter Gunderson as he had just arrived from Sweden and had not yet sought employment.

There was now a total of fifty souls crowded aboard the *Otter*.

Any possible doubts about the *Otter's* new role as a privateer had been completely erased by news of the most recent events. Colonial resistance to the crown was growing to a white hot heat.

British forces still blockading Boston from the sea were, in turn, cut off from the countryside by the surrounding colonial troops, troops which had been adopted into the new Continental Army only the month before. Running low on wood for fuel and fortifications, British General Gage had dispatched two timber sloops, under the protection of the armed schooner *Margaretta*, to Machias in the eastern district of Massachusetts, as Maine was known at that time. Although the provisions offered in exchange for the wood was badly needed, a group of woodsmen armed with pitchforks and axes captured all three vessels. The captured guns and ammunition were then used to bring in other British prizes.

At the same time Rhode Island voted to create The Rhode Island Navy and commissioned the twelve gun sloop *Katy*, which, only three days later, captured the British Sloop *Diana*.

The biggest event occurred two days after this. British troops, numbering twenty-five hundred, had to make three assaults to finally wrest the Charlestown Peninsula from only twelve hundred fortified colonials, and then only after the Americans ran out of ammunition. The fierce tenacity with which the colonials held on cost the British over a thousand in killed or wounded compared to about four hundred American losses. Although the British won the day, in what was to become known as the Battle of Bunker Hill, there were many on both sides of the Atlantic who considered it an American victory. Either way, an important lesson was learned that day—the Americans could fight and were not afraid to do so. No British officer who was present that day ever again went into battle with the same degree of arrogance.

With the passing of these events and numerous lesser ones the stage had been set. The *Otter* and those aboard were now players, reluctant or eager, players just the same.

"Fire in succession!" yelled Christopher through his speaking trumpet. As each Gunner's mate in turn lowered his smoldering wick to his gun there was a hiss and puff of smoke emitted from the touchhole. Immediately the air was rend by a series of deafening roars as shafts of flame and smoke streaked out from the ship's side and the heavy, black cannons lunged backwards against their restraining block and tackle, first one, then another, and another. All eyes watched as the three black balls sped, disappearing, toward their target. Suddenly a geyser of water shot upward as the first ball ended its journey, and then another. A split second later this was repeated as a third column of water shot into the air except this one carried with it with pieces and splinters of wood, which then fell splashing back into the sea. A cheer arose from the gun crew that had earned the reward of an extra tot of rum for hitting the barrel.

"Well done!" exclaimed Christopher not being able to hide his own excitement. "That will be all for today. Clean your pieces and secure from drill."

"Christopher, you've done a remarkable job with these men," said Captain Pierce smiling. "And in just one week," he added. Most of them had never seen a naval cannon before. Frankly, I had reservations about recruiting so far inland but my mind is at ease now. They've even done well at handling the sails. I was afraid you and Juan were pushing them too hard."

"They're eager, sir. It's been a week well spent."

"Would have been suicide to have done otherwise," added the Captain.

The decision had been made early to sail directly out beyond the usual ship lanes to an isolated area where they could, unmolested, have time to learn the basic skills of privateering. Juan was assigned the task of teaching the landlubbers the rudiments of sail handling; Christopher was given the job of sharing what he'd learned about gunnery from Colie aboard the *Briareus*. All day, every day, for a week the crew was at one drill or another. Under most circumstances men would find such repetition cause for constant grumbling but the vision of sharing in the prizes to be taken encouraged them in their tasks and even fostered an air of competition among the gun crews. They were ready.

Captain Pierce leaned against the quarterdeck rail deep in

thought. In his mind he visioned the *Otter* up against various foes. Some would be easy, others formidable. But he knew the *Otter* could out sail the larger, and out fight the smaller. As he watched the last bit of gun smoke drift off to leeward he calmly announced, "I think it's time we go hunting."

"The men will be pleased to hear that, sir," said Doyle, who had just joined them.

"Very well then," said the Captain, "assemble all hands after the gun crews are finished. Call me when they are ready. I'm going below to plot a course that'll take us back to where we can ply our new trade, south of the Nantucket Shoals."

Christopher and Doyle looked at each other knowingly, both recalling that was the area where Jacob had been killed. They both knew that beyond patriotism and prize money the captain had another motive and they wondered where and how far that motive would take them.

Three days had gone by since their arriving off the Nantucket Shoals; not a thing had been seen. There had been daily drills but not with the intensity of those the week before and disappointment and boredom was beginning to set in. The carpenter had just that morning finished building fighting tops on both masts and Elias and his 'Marines', the four gentlemen volunteers, were going over how best to use these high perched platforms in combat. It was a clear day. The sun had passed its zenith and had started its descent toward the western horizon. A light but steady breeze from the southwest pushed the *Otter* along on her course, west by northwest. Then the long awaited cry came from above, "Sail Ho! Off the starboard beam!" All eyes turned toward the north.

"Do you see it?" asked Christopher to those around him. No one answered.

Doyle took the telescope from its rack by the wheel and started toward the ratlines. "I'll take a look from aloft with the glass." They all continued to scan the horizon in vain as Doyle climbed up for a better look. After a few moments he called down, "One sail, bright in the sunlight. Maybe a cutter or a sloop."

Captain Pierce turned to Juan who was standing by the helmsman and ordered, "Have the tops'l furled, Mister Tortosa." Christopher was surprised to hear the captain address Juan with the title "Mister" unconsciously emulating the formality of a man-o-war.

"Why do you want to lighten sail?" asked Christopher.

"Perhaps they haven't seen us yet." Captain Pierce explained. "We want to keep a low profile as long as we can. We'll hold this course until we see what she is."

As the *Otter* proceeded at a slower pace and normal work was resumed the thoughts of all those on board were directed toward the stranger on the horizon. Could this be a rich prize that would add substantially to each man's coffers or a British Man-o-War promising imprisonment or death. Perhaps it was just another privateer. These possibilities raced through every man's mind as they mechanically went about their tasks and waited for further word from Doyle.

After about a half hour Doyle's voice rang out from above, "Deck there!" All eyes looked up as he continued, "Still only one vessel . . . single mast . . . on a steady westerly course." The strange vessel was sailing along the southern edge of the shoals and headed due west, putting it on a slightly converging course with the *Otter*.

"Apparently they still haven't seen us," commented Captain Pierce as he contemplated the possibilities and his next move. "From her size she's probably not a merchantman of any consequence; most likely a mail packet headed for New York with dispatches from Boston or Halifax. If she's sloop or a cutter rigged she'll be fast but we've got the wind gauge and if we play it right we can keep her between us and the shoals. We'll hold this course a while longer."

A half hour later the strange sail was visible to those on deck and growing larger. From that moment on each man kept one eye in that direction. The *Otter* was still on a course taking it closer to the Nantucket Shoals, still a good ten miles away. All the while, Captain Pierce was deep in thought. Those around him, knowing their very lives might depend on the success or failure of whatever he was planning, chose not to interrupt him.

When Captain Pierce, spoke everyone turned to listen. "I'm certain they've seen us by now. As long as we hold this course they can only guess our intent. Let's hope they're slow in recog . . . " The captain was interrupted by Doyle's excited voice from his perch on the tops'l spar.

"She's changing course . . . I can see her colors now . . . British!" After a pause he added, "Looks like she's doublin' back."

"Mister Tortosa," said the captain, "have Mister Renck and his marines come down. Bring us about on an opposite course. We must keep her downwind and between us and the shoals. "Mister Hall, as soon as were on our new course have your gun crews prepare for action. Load one gun on each side with solid shot, the others with chain. We want to capture her, not sink her."

Christopher smiled at hearing the captain again using such formality. "Aye, aye, sir," he replied, as he felt his heart beginning to beat faster with the excitement.

Juan picked up a trumpet, directed it upward and passed the word to Elias. "Mister Renck, bring your men down. We're coming about."

In a scant few seconds Elias and his four marines, demonstrating the agility they had acquired in their short time at sea, were standing safely on deck. Doyle came down right behind them to discuss in greater detail what he had seen from above.

Having the tops'l furled, made turning the *Otter* completely around on her course simpler and faster. "Stand by on the main and heads'l sheets!" yelled Juan at the men clamoring to their stations. When he saw that they were ready he turned to the man at the wheel, "Helmsman, ease down your helm! Bring her around."

Another crewman rushed to help the helmsman and together they began the struggle of turning the wheel to the left. The rudder fought back as the rush of sea water applied tons of resistance to it but the system of pulleys in the steering gear gave sufficient mechanical advantage that the *Otter* began to turn to the left. As the bow swung into the wind the sails began to luff. "Haul in the courses, let go the heads'l sheets. Ready on the lee," yelled Juan. As the bow passed through the eye of the wind and started to fall off to the left, Juan continued his string of orders, "Ease out the courses on the larboard, haul in and make fast lee heads'l sheets." The sails again billowed out with the wind and the *Otter* began picking up speed racing back in the direction from which it just came.

Several adjustments had to be made in the setting of the sails as the *Otter* increased its speed. When Juan was satisfied they were getting the maximum pull from the wind he ordered the men aloft to unfurl the tops'l.

With the tops'l set and the wind on their starboard quarter the *Otter* almost leaped forward on its new course to the east-southeast. They raced along faster than Christopher had ever seen the *Otter* move. Well heeled over to the larboard the schooner with its sharp bow knifed through the water throwing spray high into the air as each swell was met. The slanted deck was becoming increasingly wet from the spray, making the handling of the heavy guns very difficult and dangerous. Christopher had the six crews double up and prepare first the guns on one side and then the other. As the final wad was being tamped down in the last gun a sheet of water came flying over the rail soaking Christopher to the skin. He paid little attention to this except to remind his crews, "Keep your touchholes covered and your linstocks away from the spray. A wet match is no use to us." He then turned to face the quarterdeck and shouted in a loud and proud voice, "All guns are ready, Captain."

Captain Pierce smiled, "Thank you, Mister Hall." He then braced himself against the quarterdeck rail, extended the long brass telescope and lifted it to his eye. After a moment he lowered the telescope, turned with a puzzled expression and said, "Very odd, very odd indeed."

"What, sir?" asked Juan.

"She's a cutter all right . . . mail packet by all appearances . . . four guns," answered the Captain.

"What's so odd about that?" asked Elias.

"It's her course," Captain Pierce began to explain, "they seem to be sailing southeast. I would have expected them to veer off more to the north when we reversed course. I thought they wanted to avoid us; we out gun them. Instead, they're converging with us."

For almost half an hour the two ships continued under full sail coming ever closer. More and more detail could be made out by the naked eye. It was a beautiful vessel with a single mast, freshly painted red hull with black rail. Its large gaff-rigged mainsail and three headsails looked like new. Everyone on the *Otter* watched as the two ships drew closer. That is, except Christopher, who was again going from gun crew to gun crew to make certain everything was in readiness and that he'd not forgotten something in his training of the crews.

Suddenly the cutter's profile became smaller and its sails began to flutter. "She's changing course," exclaimed Doyle. The cutter's bow was slowly turning toward the *Otter* with her sails luffing. For a moment everyone on the *Otter* thought the other ship was heaving to and giving up the race. Then its image grew larger and its sails billowed out on the other side. The cutter had changed course and was heading due west.

"That explains it," said Captain Pierce. "Doyle, Bring us about! Course northwest."

Without a reply Doyle set the crew to the task of changing course again. "Ready about! Stations for stays!" Doyle's face revealed his frustration for the maneuver this time would be complicated by the topsail being set. The momentum required to swing the *Otter* far enough around for the wind to come in on the other side could be dampened by the big square sail atop the foremast. Timing was important.

When the hands were set to handle the lines he gave the order for the helmsman to bring them into the wind. "Ready! Ease down the helm!" Then the orders were given for the main and headsails to be brought over to the starboard side. As the topsail began to luff Doyle gave the command to those handling its lines, "Brace to! Tops'l aback!" At this point the yard was positioned so the wind was striking the front of the sail. This helped swing the bow around but at the same time slowed their forward motion. As the turn was being completed Doyle ordered the tops'l yard brought back around and with a thunderous clap the sail filled with air and began to pull.

"Explain what, sir?" asked Christopher who had in the meantime returned to the quarterdeck.

"The reason he didn't run to the north was he's dead set on reaching his destination, probably New York. He only took that last course to get some distance from the shoals and draw us further south, hoping to gain room in which to slip past us," explained Captain Pierce. "Whatever or whomever they've got on board must be of unusual importance."

Soon the *Otter* was gaining on the cutter. The topsail, which had been a hindrance in tacking, was again their advantage. The two ships were converging rapidly now. After a while, it became apparent to the captain of the cutter that if he maintained his present course the *Otter* would cut him off. He changed his course to northeast in a desperate move to buy time in the hopes of a wind change. It didn't come. The two raced on; the *Otter* was almost abreast of the cutter, which was now no more than a cable's length away.

"Mr. Hall, fire a shot across their bow."

"Aye, Aye, sir," replied Christopher with great excitement. He ran to the forward starboard gun and directed the gunner's mate to aim just ahead of the cutter and fire when ready. All hands watched as the gun crew swung the heavy piece around. The match was lowered to the touch hole; the gun roared and sent its ball racing across the gap between the ships. As a spout of water rose in front of the cutter everyone on the *Otter* gave out a cheer. This was their first shot not fired in practice.

However, the cheering quickly stopped when two puffs of smoke appeared along side the cutter. Everyone fell silent as they waited for the two balls of iron racing toward them. A harmless column of water rose in the air behind them. Then there was whine and a loud crack as a large portion of the starboard focs'le rail disintegrated into flying splinters and the second ball, having done its damage, continued on into the sea beyond them.

"Very well, then," said Captain Pierce. Then to Christopher, "Fire at their rigging and reload with more chain."

In anticipation of the order, Christopher had already had the other two gun crews elevate their guns and gave the command to fire almost immediately. The two guns fired almost simultaneously and the chains could be heard singing as they flew spinning toward the enemy. The first tore a large hole in the cutter's fore staysail and severed the jib sail's sheet permitting the sail to fly loose in the wind. The second chain did more damage, flying higher than intended it luckily cut through the mainsail gaff halyard. The spar came crashing against the mast, dropping the mainsail into a useless heap.

Confusion now reigned aboard the cutter as its crew worked furiously to free the tangled mass of lines and canvas. With only the two remaining headsails to drive it, the stricken vessel slowly lost headway and was barely moving. Unable to come about and bring his starboard guns to bear, the captain of the cutter realized the futility of further resistance.

"Saints be with us!" exclaimed Juan. "They're striking!"

Instead of a cheer, silence fell over the *Otter*. Each man stared in awe as the ensign was lowered on the British vessel. It was when the red flag was finally down and out of sight that all hands broke into an uproar of jubilation, shouting, dancing and slapping each other with their hats.

"Order!" bellowed Captain Pierce, upset with his crew's lack of dignity but sharing their glee. "Mr. Doyle, get your men under control and bring us about, then heave to, windward of the cutter. Mister Tortosa, be ready to lower a boat as soon as we heave to."

Then turning to Elias, "Mister Renck, be ready to take your marines and enough of the crew over to secure our prize. Have their captain brought back here."

The enemy cutter had fallen behind as the *Otter* continued its forward movement. But the privateer crew, excited by victory and eager to see what they had captured, soon had the *Otter* dead-in-the-water and abreast of the enemy.

Christopher and those remaining aboard watched as the launch bounced over the waves on its way to the enemy vessel. Christopher turned to Captain Pierce and asked, "Aren't our men in great danger? What's to keep the British from attacking them when they go on board?"

"They could do that, but they also know what the final results would be in their crippled and helpless condition. No, very unlikely they would choose to pro . . . DAMN!"

"What?" asked Christopher, startled at the captain's sudden expletive.

"Someone just threw overboard what looked like a large dispatch pouch."

"Can we retrieve it?" Christopher asked.

"No," answered the captain, "it would be weighted. It's probably half way to the bottom by now. I'd sure like to have had a look at what they considered so important."

A short while after Elias and his boarding party went on board the cutter the launch returned to the *Otter*, but without the cutter's captain. As the launch came along side Captain Pierce leaned over the rail and angrily queried the coxs'n, "Where is their captain?"

"I'm sorry, sir, but he refuses to come. The man's actin' crazy like, rantin' an' ravin', carryin' on sumpin' awful. Never saw anythin' like it before."

The captain, filling up with irritation, drew a long breath to calm himself then replied, "Very well then, I guess I'll have to go to him. Stand by, coxs'n." Turning to Christopher he said, "Come along. I'd like you to take a look at their ordnance."

As they drew near the cutter Christopher could see work was

well underway to repair the damage rigging. "Looks like it won't be long before she can be under sail again," he commented.

"It had better not be long," answered Captain Pierce. The wind is starting to pick up. Don't forget those shoals are down wind of us."

As the launch passed the stern of the vessel to come around to the lee side, both the captain and Christopher looked up to see the name in large gold letters, *Gander*. Then they were along side the cutter. Even before the line could be made fast Captain Pierce was up the ladder and on board. Christopher had to scurry to keep up with him. Once on deck they were surprised to see two junior officers in Royal Navy uniforms. Christopher at once recognized the condition of the vessel to be more consistent with that of the Royal Navy rather than a merchant or mail packet and commented to that effect to Captain Pierce who had come to the same conclusion.

"It appears we've caught a bigger fish than we thought," said Captain Pierce.

They were greeted immediately by an apologetic Elias. "I'm sorry, Cap . . ."

"Never mind. Where is this mad man?"

"In his cabin, sir."

"Lead the way."

Christopher, not knowing what else to do, assumed it was all right to follow. Besides, he was curious to see this person who could make such a fuss. As the trio walked aft toward the door leading below to the captain's cabin, Christopher noticed a strange man standing on the far side by the rail. He was alone and apparently not a member of the crew. He was a thin man in gentleman's attire, all black except for white knee stockings and a white jabot that formed ruffles on the front of his shirt. Over this he wore a black cape. He held a silver tipped walking stick in his right hand. He appeared to be paying attention to no one and did not seem overly concerned about what was happening. There was something about this man that made Christopher think he'd seen him before. But where?

Christopher followed the Captain and Elias down the ladder to a very cramped but eloquently appointed cabin in the stern. What they found was not what they had expected. Instead of a ranting and raving, hysterical captain there was now only a pitifully dejected human being, sitting at his table, head face down on his folded arms. His sword lay on the table before him. It had finally become apparent to him that the British Empire, no matter how mighty, could not help him now. The privateers would not be deterred from their actions by threats, which obviously could not be backed up in the present situation. And the realization that he had failed had plunged this once proud man into hopeless depression.

When all three Americans were in the cabin Captain Pierce spoke. His voice was firm but with a detectable trace of compassion for the man before him. "Sir."

The Englishman slowly raised his head; his face portrayed his every feeling. Then, summoning a dignity that had been passed down from generation to generation, he rose to his feet, saluted Captain Pierce and introduced himself. "Captain Philip Cravens, His Majesty's Royal Navy. At your service, sir." He picked up his sword and held it out to Captain Pierce.

"I've no need of your sword, sir. Please keep it."

"Thank you. That's very gracious of you." The Englishman motioned to a settee at the side of the small cabin. "Please make yourself comfortable."

As Captain Pierce accepted the invitation Elias said, "Beg your pardon, sir, but I think I'd better see how things are going topside."

Christopher followed Elias' cue saying he was going to inventory the ordnance.

For twenty minutes Captain Pierce questioned Captain Cravens but learned nothing about their mission. Dispatches had indeed been jettisoned and a search of the cabin turned up nothing. There was no vital information to be found and there was no valuable cargo that could be sold. However, the vessel itself, being in excellent condition and having sustained no significant damage, should bring a handsome figure.

Finally Captain Pierce questioned Captain Cravens about the passenger they had seen when they came on board.

"The man's name is Ashton, Harold Ashton, a civilian who just wanted passage to . . . to our destination," replied Captain Cravens, almost revealing their destination.

"I'd like to talk to him, just the same," said Captain Pierce. He went to the door and asked a seaman to summon the stranger.

Meanwhile, Christopher was on deck making a final tally of the ordnance he'd found. There were four brass cannons in mint condition, two hundred balls, six barrels of powder, two swivels with balls and powder, and numerous muskets, pistols, swords, boarding pikes and axes. He was just finishing his inventory when the seaman asked the stranger to follow him down to the captain's cabin. As the man turned to follow the seaman, Christopher happened to look that way and was stunned at what he saw. The man's cane had a silver handle in the shape of a wolf's head. Now he knew where he'd seen the man, or at least he thought he did. One thing was certain, he had to speak to Captain Pierce about it, and now.

Christopher stopped what he was doing and followed them immediately. If this man was who he thought he was Captain Pierce should know about it before interrogating him. Captain Pierce looked up, surprised, as Christopher entered the cabin behind the others. Christopher addressed the captain right away, "Beg your pardon, sir. May I have a word with you?"

"Can it wait?" Mild annoyance was in the captain's voice.

"I'm afraid it might be urgent, sir."

"Well, what is it?"

"I think we best speak in private, if you don't mind."

Captain Pierce rose and followed Christopher out.

When they were up on deck and away from others, where they could talk without being overheard, Christopher asked, "How many walking sticks have you seen with a wolf's head handle?"

Captain Pierce came very close to losing his temper. "Christopher! We've not much time. We can't be wasting it on riddles.

We've got to get these vessels underway before we're both washed up on the shoals."

"I'm aware of that, sir, and I wouldn't have taken you away if I didn't think it important. Please, sir, isn't such a cane a rarity?"

"Why yes, I've never seen one."

"That passenger, if that's what he is, is carrying one." Then Christopher, as quickly as he could, proceeded to tell Captain Pierce about the man he had seen on the boat to Annapolis and the walking stick he'd seen at Mister Hampton's house so long ago. "I'm sure it's the same man, sir."

The captain slowly stroked his beard; his mind was working hard to understand the situation. "If he is the man you speak of, and I believe he probably is, what is he doing on board this ship and on such friendly terms with the English?"

"I thought you should know, sir."

"You did right, Christopher. Come, I want you in on this." With that, the captain turned to go back below.

Back in the cabin, Captain Pierce continued his interrogation of Captain Cravens. Christopher listened intently as the Englishman very skillfully carried on a continuing conversation without revealing any information of value.

When further efforts seemed futile Captain Pierce turned to the passenger and asked, "What is your business aboard this ship?"

I am a broker, a broker of wheat and other grains. A simple business man, nothing more, nothing less. I am on my way from Boston to New York to arrange purchases.

At once they had obtained more information than the tightlipped Captain Cravens had offered. At least, they now knew the ports of origin and destination.

"Are you American or English?"

The man answered wryly with the question, "Are not all Americans English?"

"Are you a Tory?" asked Captain Pierce, annoyed with the man's evasiveness.

"I have found, sir, that politics is bad for business. Don't you agree?"

Captain Pierce did not answer but suggested to Captain Cravens he go up on deck and assure himself his men were being treated properly. Captain Cravens, thinking this was the real reason, thanked Captain Pierce for his decency and graciousness, then left.

As soon as Captain Pierce and Christopher were alone with the strange passenger the man seemed to relax. Captain Pierce began, his voice showing his impatience, "Now just who are you, what is your politics and what really is your business?"

The man smiled and answered in a low voice, "My name is William Mundy, member of the Maryland Committee of Correspondence and an agent of the Continental Congress. To the British I'm Harold Ashton, broker of grains, on my way to New York to buy wheat for the British troops in Boston."

"If you're who you say you are, why would you do that?" asked Christopher.

"They'll find someone to do it in any case. By my doing it I've won their confidence."

"Did you ever have a stone?" asked Christopher.

"A what?" asked Captain Pierce in utter bewilderment at Christopher's question.

"You mean a kidney stone?" the man asked, also puzzled by the question. "Yes, but what's that got . . . ?"

"Where? Where were you when you had it?" continued Christopher.

"Why, in Annapolis, last year."

Captain Pierce let Christopher continue with his strange line of questioning. He was curious and by now convinced Christopher knew what he was doing.

"At who's house?" continued Christopher.

"At the home of Mister Charles Hampton," answered Mundy, wondering where this was leading.

"Do you know Thomas Owings?"

Mundy's face lit up. He knew they were making connections. "Why yes, of course I do! He's a member of our committee."

"What's his wife's name?"

"Her name is Matty. They live in Annapolis."

"I am Matty's brother."

Mundy's smile suddenly faded into an expression of concern for he had news of Christopher's brother-in-law, news that was not good.

At this point Captain Pierce became cautious and interrupted, "Granting the fact you know these people, how do we know you haven't been working for the British all along?"

Mundy carefully unscrewed the wolf's head handle from his walking stick and extracted from it a rolled-up piece of paper. Handing the paper to Captain Pierce he said, "Perhaps this will convince you."

Captain Pierce took the paper, studied it for a while, looked up and asked, "Where did you get this?"

"It's not original, of course. It's in my own writing but it's information I obtained in Boston and from our friend Captain Cravens, who by the way, became rather loose tongued after I convinced him I had no use for the bloody rebels and their hopeless cause."

Captain Pierce handed the paper to Christopher. The first part described the present condition of British troops in Boston, listing strengths, weaknesses, supplies and armament. Boston was vulnerable from two directions, from the heights of Breed and Bunker Hills on the Charlestown peninsula on the north, and from the Dorchester Heights on the south. The Charlestown peninsula had been secured but at a tremendous price. With a significantly weakened garrison General Thomas Gage was now concerned about the possibility of attack from the south. He was requesting reinforcements.

Christopher began to read the second part of the paper, which dealt with the disposition of several Americans being held as spies in a Boston jail. The paper went on to say that one in particular was considered dangerous and was to be transported to England for trial July 15. His name—Thomas Owings."

"Thomas! A prisoner?" shouted Christopher. "He's alive? You know where he is?"

"Yes, in a jail near Dock Square."

"Hasn't anyone tried to get him out?" Christopher was on the edge of his chair, elated that Thomas was alive, but horrified at the thought of his being taken to England for trial. The outcome of that would almost be certain.

"I assure you considerable effort has been made to free him. Even John Adams did his best to get the trial held in Boston but with no luck. Gage was adamant in his refusal. If Hutchinson were still Governor we might have had a chance. But, as you probably know, he turned over that office to General Gage last year."

"How about an escape?" Christopher could not believe everyone could sit still and let Thomas be taken to London.

"He's in a large stone building the military took over to hold political prisoners and spies. It's impregnable. It's so heavily guarded one can only get in with a pass from General Gage himself. I'm afraid there is nothing anyone can do."

Christopher was aghast. "I can't believe you people are going to let this happen. We must do something. If Thomas is tried in London they'll hang him for certain." Turning to Captain Pierce, Christopher pleaded, "I've got to try. I don't care if others have failed, I've got to try!"

Mundy spoke before the captain could answer, "He's right, sir. I think I can help. It's a slim chance and time is short but, we should try."

Captain Pierce agreed, "Very well then. I'm having Juan take this vessel back to Newport with a prize crew. Christopher, you and Mister Mundy can return with it. There's a man in Squansett Cove who, I believe can be of great help to you. His name is Zachariah Davis. Rena can help you get in touch with him. Now let's get these ships away from those shoals or no one will be going anywhere."

"Sir," Mundy spoke, "this information should get to Congress as soon as possible." It was as much of a request as it was a statement.

"Don't worry," said Captain Pierce. "We'll see that it gets delivered, one way or another."

CHAPTER X

The trip from Newport to Squansett Cove was easier this time and certainly under more pleasant circumstances. Although the condition of the road was not much better than before, the two were making much better time on horseback than they would if they were traveling by coach. William Mundy seemed quite at home in the saddle, and was obviously an experienced rider. However, it was not so with Christopher whose traveling experience had been limited almost entirely to boats and ships.

Christopher had reason enough to want to go on, for his anxious thoughts were not just on rescuing Thomas but also on seeing Marion again. For this he would be more than willing to let his anatomy suffer on, but he did realize the horses had to be rested and was quite agreeable when Mundy asked if there was an inn nearby where they could spend the night.

"Taunton is only a short piece ahead," answered Christopher. "There's an inn there, William—a decent enough place. I stopped there for food when I brought Captain Pierce's son, Jacob, back home."

"Good enough," said Mundy, "we've done well today. And please call me 'Will'. That's what my friends call me."

"All right, Will," answered Christopher, happy with the new friendship.

They had done well, leaving Newport at daybreak and covering almost forty miles. This was not a great distance for an ordinary day's journey; however, they had to first travel the length of Rhode Island (note 2) then wait for Howland's Ferry to come take them across the Sakonnet River. The day was half gone by the time that was accomplished. There was no point in going on. They would easily reach Squansett Cove the next day. Besides there were the horses to consider.

Very much to Christopher's surprise, Will Mundy was not at all like the image he'd been portraying. He was not the quiet, aloof person Christopher had observed before. On the contrary, Will Mundy was a friendly, rather talkative person and a very pleasant traveling companion. He explained to Christopher the advantages of the facade. The quiet, almost rude, image allowed him, for the most part, to limit his conversations to only those he chose. The less he talked, the less he might accidentally reveal.

They had ridden only a short distance more when the inn came into view. "There . . . there on the left. That's the place I was telling you about," said Christopher.

"Looks like a good enough place all right," commented Will as they rode through the gateway and into the yard.

A dirty but smiling stable boy had seen them approach and ran out to greet them. "Let me take your horses, sirs," he said as he took their reins. "Are you staying the night?" he asked.

"We are, provided there is room available," replied Christopher.

The boy's smile grew bigger as he said, "Yes, sir, I'm sure there's room for you. I just heard Mister Tanneman say we weren't full for the night." The boy knew there would likely be a nice tip in store if he had the opportunity to care for the horses overnight. "I'll give them a good rubdown and feed and water them. I'll take very good care of them for you, sirs. I can tell gentlemen of your station and means would want the best care for your mounts."

Will smiled at the lad's obvious solicitude. "Don't worry, young man. You do your job, do it well, and you'll be adequately compensated. Just be sure they're dried off thoroughly."

Christopher and Will dismounted, removed their bags and entered the inn. The sitting room was clean but modest, both in size and furnishings. Two other travelers, sitting by a small, unlit fireplace, looked up to see who had entered, then nonchalantly resumed their conversation. As Christopher and Will looked around the room, the innkeeper, who had heard them enter, came in from the kitchen, smiling and drying his hands on his apron.

"Welcome, gentlemen. Welcome to White Birch Inn. My name is Tanneman, James Tanneman, owner and proprietor. Can I be of service?"

"We wish food and lodgings for the night," said Christopher. "Can you accommodate us?"

"Yes, why yes. I've one room with a bed large enough for the both o' ya. Ye're lucky, there's no one else in it and don't appear there will be. Ye'll have it all to yerselves."

"Can we get something to eat?" asked Will. "It's been a long ride."

"Yes, yes, of course. Just make yerselves comfortable. There's clay pipes on the mantle and tobacco in the tin. Help yerselves, gentlemen."

The two men by the fireplace had finished their conversation and were leaving to go upstairs. As they passed by they simply expressed a cordial greeting and went on. "Just as well they're leaving," whispered Will to Christopher. "Can't be too careful whom we talk to."

Christopher led the way over to the fireplace and took one of the chairs, still warm from its recent occupant. Will carefully selected one of the long clay pipes from the stand and broke off about an inch of the stem to remove that part used by the previous smoker. He carefully filled it, then lit it from one of the candles on the mantle. "You smoke?" he asked Christopher.

"No."

"You might give it a try. It'll relax you."

"I think I will," said Christopher bravely and surprised at his acceptance of the suggestion. "I like the smell of it." He took another pipe from the stand and emulated Will's ritual. When the pipe was filled he took the candle and tilted the pipe's bowl to the flame. The tobacco glowed to a cherry red as he took a long deep draw. Christopher's lungs filled with smoke then revolted instantly and violently. He went into uncontrollable convulsions of gagging and coughing as Will watched, laughing.

When Christopher regained control he looked at Will with disgust and said sarcastically, "Thanks, but I believe that will be all I need of that." Then he dumped out the remaining tobacco into the fireplace and replaced the pipe in its stand. "It smells a lot better than it tastes. I'll be content to let you do the smoking. The aroma will be enough for me."

Will was still smoking his pipe when the innkeeper brought in their dinner consisting of cold mutton, baked potato, hotspur peas and brown bread. He set the food on a nearby, bare table. "Wu'd there anything else ye'd like gentlemen?"

"We might follow this with some flip when we're finished," suggested Will as he looked to Christopher for a sign of confirmation.

"Sounds good to me," agreed Christopher who had never tried the drink but was curious and willing to try it.

As they ate their dinner they traded stories about their backgrounds and what events had led each to this place at this time. Will was still amazed that Christopher, whom he had met under such unusual circumstances, was the very person commissioned by Charles Hampton to take his place as courier while he himself lay helpless upstairs with a kidney stone. Christopher was still somewhat amazed at the dissimilarity between the William Mundy he'd first observed on board the *Nancy* traveling to Annapolis and the William Mundy who sat across from him now, a friendly, outgoing person who was fast becoming his good friend. It turned out that Will and Christopher's brother-in-law, Thomas, had become close friends while attending William and Mary College in Williamsburg. Will and Thomas had shared like political views, and both, reacting strongly to England's oppressive acts, had become swept up in the events leading to the present revolution, although it was not yet officially called that.

When they had finished eating, the stable boy who had met them on their arrival, appeared and cleared the table, reminding them all the while of the excellent care their horses were receiving. No sooner was he gone than Mrs. Tanneman, a middle-aged woman with graying hair, entered carrying two large mugs. "Your flip, sirs."

"Thank you," replied Will as she turned and left the room.

"What's in this?" asked Christopher eying the hot drink in front of him. "I've heard of it but I confess I don't know what it is."

Will smiled, "You'll like it. It's hot, spiced wine whipped up with egg."

Christopher winced at the description but carefully lifted the mug saying, "I hope I like this better than than that pipe." He took a sip and cocked his head to the side while he tried to decide whether or not he liked it. Then nodding an affirmative, he took a larger drink.

After casually finishing the drinks, they agreed it would be well to retire and get a good night's sleep.

The next morning Will and Christopher were up, breakfasted and on their way by the time the sun cleared the treetops. The air was crisp and a light ground fog accented the multitude of sun's rays penetrating the foliage along the road. It seemed to be a perfect day for traveling. Their horses were well rested and moving eagerly along, and the road was getting better the farther they went. After two hours Christopher felt confident enough to say, "Looks like we'll get to Squansett Cove by early afternoon at this rate."

"Have you looked over your shoulder lately?" asked Will.

Christopher turned in his saddle to look to the west. What he saw immediately dampened his enthusiasm. The whole western horizon was growing dark with ominous, anvil shaped pillars of clouds rising high into the sky. Occasional flashes could be seen within the clouds but they were still too far away for thunder to be heard.

"I don't like the looks of that," remarked Christopher. "Maybe it will pass us," he added hopefully.

"Don't think so," said Will. "I'd wager we'll get this one square on. Anyway we need to keep moving. Maybe we'll find shelter before it hits."

As if by silent signal they both returned their attention to what lay ahead, increasing their horses' gait as they did so.

For another forty minutes they rode on, forgoing several opportunities to seek shelter confident others would present themselves before the storm hit. They were wrong. When the first, large, cold drops of rain came they were on a stretch of road that lay between expansive fields. No house, no barn, no bridge, no shelter of any sort was in sight. However, this did not disturb Christopher as much as it did Will for Christopher's experience at sea had exposed him to such conditions many times before.

"We're all right, Will, it's just water," said Christopher jokingly.

But he was wrong for soon it was more than just water. When the full force of the cold front hit, the temperature rapidly dropped and the drops of rain turned to hail stones, some as large as grapes. Soon the horses began to whinny and act excited as the pelting hail became accompanied by numerous flashes of lightening and rolling thunder.

"Up ahead, look," yelled Will, "there's a grove. Let's get out of this barrage."

Together they sped their nervous horses toward the stand of trees knowing it offered very limited shelter, but hoping the branches would soften the hail and perhaps lessen it and the lightning's frightening effect on the horses. Just as they reached the stand of trees the probing fingers of the electric sky found a target in the towering oak just ahead of them. There was a blinding blue light of unimaginable intensity and an earsplitting report louder than any cannon Christopher had ever heard. The concussion nearly knocked them backwards off their mounts as the lightning bolt split the giant tree from top to bottom. Half the tree fell in front of Will's horse and the frightened animal reared up, throwing Will to the ground.

Christopher quickly grabbed the startled horse's reins, dismounted and tied the two mounts to a nearby sapling. Running to Will who remained motionless on the ground he yelled, "Will, you all right?" There was no response and he was frightened by his friend's lack of movement. Rain was pouring down around them but he paid no attention to it; Will was his only concern now. Will was lying face down, with his left arm underneath him; he was soaking wet and covered with mud. As Christopher reached down to lift Will's face out of the mud he was relieved to hear him groan. He knew he was alive; the worst was no longer to be feared.

"Take it easy," admonished Christopher, "you may be hurt worse than you think. Do you feel any pain?"

"No, not real bad pain. Help me up."

"Go slow, Will. Roll over, let me have a look at you before you try to get up."

With Christopher's help Will rolled over onto his right side then on his back. As he did so he cried out with pain.

"What is it, Will?"

"My arm, my left arm. I think it's broken."

Christopher looked at Will's arm and saw Will's self diagnosis had been correct. The left forearm was unmistakably broken, for midway between the elbow and wrist it took a grotesque turn away from from the torso. "You're right, Will, it's broken. Now take it easy. It could be worse, I don't see any break in the skin." Christopher examined the arm more closely and confirmed the fact that it was only a simple fracture.

"The best I can do for you here is to immobilize it. Stay put while I look for something to make a splint." Fortunately, he'd watched the ship's surgeon on the *Briareus* work with fractures so he had some idea of what had to be done.

Looking around, Christopher saw that when the lightning hit the tree it produced several flat slivers of wood that with some trimming could make an acceptable splint. He went right to work on it and before long he was ready.

"I'm not going to try to set it; I'll leave that to more skilled hands. All I want to do now is straighten it a little so we can get it splinted. Now I'm going to try to ease the break a little by pulling out on your arm. It'll most likely hurt. Yell if you want to."

"Just get it over with," said Will. "My horse?" he asked, suddenly realizing it might have been injured also.

"It's all right. It didn't fall. They're both tied to that sapling over there." He motioned to where the two horses were securely hitched. "Now hold still."

Christopher held Will's elbow in his left hand and gently pulled on the wrist as he straightened the arm as best he could without causing further damage. Will was surprised it didn't hurt any worse than it did. "That wasn't so bad," he bragged.

"Wait 'til later, we'll see how tough you are. Now I've got to splint your arm and make a sling."

By the time Christopher finished, the worst of the storm had passed, leaving only a steady but cold drizzle to contend with. It was the cold that worried him the most for Will was wet through and through, not a good thing for an injured man suffering, partially at least, from shock.

"We've got to get you someplace where we can get you warmed up and into some dry clothes, and if we're really lucky, where there's a doctor. Do you think you can travel?"

"I can if you'll help me mount."

Christopher untied Will's horse and brought it to where Will was still sitting on the ground. Holding the reins of the horse in one hand he used the other to assist Will in getting to his feet. As Will stood up, his face went ashen and things around him seemed to be moving when they should not have been. He reached out with his right hand to steady himself against the horse.

"Take it slow, Will. Give your head a chance to catch up with you. You let me know when you want to try getting on your horse."

Will shook his head as though he were trying to rid himself of the dizziness then said, "I'm ready, just give me a boost."

Working together they managed to get Will in the saddle.

"Hold on to the pommel with your right hand," said Christopher. "I'll keep the reins. Just don't fall off. We don't want any more broken bones today."

Christopher mounted his horse, looked back to make sure Will was all right, then nudged his mare and they were on their way again.

It was not long before the storm completely passed them by and the sun reappeared. By the time they came to a town Will's clothes had fairly well dried and he insisted they continue the journey to Squansett Cove. Christopher was reluctant to agree but had to admit it would probably be better for Will to be in Dr. Finlay's hands rather than those of an unknown. So, on they went.

When they finally reached Squansett Cove they went straight to Dr. Finlay's home, where he maintained his office. It was late in the afternoon, for traveling had been much slower after the accident. Christopher had tried to keep the pace down as he led Will's horse by its reins; Will just held on to his saddle with his one good hand. Now standing next to Dr. Finlay, watching him set Will's arm, Christopher was convinced that pushing on had been the right thing to do. He had acquired considerable confidence in this man in the short time he'd known him.

"Fortunately you did a good job with the splint, Christopher," said Dr. Finlay as he laced up the leather cast, which would hold the bones in place while they knitted together in the healing process. "You'd be surprised how many people are permanently crippled by well-meaning but ignorant friends. They jerk broken limbs around so clumsily they tear the flesh to shreds, to say nothing of the bones they shatter beyond repair. Your friend has much to thank you for."

"Thank you, Dr. Finlay," replied Christopher too embarrassed by the compliments to say any more.

"I'll have to say 'Amen' to that, Doctor," added Will who was trying, but not too successfully, to hide the pain that was consuming him. The small dose of laudanum Dr. Finlay had given him was starting to wear off.

All the while the doctor had been working on Will, Christopher related the events leading up to the present and that they were going to try to get Thomas out of the Boston prison before he was transported to England.

"Captain Pierce said we should seek the help of a Mr. Zachariah Davis," said Christopher. "Do you know of him?"

"Oh, yes. I'd say there's mighty few people around here who haven't."

"Is this someone prominent?" asked Christopher. "Do you think he'd take the time to aid us?"

"Prominent? Yes, I suppose one could say that, at least in his own way," replied Dr. Finlay with a chuckle.

Christopher looked at him, puzzled at his response.

"Zachariah Davis is prominent all right but certainly not one of your pillars of society. Zachariah has an unusual propensity for getting into trouble. But his fame, if you want to call it that, is his uncanny ability to get out of trouble. Abraham is right, he picked the one man, if there is one, who can help you get your brother-in-law out of Boston."

"But would he be willing?" asked Will.

"If it means a chance to twist the lion's tail I'd bet on it."

"Good," said Christopher, encouraged by the doctor's response. "Where can I find Mr. Davis? We must act soon."

"He has a place out on the southern point of the cove, at the end of the road. You can't miss it."

"I'm anxious to meet this person. He sounds interesting. But first we must find lodgings for Will here; he's in no condition to go in to Boston on this mission."

Will objected immediately, "I got here with a broken arm didn't I? Now that Dr. Finlay's fixed it up I can travel as well as anyone."

"That you probably can," said Dr. Finlay, "but how many people do you pass in a day with a broken arm in a sling?"

"Hardly any, of course," answered Christopher, "but what's that got to so with it?"

"Well, I don't know what sort of a plan Zachariah will come up with but I'm sure of one thing, it will require your remaining inconspicuous. Get the point? Besides, Will here needs to rest and I want to keep an eye on him for a few days."

"I suppose you're right," admitted Will. "But Christopher

doesn't know his way around Boston. He's never been in the city."

Dr. Finlay placed his hand on Will's good shoulder as a friendly and reassuring gesture. "You can rest assured that Zachariah will either know his way around Boston or know someone who does. I'm afraid your presence would jeopardize the mission, Will."

"In any case," said Christopher, "we must find lodgings for at least tonight."

A woman's voice interrupted, "You need to do no such thing, Christopher Hall."

They all turned to see Captain Pierce's wife, Rena, standing in the doorway. "Mrs. Pierce, how did you know we were here?" asked Christopher.

"The good doctor here sent word to me right after you arrived. And you needn't be looking for a place to stay. You know our home is your home, Christopher, and your friend's also. But why are you here? What has happened? Is Abraham all right?"

"Thank you, Ma'am," said Christopher with a big smile and thinking also of Marion. "The Captain's all right. We took a prize vessel and I came back with it." He then went on to give her a brief account of the events that brought him back to Squansett Cove and the need to rescue Thomas as soon as possible.

Addressing Rena, Dr. Finlay spoke, "Abraham suggested Christopher seek help from Ol' Zach Davis."

"Well, I suppose if any one can figure a way to get out of a prison it would be Zach Davis, that is, if you can keep him sober long enough."

This last comment worried Christopher. Would Thomas' life depend on a drunkard?

Dr. Finlay noticed the concern on Christopher's face. "Now don't worry, young man, Zach has risen to the occasion more than once, especially if it's for something he believes in."

"Come now," said Rena, "Joseph is waiting with the chaise. We'll get you home and settled, then he'll take you to see your Mr. Davis." There was a hint of disgust or disapproval in her voice as she mentioned Zachariah's name.

As the three started toward the door, Christopher stopped, turned and asked with some embarrassment, "What do we owe you, Doctor?"

"We'll talk about that later. I'll come by later this evening to take a look at that arm. Now, off with the lot of you."

With Christopher's and Will's horses tethered to the chaise they departed.

When the chaise stopped in front of the Pierce's house Christopher quickly stepped out so he could help Rena, then lend a hand to Will. But by the time he turned to Will, he was already out and fussing about being treated like an invalid. Then as Christopher turned toward the house the front door flew open and young Molly came flying down the steps. Looking at no one else, she threw her arms around him, kissed him on the cheek and said, "Oh, Chris your back!" Then quickly releasing him she stepped back, turned aside and with her handkerchief to her face tried to hide her embarrassment.

Christopher was momentarily stunned by the enthusiasm of Molly's greeting. She had never shown any signs of affection before; he was taken completely aback.

Then Molly regained her composure and said, "Please forgive me, Christopher. I'm just so glad to see you again, and safe."

Groping for words, Christopher said, "That's all right, It certainly is good . . . "

Will interrupted, "Is this the young lady you've been telling me so much about?"

"This is her sister, Molly." Then to Molly he said, "Molly, I'd like you to meet my good friend, William Mundy."

Will bowed, took her hand and smiling said, "It is indeed a pleasure to meet such a fair young lady."

At that moment the front door opened and Marion appeared. When Will looked up he was overcome by that same feeling of awe Christopher experienced when he first saw her. She had that rare combination of natural beauty and bearing that robs even the staunchest men of their speech and wits. She descended the steps with grace and extended her hand to Christopher saying, "Christopher, Oh, Christopher, we've all been so worried. Is Father all right?"

"Yes, he's fine. I'll explain everything inside. Marion, this is my friend, William Mundy." Then to Will he said, "Will, I'd like you to meet Marion Pierce."

Again, Will bowed and fumbling for the right words, finally said, "Your father sails the seas seeking treasures while all the time the greatest treasures on earth are here in his home." Then to Christopher, "Chris, where did you acquire this ability to surround yourself with such beautiful women?"

"Shall we go in," interrupted, Mrs. Pierce, "the sun is getting hot."

"By all means," agreed Christopher, "it's starting to affect us in more ways than one." He was mildly annoyed at what he thought was an over display of gallantry on Will's part.

As they all ascended the steps and entered the house Will could not help but wonder why Christopher had received such an affectionate greeting from Molly while Marion, the girl he claimed to be in love with, was considerably more circumspect, conspicuously so. Christopher wondered the same thing.

When they entered the parlor Christopher was surprised to see a rather handsome, well-dressed man rise to greet them. He looked to be a few years older than Christopher. Mrs. Pierce made the introductions.

"Christopher, I'd like you to meet a good friend of the family's, Philip Wescott. Philip, this is Christopher Hall from Maryland and his friend William Mundy."

"Philip eagerly shook hands with them both and with a friendly smile inquired, "What brings you gentlemen all the way to Massachusetts?"

Christopher started to reply but before he could speak Rena interrupted, "They came to bring us news of Abraham's successes and to assure us he was well."

"I'm extremely pleased to hear that," said Philip.

Rena quickly continued, "Philip is the best lawyer in Squansett Cove and maybe all of Massachusetts—at least on a par with Samuel Adams, though they don't always see things eye to eye. Isn't that right Philip?"

"Well, I don't know about the first part," he replied somewhat embarrassed, "you're probably right about the latter."

At this point Will sensed Rena was trying to tell them something and that nothing should be said about their true mission. "Mrs. Pierce, Ma'am, I'm afraid things are catching up with me. I don't . . . " With that he feigned dizziness by grabbing hold of Christopher's arm.

"Oh, how thoughtless of me," she said, "you should be lying down. Christopher, help me get him upstairs."

When they reached the top of the stairs Rena whispered, "You really ought to be in bed."

"I feel fine," said Will.

"What's going on?" asked Christopher. "Are you ill or not?"

"Christopher," admonished Mrs. Pierce, "you must be very careful what you say and to whom you say it, even to those you trust for you don't know what they might let slip in the presence of others. And I'm not too sure of Mr. Wescott's politics."

"Oh! I wasn't thinking, I'm sorry."

"That's all right," said Will, "you're new at this, but remember, from now on you must always be thinking when there's much at stake."

"That's good advice," added Rena. "Now you go on downstairs. I'll get Will settled. He really does need rest if he wants that arm to heal."

"All right," agreed Christopher.

He reached the bottom of the stairs just as Marion came out of the Parlor. When he saw her he stopped where he was so she would come to him and be out to sight of Molly and Philip, still in the parlor.

He had waited so long for this moment. His pulse raced as she came near him and he reached out to draw her close. All he could say was her name, "Marion, Marion." He looked into her eyes with longing and the anticipation of holding her body close to his own.

But instead of surrendering to his embrace, she stiffened and whispered, "Not now." She then turned to lead him back to the parlor. He followed, disappointed.

Within a few minutes, Rena reentered the parlor to announce Will was resting well. At that point Philip suggested he take his leave and Marion saw him to the door.

As Christopher and Rena watched Marion and Philip leave the room he wondered at Marion's coolness toward him. Was it just because someone else was in the house or was it especially Philip who was present that caused her to react that way. Who was he? Did he have any special meaning for Marion?

When Marion reappeared she seemed somewhat embarrassed. Christopher wanted desperately to talk to her, to be alone with her, but in spite of his strong desire to do so he felt he should go see Zachariah as soon as possible. There was a mild tension in the air but this was soon relieved by Joseph who appeared in the doorway. He announced the riding horses had been put away and he had brought the chaise back around in order to take Christopher to see Zachariah.

"I hate to rush off," said Christopher.

"Nonsense!" replied Mrs. Pierce, "You shouldn't waste any time. If Abraham thinks Zach Davis is your best hope for rescuing your brother-in-law, you'd better go see him right away."

Zachariah Davis, a bachelor, well into his sixties, lived alone. To many he seemed to be the antithesis of every thing around him. Whereas most people lived in, or close to a town, Zachariah preferred the isolation of Burnt Point, a desolate finger of land jutting out towards the sea and forming the protective southern arm of Squansett Cove. While most homes in the area were well-kept, his was a blending of cottage and a myriad of old objects surrounding it. One could safely say the value of this melange, mostly extracted from the sea, existed only in the mind of Zachariah. Only the most discerning eye could tell where junk ended and the cottage began. When most people were striving to 'get ahead' Zachariah was the epitome of contentment and was quite satisfied with what he had, although most folks would consider that to be next to nothing. He was not a lazy man just very frugal in the expenditure of his efforts. He took nothing seriously, that is, except his freedom to say and do as he pleased. And when he felt that to be encroached upon, his reactions usually led to jail, the bottle, or both.

As the chaise passed through an open gateway formed by large, bleached whale bones, Christopher could understand why one would prefer this location. It was on a rocky rise that afforded a panoramic view of the glistening sea. The roar of the pounding surf below competed with the wind blowing through the nearby pines while sea gulls swooped back and forth adding their cries to the scene. Christopher felt this must be the closest thing to being at sea without actually being there.

Zachariah had been poking around in a pile of broken lobster traps when he heard the chaise approach. At the sound he turned and came to greet them. Christopher was surprised for this was not at all the ill-tempered old sot he had pictured from the things he had heard. Instead, Zachariah was one of those persons who seemed to effuse friendliness. He was slightly taller than most men, partly due to a longer than average neck. He had dark hair for his age, a larger than average nose that seemed even larger because of his mouth receding to where his teeth had been. When he smiled, which was most of the time, his brow wrinkled in a funny sort of way just above his nose and deep crow's feet radiated from the corners of his eyes. Christopher, at once, liked this man.

"Well, Joseph my friend, haven't seen you for quite a spell. What brings you all the way out here?" asked Zachariah as he took the reins and secured them to a hitching post. Even before Joseph or Christopher stepped down he was holding out a large, powerful hand to greet them.

"Hello, Zach," answered Joseph, "This here's Christopher Hall, a close friend of Captain Abraham's and his family. The captain advised him to come see you for help with a problem."

"A problem hey? And just what kind of a problem would it be that two strong men like you can't solve without the aid of old Zach?"

"A problem with the British, Zach," answered Joseph, knowing that would get his interest.

"Well now, this sounds interesting. Come in, come in," he added, motioning to the door of the cottage. "Let's hear about it. Yes, let's hear what the rascals are up to now."

The interior of the cottage gave the same impression as the outside but for some reason Christopher felt comfortable in this strange collection of clutter. Everything there seemed to reflect the unusual charm of their host. After offering them a tot of rum, which they each declined, he poured one for himself and sat down at the table with them. Christopher then told him the whole story of Thomas' disappearance, his being in a Boston jail near Dock Square, and the urgency of rescuing him as soon as possible.

All the while Christopher was talking, Zachariah rubbed his chin and listened intently. When Christopher finished, Zachariah pounded the table with his fist, stood up and declared, "By heaven, we've gotta get him outta there. I don't exactly know how right now, but we'll figure out somethin'." He poured himself another tot of rum, tossed it down, then continued, "We'll have to have help inside Boston, we'll need that, don't think we could pull it off otherwise. But that's no problem. I know a man, a good man, one we can trust."

Christopher was elated. "Thank you, sir, thank you very much." He could almost see Matty's face when he returns with Thomas. "When do we start and what must I do?"

"We've gotta get ourselves into Boston first," said Zachariah. "Everyday there's wagons o' produce goin' in. You and I are goin' t' become farmers. I know where I can get a wagon; we'll take a load in day after tomorrow. I'll need tomorrow to make certain arrangements. Now you're gonna have t' look the part. A man don't work the soil all day without wearin' some o' it."

Joseph said, "I'll take care of that."

"Where should we meet?" asked Christopher.

"Not in town," admonished Zach, "There's too many Tory eyes pokin' about. Have Joseph bring you out to where the Squansett road cuts off from the Boston road. Be there at daybreak, day after tomorrow. I'll have what we need."

CHAPTER XI

As the wagon rumbled along the rut-worn road to Boston, jostling Christopher and Zach first one way then the other, Christopher still marveled at the dichotomy of his companion. Zachariah Davis gave every appearance of one who had not a care in the world, happily shunning responsibility and having as little to do with the concept of governing authority as he could legally get away with—and sometimes not. Yet, his resourcefulness and dedication to a cause, once accepted, amazed Christopher. The more Christopher thought about it, the more he realized that Zach was the perfect man to plan and lead in Thomas' rescue. Who would ever suspect a man like Zach of any clandestine activity? Yet, it had been less than forty-eight hours since Christopher had met Zach and he was already impressed by this man's fox-like mind and attention to detail. Christopher was feeling relaxed and confident they would succeed. He smiled as he thought of the events earlier that morning.

When Christopher and Joseph had arrived at the junction that morning Zach was already there, waiting with a wagon loaded half with potatoes, half with hay. He greeted them with a smile that suggested of more than simple affability. His eyes showed the excitement a contestant feels going up against a hated foe and being confident of victory. "Good morning, gentlemen," he said as he climbed down from the wagon and walked over to the chaise.

Christopher got out of the chaise and extended his hand to greet Zach. But Zach walked over to the side of the road where there was a mud puddle and stuck his hand in the muck. He then walked back and shook Christopher's hand with the one he'd just dirtied. Christopher looked at him incredulously.

"Ye're too damned clean my friend," laughed Zach, "now wipe it on yer clothes."

Christopher did as he was told and wiped his hand on his shirt. "How's that?" he asked.

"Not quite good enough. We're not goin' to the Governor's ball. Lie down."

"What!" asked Christopher.

"Lie down. Here, right here in the road, lie down."

As Joseph looked on, hardly able to contain himself, Christopher lay down in the road.

"Now roll over," instructed Zach.

Christopher rolled, and rolled again. Joseph could not help himself any longer and burst into laughter. Then Christopher began to laugh at himself and rolled over another time. Now all three were laughing at the absurd scene they were creating.

"Good, that's good enough. Now ye can get up and brush yerself off," said Zach. "By Golly! Ye might pass for a farmer after all."

And so it was on that bright July morning that these two "farmers", with their load of potatoes and hay, drove their team northward toward the besieged city of Boston. Within two miles of their destination, they found themselves traveling through a shallow valley, the sides of which joined together ahead of them to form Roxbury Hill. Soon the grade began to increase; the wagon creaked and groaned as the horses strained against the heavy load. As they neared the crest of the hill Christopher could see, on the left, the star-shaped fortification the colonials had erected on the highest ground. A shiver of anxiety ran through him as the realities of warfare began to reveal themselves to him and he knew they were getting ever closer to the enemy. This was suddenly replaced by simple awe as they crossed the top of the hill and a magnificent panorama opened up before them.

On the downward slope of the hill was the Colonial encampment. Farther on, another fortification had been thrown up stretching far to either side of the road at the George Tavern. Beyond that, there was nothing but open road for three quarters of a mile to the British fortification guarding the neck of land leading into the city of Boston. This narrow strip was the only way into Boston by land for it was otherwise surrounded by water. And there beyond, lay the city itself. Christopher had only seen it before from the deck of the *Briareus* or from water level that memorable night he escaped from the *Briareus*. The city stretched out a mile wide and almost two miles long beyond the connecting isthmus. Christopher was excited at the thought he would finally get to visit this fabulous city even though it would be under rather dangerous circumstances. Again he thought of what would happen to him if captured. After all, he was still considered a deserter by the British.

As they drove down the hill Christopher noticed the Colonial troops on either side of the road. The thing one usually notices about a military force is uniformity—uniformity in clothing, in equipment, in weaponry and in procedure. But here, any semblance of uniformity lay only in their cause. They were a hodgepodge collection of citizenry thrown together by fate and their dedication to the principle of self determination.

Christopher wondered, "How could such an army ever stand up to the well trained, well equipped, and experienced British army, the mightiest army in the world?" Yet, he knew they had already exhibited that ability, first at Lexington and Concord and again on Breed's Hill. Even though the British were the victors at Breed's Hill they won useless ground that day and paid dearly for it in lives. It was even rumored that British General Clinton had said, "A dear bought victory—another such would have ruined us."

As they drove on down the hill, reining in the team to keep the heavily laden wagon under control, they elicited a variety of reactions from those along the way. Some examined them with scrutiny, some with simple curiosity, and some with complete indifference. When they reached the bottom and drew near the George Tavern, where the lower fortification crossed the road, two armed Colonials stepped out and commanded them to halt.

Zach immediately drew back on the reins bringing the wagon to a stop. "Good morning, Gentlemen," he said, smiling.

The older soldier asked, in a not too friendly voice, "Who are ye? What've ye got? And where're ye goin'?"

Zach smiled and answered, "We are simple farmers bringing potatoes to our fellow Americans in Boston and hay for their horses."

"That may be, and it may not," replied the soldier. "We're to search every wagon going in or out o' Boston—orders of General John Thomas."

Zach calmly reached into his shirt a pulled out a paper. "Perhaps ye'd like to start with this." He handed the document to the puzzled soldier. Christopher was getting nervous, having no idea what was going on.

The soldier slowly examined the paper then offered it back to Zach. "Proceed. An' God be with ye."

Zach did not take the letter but said, "Ye'd better keep it, or better yet, burn it. We shouldn't want the Redcoats to find it on us." With that he slapped the horses with the reins and they started off toward the British lines, leaving the two Colonial soldiers standing in the road wondering what kind of a mission these two strangers could be on.

"What was that and where did you get it?" asked Christopher in amazement.

"Just a letter stating we should not be delayed in any way."

"Who could write such a letter? Where did you . . . ?"

Zach was enjoying himself. He grinned and looking straight ahead answered, "Abigail Adams."

"Abigail Adams! Who's . . . ?"

"The wife of John Adams. He's in Philadelphia right now . . . one of our delegates to the Continental Congress. I rode up to Braintree last night; they have a farm there. Lucky for us she was at home. I did a bit of a favor for John once. She was more than happy to help when I explained what we were doing."

"But why the trouble? It wouldn't have taken long for them to inspect the wagon and let us go on. Getting through our own lines should have been easy."

"Perhaps, perhaps not," said Zach. "True, our own soldiers

would be no threat to us personally, but suppose they decided they needed the potatoes and hay more than the people in Boston do. Our load of supplies is our ticket into Boston, without it we might as well turn around and go home."

Christopher made no comment. He was too busy thinking what an unusual man Zach really was. He felt even more secure and confident with him than ever.

The road now stretched out before them across an open plain. About two thirds of a mile straight ahead of them was the British fortification guarding the only way into the city.

"Relax," said Zach, "this won't be as difficult as ye think. The people in Boston, whether Rebel, Tory or British, need what we have. They'll let us through. If ye want to worry, worry about how we're going to get back out, especially with yer brother-in-law."

"How *are* we going to get back out?"

"Haven't figured that out yet."

That did start Christopher to worrying for now he felt like a fly plunging headlong into a spider web.

In a short while they reached the British line and, without a great deal of trouble, were allowed to pass. Zach was right. The soldiers even seemed to welcome them. "Things must be pretty bad in the city," mused Christopher. What did trouble him was the way they poked their bayonets into the bales of hay. "How were they ever going to get Thomas out of Boston in a wagon that's supposed to be empty?"

They crossed a short causeway and encountered a second check point where they were casually waved on by the guards. They were in! But Christopher's relief was dampened by the realization they were now in an enemy held city, a city that had only one road out and a shoreline surrounded by warships. As they traveled down Orange Street, the only thoroughfare along the neck of land leading to the city, Christopher felt they were being watched from every direction. Suddenly Zach began to whistle a peppy tune and doff his hat to the people along the road. Nudging Christopher with his elbow he whispered, "Relax, after all, we're just two farmers bringing supplies to the city. No one suspects any different, unless ye keep looking like ye've just stole the crown jewels."

"Sorry, I guess you're right. I'm not much experienced at play acting though."

"It's not too hard. Just think about yerself the way ye want the people around ye to think. A farmer who doesn't think he's a farmer won't act like a farmer. A young buck like you, comin' to the big city and not havin' a care in the world, would most likely be a gawkin' this way and that lookin' at the skirts. I remember my first trip to Boston—that's been a few years back mind ye—but I remember thinkin' I'd never seen so many pretty girls. Try lookin' fer the prettiest one. That'll make ye smile."

Christopher laughed at this as it broke his spell of apprehension. Soon, houses and shops became more numerous as Orange Street became Newbury Street and then Marlboro Street. It would change its name six more times as it wound its way through the city. "Seems like they have more street names than they do streets around here," said Christopher.

Most of the timber frame houses were symmetrical with one door and one or two windows on either side. Their shake shingled roofs and silver-gray weathered boards gave them a common look. An occasional house would break the monotony with a room addition and farther in town some had overhanging second floors where streets were narrow and building space limited. In the "better" areas prominent citizens had erected large homes of brick, or more often, wood sculptured to resemble stone.

Again the street changed name, this time to Cornhill Street. As the wagon rolled on they began to see fewer houses; shops and commercial buildings, some as high as three stories, were becoming more numerous, and so were the people. In spite of the embargo by the British and the siege by the colonials, Boston was still a busy town. By now there was so much to capture Christopher's attention that Zach no longer had to remind him to look natural.

After a block of various stores and businesses they came to a wide area where Queen Street went off to the left and King Street, to the right. In the center of this area stood the Town House, the seat of local government. It was a remarkable building, three stories high with a tiered cupola towering above it. A second floor balcony protruded over the eight steps leading up to the main entrance. The most unusual feature was the two brightly colored figures high up on the top corners and facing each other. One was a lion, the other a unicorn. They gave the building a regal appearance, which was, in all probability, the exact intent.

Zach pulled on the right reins and the team turned the corner onto King Street where there were even more tall buildings, some as high as four stories. Along both sides of the street and over the doorways hung a myriad of signs, each proclaiming the nature of the business conducted within. They ranged from the elaborate, with gilded lettering, to the old and weather-beaten. People were coming and going everywhere; Christopher had never seen anything quite like it. Looking on down the street he could see a forest of masts and crisscrossing jib booms where the street ran onto Long Wharf and idle ships waited for commerce to return to normal.

"Look over there, to the right," said Zach as he nudged Christopher with his elbow. "That's where American blood was spilled by the redcoats back five years ago. Some call it a massacre."

"What happened?" asked Christopher, who had not yet heard of the event.

"Well, to tell the truth, they probably brought it on themselves. A bunch of rowdies were teasin' the soldiers, callin' 'em 'Lobsterbacks' an' worse. One thing led to another; the crowd got bigger and noisier and started throwin' things. First thing ye know, one of them soldiers must have panicked and fired. Before it was over five citizens were killed and six wounded."

"Whew! What happened after that?"

"Governor Hutchinson got up on that balcony back there at the Town House and calmed everybody down. There was a trial later on—for the soldiers, that is. John Adams defended them to show the Brits we could do things fairly over here, I guess. Only two of the eight were convicted."

"What did they do to them?" asked Christopher.

"They were burned on the hand. The fourteenth and twenty ninth regiments were removed from the city to Castle William in the harbor. But old Sam Adams—that's Sam, not John—he made the most of it, ye can bet on that. Hasn't let a soul forget it since; they made a holiday out o' it, March fifth 't is."

"Is Sam Adams John Adams' brother?"

"Nope, cousin. They say Sam was never good at much 'cept stirrin' up folks. Guess we need someone like that once in a while; too many folks are just too damned willin' to let others walk all over 'em. The whole business probably wouldn't a happened if King George hadn't seen fit to force his troops on us."

Zach pulled the reins to the left. The wagon rattled onto Market Row where produce and other products were being traded amid a cacophony of sound. Because of the shortages competition for farm products had become rather intense. Zach and Christopher had no difficulty in getting rid of their load.

"Where do we go now?" asked Christopher as Zach placed the money from their sale into his leather money pouch and tucked it back into his shirt.

"I've a friend, lives on Clark Street. We can stay there. He'll help us too," replied Zach as he and Christopher climbed back on the wagon.

As they rode off through the maze of Boston's narrow back streets Christopher wondered what was to happen next. How were they going to go about rescuing Thomas? "Do you have a plan, Zach?"

"'Course not, don't know the situation yet," said Zach. "But if Eli don't know what's goin' on he's the one that can sure find out."

"Eli?"

"Eli Yates is his name. Hates the redcoats more than anyone I know. That's why I'm sure he'll help us."

"Why is he so bitter?"

"Well, for one thing, he had a prosperous tea import business before Parliament started passin' all its confounded laws. They might near ruined him; he's barely hangin' on now. But, more 'n that, his younger brother got run through by a British bayonet on Breed's Hill."

"Oh," was all Christopher could say as he pondered how many such stories could be told and if there would ever be a healing between England and the colonies after so much hurt.

"Here we are," said Zach as he reined the horses to a stop in front of a modest but well-kept, gray, wooden cottage. He handed the reins to Christopher and said, "Wait while I see if anybody's home." He then got down and went to the door. Before he could knock, the door opened and there stood a small, dark-haired, round-faced woman who looked to be in her mid-thirties. Her wide eyes and broad smile showed both surprise and delight.

"Zach! Zachariah Davis! Whatever brings you into Boston town?" Before he could answer, she turned and yelled, "Eli! Come here. You'll never guess who's here." Turning back to Zach, she said, "I thought I heard a wagon stop outside; never figured it was you. How've you been?"

"Just fine, Bertha. And you?"

"Better 'n some; not as good as others. Can't complain though, I figure the Lord's been good to us when I consider what some folks have to contend with."

Just then Eli, a thin, half bald man, who didn't look to be much bigger than his wife, appeared. "Zach! By Golly! Come on in. You gonna stand there in the doorway all day?"

"I've got a friend out with the wagon," he replied as he motioned toward the wagon and Christopher.

"Oh. I'm sorry, Zach. Bring your rig around to the back through the ally. I'll meet you out there." Turning to Bertha he said, "Would you prepare some tea, Dear? I'll go help with their horses."

After the horses were unhitched, rubbed down, fed and watered, the men went inside. Christopher was properly introduced to Bertha then all four sat down at the small kitchen table to tea

Bertha had just prepared. Eli and Bertha listened intently as Zach and Christopher explained their reason for being in Boston. Christopher could tell by the excitement welling up inside Eli that they could certainly rely on him for help.

When they had finished describing their mission, Eli said, "You can count on me, and as many others of the Sons of Liberty that it'll take."

"Thank you, sir," said Christopher half choked with gratitude, "you'll be risking so much and there's no way I could ever repay . . . ."

"Nonsense, I'm beholdin' to you for givin' me an opportunity to twist the lion's tail. Nothin' could suit me finer than to snatch your brother-in-law out from under the noses of the lobsterbacks. Don't know how we're gonna do it yet, but believe me, we'll find a way."

Zach leaned forward and, in a more serious tone, said, "We've been told he might be in a jail near Dock Square. Do ye know of the place?"

"Aye, that I do . . . and I wish it were any place else."

A frown immediately came over Christopher's face as he asked, "What do you mean? You don't think we can get him out?"

"Oh, I didn't mean that, my friend. It'll just be a bit harder than I thought. And a bit more dangerous. First of all, we need to find out for certain that's where he is. We can't be wastin' valuable time barkin' up the wrong tree. Now you two make yourselves at home while I go see what I can find out."

"We'll go with you," objected Christopher.

"No, it's better that you don't. There's too many Tories around. Folks are used to seein' me here 'n about. Havin' strangers with me might arouse their curiosity." With that, Eli stood up, took his tricorn hat from a peg near the front door and left.

Bertha showed Zach and Christopher to the extra room that had been added to the side of the house. "Make yourselves comfortable," she said with a motherly smile, "I don't expect Eli will be very long."

It was a small, sparsely furnished room having only a bed, one chair, and a small table with the usual pitcher and bowl. The little space that remained was mostly taken up with a variety of items stored there in order to keep the rest of the house neat. It was obvious this room was not used very much but it would do, and do very nicely. Christopher sat down on the bed and let out a long sigh. He could relax for a while. It wasn't until now that he realized how much of a strain he'd been in pretending to be something he wasn't and all the while trying not to let the anxiety show. Even Zach appeared more at ease. They were secure now, at least for the time being, and beyond the reach of curious and prying eyes. Christopher lay back on the bed and casually examined the rough hewn beams of the ceiling. Somehow everything here reminded him of his sister Matty's house. They were much alike, not in appearance but in atmosphere. He felt comfortable here, so comfortable that he was soon fast asleep.

"Wake up! Eli's back," said Zach as he shook Christopher out of his deep slumber. "Boy, you sure were out."

"Huh? What? Oh." It took Christopher several seconds to remember where he was and why. "Golly, how long was I asleep?"

"Over two hours, sleepy head. Come on to the kitchen. Let's hear what he found out."

Christopher shook off the last remnants of slumber, and was off the bed in a second and following Zach into the kitchen.

Eli, who had come in by the rear door, took a piece of paper and a pencil from a drawer and sat down at the table. "Let me show what the situation is," he said. He was not smiling and this worried Christopher.

As Christopher and Zach sat down at the table Christopher asked, "Did you find him? Can we get him out?"

"Let me show you. It won't be as simple as I thought but I still believe we can do it." Eli drew a large rectangle on the paper and within it he drew three small squares in a row, touching each other but not the outside rectangle. "This is the jail," he indicated, pointing to the large rectangle. "It's just off Dock Square like you heard. It's an old stone warehouse the British have converted into a jail for political prisoners, or traitors as they prefer to call them. These three squares were originally storage bins which are now used as cells. They're open at the top but they have very high walls. What's worse is the cells have no outside walls. Your brother-in-law is in this one on the right. As you can see, there is no way for him to break out through the wall for he'd only end up in the larger enclosure which is where the guards are."

Gloom poured over Christopher as the seemingly impossible was revealed to him. He was so stunned he could not even comment on what Eli had diagramed.

"How'd ye find this out?" asked Zach.

"John Parsley has the Brass Lantern Tavern nearby. He supplies the food for the prisoners. He sends it over by his daughter, Agnes, or sometimes he takes it himself to this cell here." He pointed to the third square on the paper. "We can be pretty sure that's where Thomas is being held."

Christopher finally spoke, "We'll never be able to get him out of there." He looked first to Eli then to Zach. The expression on his face pleaded for reassurance.

"Don't be so quick to give up," admonished Eli. "The walls are high, like I said before, and no one can climb out. But a rope could be lowered by someone above."

Christopher's eyes widened as hope was being restored.

Eli continued, "John took me to a friend who used to work there when it was still a warehouse. Name's Woods, Henry Woods. He says he knows every nook and cranny in the place. He tells me the space above the cells is open and the roof trusses go right over the cells. He's positive we can get over Thomas's cell from the attic of the building next door. He's workin' on the possibility right now."

Zach leaned back in his chair and slapped the table with his right hand to emphasize the point. "By damn! We'll pluck him right out from under their bloody noses, we will!" He saw Eli's eyes move toward Bertha who was standing nearby. "Oh, sorry, Ma'am. I sorta got carried away."

Christopher's optimism was returning as he imagined the scenario of the rescue. But it went no further than just getting Thomas out of the jail. "How are we ever going to get out of Boston, especially if the word is out there's been an escape?"

"That's the important thing," replied Eli, "we've got to get him out without their knowing it. Otherwise, they'll seal up the city tighter than a barrel hoop. Our best time, I figure, will be shortly after they change the guards at midnight. They're least likely to be checking on him after that. That'll give us the most time."

"But getting out of the city, how . . . ?"

Zach interrupted, "I might have an idea or two on that." Turning to Eli, he asked, "Isn't there a burial ground outside the city?"

"Yes," replied Eli, "it's between Roxbury Hill and Dorchester Neck, just below our troop's lines."

"Good. Do ye know where we can get a coffin?"

"Believe so, if not, we can have one made in a day," answered Eli. "So, you want to sneak Thomas out as a corpse."

"Seems like a natural thing to be doin', two men in a wagon takin' a body out to be buried. You and Christopher work on gettin' Thomas out of the jail, I'll take care of gettin' us out o' the city."

"There's one other thing I found out," said Eli, "the ship that's supposed to take Thomas to England is in port. We must act soon if we're goin' to save him. Tomorrow we get ready, tomorrow night we get him out. Any later might be too late."

"Tomorrow night it is then," agreed Zach.
"Tomorrow night," repeated Christopher.

CHAPTER XII

Thomas Owings was awakened by the harsh sound of the bolt sliding back on the heavy oak door of his cell. The little bit of light that came from the open area above his cell was barely enough to show where objects were, not enough to identify them, or people. But Thomas immediately recognized the silhouetted figure of Agnes Parsley as the guard swung open the door. In the month since he'd been transferred here from the prison ship in the harbor she was the only colonial with whom he'd had any contact. Even this had been extremely limited for they were not allowed to speak to each other, except for matters pertaining to the food, and some of the guards did not even allow this. Nevertheless, there had been that special, and difficult to describe, kind of silent communication that often occurs in the presence of common hardship and compassion.

Agnes was a small girl with blonde hair that just touched her shoulders; she appeared to be in her early teens. Her smooth skin and pixie-like face revealed her youth but her rough and callused hands showed that most of that youth had been spent at hard work helping her father at the tavern.

"Up and at it, Rebel! Your breakfast is here," barked the burley guard as he escorted Agnes into the room. He then lit a taper from his lantern and with it lit the small betty lamp on the table. A soft yellow glow filled the room.

As the guard turned away, Agnes set the tray of food on the table. She did this with deliberate slowness, allowing time for the guard to move away, and time for Thomas to reach the table. Making sure the light from the lamp fell upon her face, she gave Thomas her usual smile. These smiles had come to mean a great deal to Thomas for they were the only source of cheer in an otherwise hopeless situation. But this time there was more. As he looked at her she carefully but silently with her lips formed the word, "Tonight." Then, aloud she said, "The burgoo's a bit loose this morning, there's bread to sop it with. Make sure you eat all of it." Then with the wink of the eye, she said, "I don't want to carry a mess back with me."

"That'll do, wench. 'E know's 'ow to eat," said the guard impatiently.

Agnes smiled again then followed the guard out of the cell and Thomas was alone.

"What? What was she trying to say?" he wondered as he watched the door close behind them. He stood there in the dim light, bewildered, with no thought for the food that had been placed on the table. His mind was racing. He tried to remember Agnes's face, to recall what he had seen there. "What was it?" he asked himself again as he wrung his hands in anxiety. "It looked like 'Tonight', yes that's what it was, 'Tonight'. She was saying, 'Tonight'. But what did it mean? Could it be that I am to be rescued tonight?" The thought filled him with excitement and the hope of freedom, a hope he'd all but relinquished. What should he do? Was anything expected of him to help in his rescue? Suddenly, his excitement was overcome by apprehension. Could she have been telling him that tonight he would be taken to the ship in which he would be transported to England for trial and almost certain execution. The thought that this could be his last day in America, a land he loved so much, consumed him with a dreadful chill and the whole room seemed suddenly cold. He thought of this for a long time before he admonished himself for being so negative. After all, Agnes might have only meant he was being moved to another jail. No, this was unlikely. His imagination ran from one extreme to the other, between hope and despair, from gloom to cheer.

After exploring all the possibilities, Thomas came to the conclusion that, no matter what was to happen, his own interest would best be served by appearing ignorant and unsuspecting. He must behave as though he had heard nothing and knew nothing. With that thought, he sat down, and with spoon in one hand and bread in the other, began to eat the oatmeal porridge, all the while wondering what Agnes had meant and why she made such a point of his eating all the burgoo.

The burgoo was good, but loose like Agnes had said. Although Thomas liked it, apprehension had replaced his appetite and he had some difficulty in finishing it. However, and perhaps it was only his subconscious that compelled him to do so, he took his remaining piece of bread and began to sop up the last of the porridge from the plate. Suddenly he stopped. His eyes widened. There it was again, scratched in the bottom of the wooden plate, in bold letters, was the word: 'TONIGHT'

He hurriedly wiped away the remaining porridge and stared at the plate in utter amazement. There, also scratched in the wood, were the words: 'BE READY, FROM ABOVE'

"From above". What could it mean? He looked up. His cell, originally a storage bin with heavy plank walls thirty feet high, was open at the top. In the dim light he could see that the trusses supporting the warehouse ceiling passed over his cell. "That's it!" he exclaimed to himself, "Someone's going to try to get me out. What else could it mean? If I'm to be taken to the ship it certainly wouldn't be from above. It has to be that someone is going to try to rescue me, and from up there." He was shaking with excitement now and pacing back and forth thinking, wondering who was planning his escape and how. Suddenly he realized all would be lost if the guard saw the wooden plate. He raced to the table and grabbing the spoon tried to scratch out the words. It was not sharp enough. "What can I use," he asked himself. They had taken away anything that he had that was sharp. The only thing he had that was metal was his buckle. He tried that but it wasn't sharp enough. What could he do? If the guard came in for the plate and saw the message not only would he be lost but his captors would surely set a trap for his would-be rescuers. He thought of burning it with the lamp but that would look too suspicious. Then, looking down at the stone floor, the idea came—sharpen the buckle on the stone. Quickly he began to rub the corner of the buckle back and forth on the granite. Soon it appeared sharp enough to do the job. He sat down and, holding the plate in his lap, began to scratch it this way and that to obscure the letters that had brought him renewed hope. Done. But the scratches looked new, too new. He spit on his hand and rubbed it on the floor then rubbed the plate until the scratches looked old. "Now the guard can have the plate any time he wants it," he said to himself.

He thought of the message again, "Be ready, what was meant by that?" There was little he could do. He pondered that for a while then it came to him that discovery of his escape should be delayed as long as possible. He would need to make his bed look occupied. But with what? He had nothing. Other than the clothes he wore, there was only a blanket and absolutely nothing to put under it. He felt so helpless but there was simply nothing he could do to be ready except remain alert. There would be no problem doing that; nothing else would be on his mind for the rest of the day and that night.

When Agnes brought in his noon meal he wanted to let her know he had received the message, but had to be careful the guard did not detect him doing it. Thomas was not very good at facial communication. As Agnes approached him with her tray he maneuvered so that for a moment the guard was behind Agnes and could not see between them. He took the tray with his left hand and with his right hand quickly pointed straight up. As she relinquished the tray she repeated the gesture and he knew for certain his interpretation had been correct.

When his supper was delivered that evening there was neither word nor gesture, all was understood and there was no further need to risk detection. The only thing left to do was wait. It was a long evening for Thomas Owings.

CHAPTER XIII

Throughout Boston lamps were being lit as the sun slowly slid below the western horizon. The twilight stillness that separates day from night spread an atmosphere of outward serenity over most of the city. However, within, all was not calm. There were families still grieving the loss of a loved one in the fighting the had preceded, and those still planning further resistance to British rule. There were those held captive not knowing their fate and not being very optimistic about it. And, of course, there were those loyalists who were bitter toward those colonial 'Hotheads' who, they felt, had caused all this strife. In a small home on Clark Street there were four men filled with excitement and anticipation, knowing that before the sun rose again another man would be free—or they all would be captive or dead.

While Zach, Eli, and Henry Woods sat around the kitchen table swapping yarns, Christopher paced back and forth in the front room, occasionally stopping to look out the front window. He found it impossible to relax. It had been so long since he'd left home for what was to have been a simple weekend visit to his sister. In his mind he retraced every event since that day—his being pressed into the British navy, escaping from the *Briareus*, nearly dying, meeting Marion, the encounter off Martha's Vineyard in which Jacob had been killed, privateering with Captain Pierce, Will Mundy, the return to Squansett Cove and now this. It had all led to this. Before the night would be out he would see Thomas again and if the Good Lord was with them, Thomas, Zach and he would be out of Boston and free. Yes, with the Lord's help. With this thought he bowed his head and prayed. It was not his custom to do so. He'd prayed often in church, of course, with someone leading, but only once or twice in his life had he, on his own, prayed for God's help. He did so now.

In the kitchen Henry was telling how his cousin Bessie got rid of the two British soldiers that had been quartered in her home. "Well, she didn't like it none, none at all, havin' to let them lobsterbacks sleep under her roof. But cousin Bessie, she's a sly one I'll have you know. She made on like she was mighty glad to have 'em so's they wouldn't suspect nothin'. Then she kinda let it slip that she'd tried to run a roomin' house after she was widowed. But since folks all around thought the house was haunted no one would stay there. The Brits didn't give it much mind at first but when she started a rattlin' chains at night they begin to wonder."

"How did she finally get them to leave?" asked Eli.

"Well, one night when she thought the time was right, she waited 'til the two were asleep then she had a friend come in the back way and make like he was her dear departed husband. She and the friend stayed in her room and talked just loud enough so's to wake them Redcoats and be overheard. In a creepy voice he said, 'You shouldn't have murdered me, Bessie. No other man will sleep in this house and live.' About that time she let out the most blood curdlin' scream. Well, them Redcoats didn't even wait to get their britches on. They grabbed their belongin's an' out the door they went, high tailin' it down the street. She's not seen hide nor hair of either of 'em since."

Eli roared with laughter even though he had heard the story before. He rocked back and forth in his chair, slapping his leg, until he almost fell over.

Zach was a bit skeptical. "Ye mean to tell us they actually thought it was the voice of her dead husband?"

"Well, there's one other thing she did to make it convincin'. I forgot t' tell ye she brought in a decayed cat and let the smell go all through the house. One sniff o' that an' they were sure somethin' was dead."

With that, they all began to laugh, including Christopher who had just entered but had heard enough to allow him to join in the mirth.

When the laughter subsided, Zach said, "Let's check once more to be sure we have everything. I've got the coffin out in the wagon and enough straw to cover it. How about you, Eli?"

"Got everything you asked for: two shovels, a pry bar, hammer, nails, hollow reed, and the Jesuit's bark and sulfur powders."

"Sounds good," said Zach. "Henry, ye've got the rope and scarecrow?"

"Yup, got 'em both."

"And the dead animal? Did ye get that idea from yer cousin Bessie?"

"Sure did, if it worked once it oughta work again. Jesse, my youngest, and some of his friends are lookin' for one. Don't worry, they'll come up with somethin'."

After a while there was a knock at the back door. Zach, Henry and Christopher retreated to the spare room, leaving Eli at the table. When they were out of sight Bertha unlatched the door and pulled it open to reveal two small boys both beaming triumphantly and one holding up a dirty cloth sack. She immediately jumped back, holding her nose. "Get that, whatever it is, out of here!" She slammed the door and turned to Eli, "Go out there and do something with that, but don't bring it in my house! Land sakes, that's enough to gag a maggot."

Eli grinned and called to the others, "It's all right, come on out. It's Jesse and I do believe he's been successful." He then took a deep breath and went outside.

In a few minutes, Eli returned and announced that their list was now complete. "I put it in the coffin and put the lid on. No need in making the whole neighborhood sick. We now wait until after midnight."

"Good," exclaimed Zach, "Ye did arrange fer a distraction?"

"Yes," replied Eli, "around one o'clock a dozen of the Sons of Liberty will cause a loud commotion outside the jail. That'll be our signal and you'd better hope they make enough noise to cover any sounds we make."

The rest of the evening Henry dozed on and off while Zach and Eli brought each other up to date on recent events in their respective communities. Christopher paced.

At midnight Thomas lay in his bed, wide awake, listening to the changing of the guard. When the new guard opened the door to check on his prisoner he was satisfied all was well. Thomas, with his back toward the door, did not move but pretended to be asleep. He watched his own shadow move back and forth against the heavy timbered wall as the guard swung his lantern around to inspect the room. Then, when the shadow ceased to move, he sensed the guard was looking straight at him. He could not resist a small smile when he heard the guard mutter, "Sleep well, Yank, for tomorrow you sail for England." The guard then turned, went out and closed the door.

"Would this really be the last time I hear that door close?" he wondered, still smiling. Then the smile quickly faded at the sound of the bolt being rammed shut. It reminded him once again of how desperate his situation was and how little chance there was of a rescue attempt being successful.

"I've got to believe someone will come," he said to himself. "I have to keep faith that someone is trying to get me out of here. But who? Who would take such a risk?" These are thoughts that plagued Thomas as he lay in his bed studying every feature of his cell by the dim light that trickled over the high walls.

After what seemed like an eternity Thomas was startled by the sounds of a commotion out in the street. There was much yelling back and forth, accompanied by the clatter of nervous horses stomping on the cobble-stoned street. Instinctively he stood up but was immediately knocked down by a mysterious figure that seemed to have come from out of nowhere. He jumped to his feet ready to defend himself, no matter what. He might be outweighed or outnumbered with no way out but he was determined to go down fighting. He looked about for his attacker, ready to strike before being struck. Then to his surprise he saw his assailant lying motionless on the floor. He knelt down to examine the figure. What he saw almost made him laugh for it wasn't a person at all, but a dummy, dressed in clothes very much like his own. Attached to the dummy was a rope leading straight up into the darkness above. At first the whole situation was incredulous, then suddenly it dawned on him that the dummy was meant to replace him and that the rope was for his escape. His heart was beating faster than it had ever done before. He knew then that the commotion outside was to distract the guards. He also knew they would soon have things settled down so there was no time to waste. He quickly untied the dummy and placed it on the bed in the same position he'd been in. He stepped back to examine it. Satisfied that it would pass for him and not arouse suspicion, he grabbed the dangling rope and started to climb hand over hand. The months of captivity had taken their toll on his muscles. His arms ached as he climbed and he would have given up under any other circumstances but he was on his way to freedom and that thought provided him with the extra bit of strength needed to keep climbing. Once or twice he had to grip the rope with his feet and rest to catch his breath. Then slowly, upward he went. This was his only chance.

Reach, grab, and pull. Reach, grab, and pull. Over and over it went with each pull straining him to the limit. His arms ached as they never had before. Then after a few minutes, but what seemed an eternity, his hand touched a knot and then the rough wooden beam to which it was attached. Out of the darkness strong, helping hands took him under the armpits and lifted him up onto the truss. He started to speak but a quick "Shhh" admonished him to keep silent. In the dim light all Thomas could see were two dark figures on the beam with him. One was tugging on his sleeve indicating he was to follow while the other quickly retrieved the rope. Carefully the trio crawled along, feeling their way in the darkness.

Then they noticed the sounds from the street had stopped. Apparently the guards had dispersed the noise makers and were returning to their posts inside. The voice of one guard echoed throughout the cavernous building, "I best check on the rebel. I hope the ruckus didn't disturb his beauty sleep."

"What if it did," added the other guard. "His looks won't help him much when the courts in London get through with him."

The three on the truss froze in their positions, breathing as lightly as possible. Below them they saw the cell door open and the inquisitive guard swing his lantern around to inspect the room. Faint rays of light strayed upward, enough to reveal the three perched there if the guard looked up. Finally, the guard looked at the bed then turned away. He stopped and turned to look at it again. A wave of panic raced through the three figures above. Then the guard turned away again and shook his head muttering, "Don't see how these rascals can sleep so sound."

When the guard turned to go out, a faint ray of light from his lantern momentarily flashed on the face of one of Thomas's rescuers. He gasped in surprise to see it was Christopher, his own wife's brother. He could hardly believe his eyes and even began to doubt what he had seen as darkness overcame them again. "It couldn't be," he told himself as they continued to crawl along the truss. "It couldn't possibly be Christopher, how in heaven's name could he be here?"

They continued to crawl, slowly and carefully, along in the darkness and after some distance they came to a wall on which the truss rested. Here was a small opening just large enough for a man to crawl through. One by one they squeezed through. Once on the other side they were in the attic of the adjoining building and standing on a solid wooden floor. The large room was dimly illuminated by a single candle Henry had left sitting on the floor and away from the opening.

Henry picked up the candle and it cast its soft light upon the three faces. Thomas whispered in amazement, "Christopher! My God! Is that really you?"

"Yes," answered Christopher as softly as he could, "and this is Henry Woods."

Emotion overcame Thomas. He embraced Christopher and

tried to speak, "I . . . I never thought . . . I prayed but I never . . . Christopher, it's . . . it's really you. How . . . ?"

"Save the talk for later," whispered Henry. "Let's get out o' here. There's a ladder on the other side. We'd best stay close to the wall; the floor's less apt to squeak there."

The three, one after the other, very carefully made their way around the room, pausing after each sound that emanated from the ancient floor boards. They listened carefully for any unusual movement from where they had come; when they felt they had not been heard they proceeded. When they reached the ladder on the other side Henry quenched the candle and said, "Wait here, I'll go down and see if it's clear."

Though Christopher and Thomas were now in total darkness and still far from free, Thomas was, for the first time in many months, experiencing some feeling of freedom.

Within a few moments they heard movement on the ladder below them, then Henry's whisper, "All right, come on down." Feeling their way, rung by rung, first Thomas then Christopher descended into the darkness below. When they reached the bottom they could see nothing; but the feel of a stone floor under their feet told them they were now on the ground floor.

"Take my hand," said Henry, "I know where things are in here." Christopher did so and held his other hand back for Thomas to take. Thus, the trio snaked their way through the black room to a door that opened into another room on the rear of the building. Here they could see by the little bit of stray light that came through the window from a building across the ally. Henry motioned them to stay back from the window as he watched down the ally.

They saw Henry quickly drop to the floor at the sound of approaching boots. They cringed in the darkness breathlessly as they waited for the patrol to pass. Six figures in red marched by the window. The light from across the ally reflected on the brass buttons of their uniforms and, more ominously, the bayonets attached to their muskets.

When the sound of the soldier's feet had diminished to nothing, Henry carefully opened the door. Seeing nothing in either direction he motioned for the others to follow. He led them to the left, in the direction from which the soldiers had appeared. "Stay close to the buildings," he admonished.

Outside, at last! Thomas looked up at the clear black, star-filled sky. It was magnificent! "It's amazing," he thought, "how little one appreciates the outdoors until completely deprived of it."

Down one block and over two the trio crept, once having to duck into a door way to avoid a passing carriage. Suddenly, Henry ushered them into a narrow ally where a wagon was entering from the other end. When it came closer Christopher could see it was the one he and Zach had driven into Boston. Zach and Eli were on the seat.

"How did it go?" asked Zach.

"Great," answered Henry, "so far, so good. It's up to you now."

"All right, let's get him up here," said Zach as Eli moved to the back.

Introductions were quickly made as Thomas and Christopher climbed into the back of the wagon. Thomas was startled when he saw the wooden coffin. "Who is that?" he asked.

"That's you," answered Eli with a grin as he lifted the lid. Now, in with you, friend, and you'll be on your way."

Thomas reeled back as the most awful stench welled up from the coffin. "My God! What is that?"

"Just a dead 'possum," answered Eli, "He'll be your company on your trip out of Boston. You gotta smell dead if you want the Brits to believe you are."

"Fine, but I'll suffocate in there," complained Thomas.

"We've taken care o' that," said Zach, as he handed Thomas the hollow reed. "There's a tiny hole in the side of the coffin. Breathe through this but if we stop, hold yer breath and pull the reed in until we're a movin' again."

Thomas reluctantly climbed into the coffin with the dead 'possum, consoled by the belief it would help in their flight to freedom. Quickly the lid was nailed down, and Eli joined Henry on the ground.

"There's no way we can thank you enough," said Christopher. "You've risked your lives for us."

"Think nothin' of it," replied Eli, "I just wish I could see the look on the guard's face when he discovers Thomas is gone."

"Now be off with you," added Henry, "Ye've no time to waste."

With that, Zach gave the team a slap with the reins. The horses began to strain against their traces and the wagon started to move. Christopher looked back and could see Eli and Henry disappearing into the darkness. These men, whom he had never known before, had risked everything to help him. Without them he surely would not have succeeded. They never once hesitated to help Thomas, someone they had never met, regain his freedom. Suddenly he realized that it really didn't matter whether they knew Thomas or not, it was freedom itself to which these men were so dedicated. As the wagon slowly rolled through the dark streets of Boston Christopher thought on these things. Gone was that last thread of confused indifference and indecision. Christopher too had come to believe that freedom was worth whatever price it demanded.

At the end of the ally Zach reined the team to the right, taking them west on Queen Street and away from the Town House and towards Beacon Hill. "We best keep away from the Town House," whispered Zach, "It'll only be a little out of the way."

The stillness of the city at this hour seemed to amplify the sound of the horse's hooves and the rattle of the wagon. Christopher felt as though there were eyes peeking at them from out of every window, and could imagine a British patrol at this very moment being dispatched to intercept them.

"Shouldn't we have muffled the horse's hooves with rags?" asked Christopher.

"Thought of that but, then again, I figured there was too big a chance of our gettin' stopped. It'd make us look too suspicious."

Slowly, they moved on. At Tremont Street they became engulfed in a fog that had rolled in over the mill Pond and was creeping into the city streets. Zach turned the team to the left onto Tremont and slowed enough to stay in the fog.

On the left the outline of the Church of England with its tall steeple loomed up in the broiling mist; on the right the fog was sliding along the ground, surreptitiously swirling around the crop of gravestones that dotted the Burying Place across the street. It was an eerie scene.

Christopher constantly peered right and left, expecting danger from every corner, while Zach seemed to be completely unconcerned. However, Zach's appearance belied his inner emotions. He too was apprehensive, but knowing how much their success depended upon appearances, he tried to consider every possibility and scenario, rehearsing, in his mind, his reaction and words in every case.

Thomas, of course, bouncing along inside the coffin, could see nothing and had no way of judging their progress. His main concern for the moment was staying alive and not becoming ill from the stench of the dead 'possum. He held his nose with one hand and with the other tried to keep the reed sticking out the hole in the side of the coffin but not too far. With this hollow tube he continued to draw in fresh air from the outside.

On they rumbled. At the end of the Burying Place they turned left onto Rawson's Lane which in one block would take them to Marlboro Street, the street that would lead them out of the city. Zach wanted to avoid this main thoroughfare as much as possible and could have continued for one short block more before cutting back to it, but that would have exposed them to the Commons and the watch house that sat on the rise.

Now it was straight to the check point on that narrow strip of land that connected the city of captivity to a land of freedom and loved ones. As they moved on, past Summer Street then Pond and Essex Streets, the neck became increasingly narrower. Marlborough had changed its name to Newbury then to Orange Street. With fewer side streets the only houses were those along the street they were traveling. They were now more exposed than ever.

By this time the fog had completely covered the isthmus and had painted the city with a glistening dew. It had become so thick it swirled behind the wagon as it rolled steadily along. Christopher was becoming increasingly edgy. The engulfing mist made him feel confined; he had the sensation of a trap slowly closing upon him.

"I don't like this," Christopher said, nervously. "Can't we hurry?"

"I do," replied Zach, "Ye'd better bless this soup we're in. Without it we'd stick out like a sore thumb. If we can't see them, they can't see us. And if we go slow we won't make too much noise. We'll get there soon enough, we've only a quarter mile to go."

For Christopher the minutes passed like hours; for Thomas, in the black confines of the coffin, they passed like days. On they rambled. Christopher watched the horses' heads bob up and down as each step was exerted to move the wagon forward. They reminded him of a ship's bow rising and falling as it works its way through the swells of the sea. He wondered if he would ever again experience that feeling of freedom he had found on the open ocean.

Suddenly the dense fog ahead of them gave way to the dim outline of a guard house on the right then to a gate stretching across the road before them. "Whoa!" cried Zach as he drew back on the reins, "Whoa, there!" When the team came to a halt he pulled the long brake handle back and wrapped the reins around it. The door of the guard house slowly opened. Yellow light from the lamp within cut through the fog and cast its glow upon the wagon and its occupants.

"Who goes there?" grumbled a silhouette in the doorway.

"Burial party," answered Zach with no elaboration.

The figure, in white waistcoat and breeches, stepped forward as he donned his red coat with yellow facings. As a corporal in the Battalion Company, thirty-eighth regiment, he had fought on Bunker Hill and seen his best friend fall at his side with a rebel musket ball embedded in his forehead. He had no love for these colonials, even though most were of British descent. He figured there must be something wrong with them for wanting to settle in such a godforsaken land, as he saw it. Now some idiot American arrives in the middle of the night for who knows what! As the soldier approached the wagon another replaced him in the doorway, this one held a musket—the hammer was cocked.

"Burial party?" barked the corporal, "Likely story! Get ye down off o' there and stand in the light."

Zach and Christopher carefully got down from the wagon and moved into the light streaming around the figure in the doorway.

"Get out o' the door, ye damned fool," demanded the corporal of the private holding the musket. "I can't see their bloody faces with you standin' in the light."

One thing was certain, this guard was not friendly, and definitely not in a good mood. As the other soldier moved on outside Christopher could feel his knees begin to shake. Zach had told him that if that happened the best thing to do was to say something or do something. Just standing and doing nothing allows your emotions to catch up with you. But he couldn't think of anything to say and he was afraid to make a move. It was Zach who broke the spell.

"Yes sir, got a body needs buryin' right away."

"Since when can't the dead wait 'til sun up to get buried? I'm goin' t' have t' take a look."

"This'ns waited long enough I reckon, 'cordin' t' the doctor," replied Zach. "A patrol found him under Gibb's Wharf over by Fort Hill. Seems 'e's been dead quite a spell."

The corporal was getting impatient. "I don't intend t' stand out here all night yakin' with you rebels. Now get up there and open it up. I have t' take a look before I let you pass."

"Suit yerself," said Zach, "But I ain't gonna open it. You might as well just shoot me."

The corporal was momentarily taken aback by Zach's refusal, then assuming Zach was just afraid of the dead, he laughed contemptuously, "You stupid colonials, so damned superstitious. A dead man can't hurt you."

"This'n can. That's why he's t' be buried outside the city. The doctor thinks 'e died o' camp fever (typhus). Don't know how they can tell when a body's as far gone as this'n. We didn't want anything t' do with it but times are hard and work's hard t' find. Besides, the doctor said if we took powders it'd ward off the sickness. He even gave us extra for anyone who might come in contact with the body." With that, Zach reached into his coat, withdrew a small paper envelope and held it out to the corporal. "Here, it's Jesuit's bark and sulfur. The doctor said t' make a caudle of it 'fore you take it."

The corporal, a little less arrogant now, reached out and accepted the paper of powders. Realizing there was no way he could get Zach or Christopher to open the coffin, and under the circumstances had no desire to do it himself, he turned to the private, "You, get up there and take a look and be quick about it."

"But . . . ," the private started to protest.

"Damn yer bloody ass, do as I say," commanded the corporal.

Fearing his superior more than death itself, the private reluctantly climbed into the wagon. As he did so, Zach and Christopher moved back as though Pandora's box was about to be opened. The private picked up the pry bar that had been left lying in the wagon and started to pry up one end of the coffin's lid. Inside, Thomas held his breath, lay absolutely still and prayed.

To the groaning sound of nails being pulled from the wood, the lid slowly began to lift. As it did, the smell of death came pouring out of the coffin and over the edge of the wagon, permeating the air around them. In horror, the private dropped the pry bar and jumped down from the wagon; the corporal, Zach and Christopher, all three, moved even farther away.

The scene had been successfully set. The corporal, now convinced their mission to the burying ground was legitimate, yelled at Zach, "Get that damned thing out outta here!" Then, retreating to the guard house, he ordered the private to open the gate.

Zach climbed back onto the wagon and loosened the reins from the brake handle as Christopher, acting repulsed and afraid, held his nose and nailed the corner of the coffin back down. When the gate swung open Zach released the brake, gave a whistle and slapped the rumps of the horses with the reins. The two mares began to trudge forward and the wagon began to roll toward the colonial lines.

Thomas, nearly suffocating from holding his breath, pushed the reed out the hole in the coffin's side and breathed clean air, free air.

Half way across the open space between the two opposing forces the road to the burying ground and tan yard forked off to the left. At this point they continued straight for the colonial lines at Roxbury—the charade was over. Zach gave the horses a hard slap with the reins and they began to run. As he drove the team racing across the rough road, it was all Christopher could do to hold on to his seat while Thomas bounced around mercilessly inside the coffin and could hardly keep the reed in the hole for breathing. On they raced, to freedom, laughing and cheering. They were all feeling light hearted as though a great weight had been lifted from them.

The guards at the colonial lines seemed to sense the wagon racing toward them out of the fog shrouded night was friend and not enemy. They had opened the gate and Zach drove the team through at full speed. They were safe.

Pulling back hard on the reins and brake handle at the same time Zach brought the wagon to a sliding halt in front of the George Tavern, throwing gravel and dust into the air around them. He stood up, threw his tricorn hat high into the air and shouted, "Yahoo, we got 'em again. To hell with King George!"

Christopher was just as elated but quickly went to the back of the wagon and began removing the lid from the coffin. When he lifted it off, and the foul stench was released, the few onlookers that had gathered around quickly moved away. But curiousity kept them within viewing distance. They were convinced the coffin contained a corpse and when Thomas stood up they could hardly believe their eyes.

Then someone in the crowd must have realized what had really occurred and let out a great cheer. When the word got around they all began to celebrate with much cheering and back slapping.

Christopher embraced his brother-in-law in spite of the odor he had acquired. Thomas was yelling, "I can't believe it!"

Christopher was yelling, "Neither can I!"

Zachariah Davis could believe it. At this moment nothing could have made him happier.

CHAPTER XIV

Although it was still several hours before sunup at the garrison guarding the southern, and only land, approach to Boston, news of what the three had accomplished spread through the troops like wildfire. Militiamen by the score crowded around the George Tavern to hear the details of Thomas' rescue. Fortunately, there had been facilities at the tavern for Thomas to bathe and rid himself of the dead 'possum's smell. One of the militiamen there had an extra pair of breeches and a shirt, older but less odorous, that he offered to Thomas in exchange for his clothes bearing the stench of the dead animal.

After Thomas was cleaned up and the coffin disposed of, the three were given a hero's welcome and a sumptuous breakfast. Only the Provost Major, a lieutenant, a sergeant and two corporals were allowed in the room as the three ate and related the story of the rescue, but the door and both windows were packed with listeners who passed every detail back through the crowd. Their story, repeatedly interrupted by a chorus of 'huzzahs' from outside, eventually got told. Their breakfast they were able to consume intermittently during the frequent periods of cheering.

Christopher, being eager to return to Squansett Cove, turned to the Major and said, "We cannot thank you enough, sir, for your kind help and hospitality, but I feel we should now take our leave for there are those who are anxious about our return."

"Of course," replied the Major rising from the table indicating it would be quite all right for them to leave. "It would be most inconsiderate to keep them in suspense needlessly. Is there anything else we can do for you?"

"Thank you, no, sir," replied Thomas as he and Zach rose

from the table. "You've helped us immensely, but Christopher is right. We should be on our way."

The Major escorted them outside to their wagon, which was surrounded with well-wishers. After a round of farewell handshakes Zach climbed up and took the reins; Christopher and Thomas took their places beside him. Then to the accompaniment of a chorus of cheers, Zach released the brake and gave a slap of the reins. As the crowd opened up before them the two chestnut Belgians leaned into their load and the wagon began to roll south into the predawn darkness.

They traveled along the rutted road for more than an hour before a faint glow began to appear in the eastern sky. Soon the roadside gradually became more detailed and as the day grew brighter only a few remaining patches of fog lay cowering from the sun's rays piercing through the foliage. These last remnants of the night would soon be burned off as the whole countryside warmed up to this mid-July day. But the spirits of the three men riding along the road from Roxbury needed no further warming. In spite of their exhaustion from being up all night they reveled in what they had accomplished and the joys that lay ahead.

So many questions had been asked concerning the rescue from Boston, Christopher just now had the opportunity to hear how Thomas came to be captured.

"You know, of course, there was more to my trip to Philadelphia than just tobacco business," said Thomas. "While I was there I met Samuel Adams. Imagine it, Christopher, Sam Adams, the firebrand of New England! He invited me to go to Massachusetts to meet with the Committee of Correspondence and the Sons of Liberty."

"But Matty was worried so," said Christopher with a hint of reproach.

"It was an opportunity I couldn't resist," Thomas continued. "To get a first hand account of what was happening there and bring it back to Annapolis . . . I had to go. I wrote to Matty saying business was taking me to Boston and that I'd be gone longer and not to worry."

"She never got the letter, at least not before I went searching for you. Thomas, she probably thinks you're dead by now. Even if she got it after I left, that was last year. Poor Matty." Christopher thought for a moment of how heartbroken his sister must be, then asked, "But why did the British put you in prison?"

"I was asked to carry some dispatches to the committee in Boston. I was given a horse and advised to stay off the main roads but at Hartford I had to use the ferry to cross the Connecticut River. It was there I was intercepted by a British patrol. They searched me, found the dispatches, and accused me of treason against the crown. I was imprisoned in Hartford until April. After the fighting at Lexington and Concord they transferred me and most other prisoners to Boston. That's were I've been ever since. But I was told I was soon to be shipped to England for trial."

"That's what we heard also," injected Zach. "Looks like we got you out just in time."

"Christopher, Zach, I can't . . . I don't know . . . ," Thomas could speak no more; he couldn't say what was in his heart he was so choked with emotion. After that, no one spoke for a long time.

Finally, Thomas broke the silence. "But Christopher, I still don't know your story. How did you come to be here? How did you find me? You said you were in the British Navy?"

Christopher then related to Thomas all that had happened to him since that day in Annapolis when Mr. Hampton asked him to deliver the letter to New Castle, and how one event led to another until the present.

"And you didn't know it was Will Mundy who was too sick to deliver the message for Mr. Hampton?" asked Thomas, amazed at such a turn of events.

"No. How was I to know? He was upstairs all the time; I never met him. I did see him on the boat over from St. Michaels but I had no idea who he was. He kept to himself all the time."

"You've been through quite a lot, Christopher."

"A lot more than I expected when I started out for that weekend trip to see you and Matty. You know, I was really mad when they pressed me into service. I thought it was the end of the world; I thought it was the end of my life when I almost died escaping from the *Briareus*. But, you know, if those things hadn't . . . ."

"I know. If you hadn't gone through all that I'd most likely be on my way to London today or tomorrow and eventually the gallows."

"Strange how things work out sometimes," said Christopher. "Maybe a person ought to reserve judgment on the things that happen to him until he sees the whole picture." He pondered that thought for a while then added, "Crazy as it sounds, I'm glad now that all those things happened to me."

They both remained silent; a new bond had been formed between Christopher and his brother-in-law.

As the wagon carrying the three men crested the hill and started down the road into the small town, Christopher was again impressed by the beauty of Squansett Cove. It suddenly occurred to him that he had traveled this way only two times before and each time, as now, he was bringing someone here. The first time he had the dreadful experience of bringing Jacob's body home, the second was bringing Will Mundy here with his broken arm, and now, for the third time, he was bringing Thomas here. Three trips, but three different circumstances: sorrow, anxiety and joy. And it was a double joy, indeed—he had helped rescue Thomas and he'd soon be with Marion again.

As the wagon rattled down the hill and into town Thomas' thoughts were of Matty and his son Michael, Christopher's of Marion, and Zach's of what a joy it was to have put one over on the British. Suddenly and much to the surprise of Christopher and Thomas, Zach burst into song. What his voice lacked in quality it made up for in exuberance.

> "Lift up your hands ye heroes,
> And swear with proud disdain,
> The wretch that would ensnare you,
> Shall lay his snares in vain.

> Should Europe empty all her forts,
> We'll meet her in array,
> And shout and fight, and fight and shout,
> For North Amerikay.
>
> Torn from a world of tyrants,
> Beneath this western sky,
> We've formed a new dominion,
> A land of libertye,
>
> The world shall own we're masters here,
> Then hasten on the da-ay,
> Huzzah, huzzah, huzzah, huzzah,
> For free Amerikay."

"That's quite a song, Zach," said Christopher, "What's it called?"

"It's called 'Free America'. A fella named Warren wrote it, Doctor Joseph Warren (note 3). He was a pretty big man around here 'til he got hisself killed at Bunker Hill. They say the tune's the same as 'The British Grenadiers'. I don't know those words though. Guess I don't care too either."

Both Christopher and Thomas laughed at that.

As the wagon rolled to a stop in front of the Pierce's home Christopher heard neither Zach's command to the horses nor Thomas' comment on the beauty of the house. His pulse was racing with the thought that in that house, behind those walls, was Marion, the woman that had come to mean so much to him, almost as much as life itself. He relished the thought that within a few minutes he would see her again. But what he really wanted was to be alone with her, to hold her, to tell her how much she meant to him. When would that be? How long would they have to wait to share the tenderness of an intimate moment together?

"Wake up Christopher, we're here," chuckled Zach.

Thomas just grinned at Christopher's embarrassment then turned to Zach. "Zach, there's no way I can ever . . . "

"Don't want to hear 'nother word 'bout it," interrupted Zach, "Ain't had so much fun since the time we tarred 'n feathered the stamp agent back in sixty-five. Shoulda been there, the rascal looked just like a giant chicken."

"Well, I owe my life to you and Christopher — and to the others too," insisted Thomas.

"Well, the way I figure it, if you just keep working to pry us loose from King George, that's more 'n enough reward for me."

As Christopher climbed down from the wagon the front door opened and the servant Joseph appeared. Behind him was Will Mundy. Immediately, Thomas leaped down from the wagon and raced up the steps. Joseph stepped out of the way just fast enough to keep from being caught between the two old friends as they embraced each other. "Watch the arm," said Will.

"Oh, sorry, Will. Christopher told me about your breaking it. How's it doing?"

"Fine, but still a little sore. Man! It's great to see you again. It's like seeing someone returning from the dead."

"I feel like someone returning from the dead, which is where I would be if Christopher and Zach hadn't rescued me."

Christopher, having tried in vain to see if Marion was present, turned and extended his hand to Zach who remained in the wagon's seat. "Zach, thank you. That doesn't sound like much, but believe me, no one ever felt more grateful than I do. I'll never forget what you've done for us. I not only got Thomas back but I've found a new friend, a fine friend."

"Well, don't know about the fine part but ye've got a friend all right. Take care, Christopher." With that, and a wave of his hand, he gave the two horses a slap of the reins. They all watched as the wagon and Zachariah Davis disappeared down the street.

Christopher, disappointed and somewhat puzzled that only Joseph had met them, went up the steps to join the others. They all went inside as Joseph followed, listening and smiling, as the three continued to greet each other. When the excitement finally died down Joseph announced to Christopher that Mrs. Pierce and the girls were visiting the Wescotts and should return later that afternoon.

A little less than two hours later, although it had seemed like an eternity to Christopher, the sound of a carriage announced the return of Captain Pierce's wife, Rena, and two daughters. It was difficult for Christopher to refrain from rushing out to meet them, but he felt it wise to maintain some degree of decorum. He certainly did not want to embarrass Marion although he was not certain such actions would. The three waited in the parlor. Thomas and Will remained seated as Christopher stood watching out the window.

There, at the foot of the front steps, was an expensive looking, four-wheeled chaise pulled by a beautiful but anxious black mare. Joseph was holding the fidgeting horse while the ladies were being helped out by a well-dressed young man. First Rena then Molly was assisted safely to the ground. Then Marion stood up to be helped out Christopher was consumed with a warm and pleasant feeling that seemed to radiate from her loveliness. She was even more beautiful than he had remembered.

He could hardly take his eyes off her but when he did his heart skipped a beat. The young man was Philip Wescott, the lawyer he had met earlier. A wave of jealousy swept over him but he could not tell himself why except that Philip Wescott with his law practice and family position in Squansett Cove could present a very formidable rival if he chose to do so. Christopher was not convinced this was not already the case. As Marion stepped down Philip did not release her hand right away but lifted it to his lips and kissed it a very continental fashion. Marion smiled and whispered something to him before he got back into his chaise and drove away. Christopher felt sick. Was his dream being lost or was it more than he had a right to dream of in the first place?

As the three ladies ascended the few steps and moved out of

Christopher's view he shifted his attention to the carriage carrying Philip Wescott away. He naively wished it would carry him away for good but knew that was certainly not going to happen.

His spell of increasing despair was broken by the sound of female voices in the hall. They were chattering away, not yet aware of Christopher's return for Joseph had considered it prudent not to mention it in the presence of Philip Wescott. Suddenly the talking stopped as Joseph, who had followed them into the house, informed them of Christopher's return.

Quickly the parlor door opened revealing Mrs. Pierce with Marion and Molly behind her. Thomas and Will stood up to greet them.

"Praise God! You're back safe," exclaimed Mrs. Pierce, "Christopher, we've been so worried about you."

Marion and Molly both rushed to simultaneously embrace Christopher while Thomas smiled at his brother-in-law's suddenly being the object of so much feminine attention.

When the exclamations of joy finally settled down, Christopher said, "Mrs. Pierce, Marion, Molly, I'd like to present my sister's husband, Thomas Owings."

Mrs. Pierce did not offer her hand but instead warmly embraced Thomas saying, "You poor young man. What you must have been through. We've prayed constantly for you and Christopher. You must consider our home your home. I'll have Joseph find you some more suitable clothes."

"It is my pleasure to meet you, Ma'am. Christopher has told me how Captain Pierce saved his life and you nursed him back to health. And now you've helped me escape from the British noose. Seems like our family is greatly indebted to you folks."

"Nothing of the kind," insisted Mrs. Pierce, "we consider it our good fortune to have had the opportunity to help. Now let's get you settled. I'm certain you three men want to get home to your loved ones as soon as possible but you must rest a day or so with us before you go rushing off."

Marion added, "And a few days more healing of Will's, I mean

Mr. Mundy's, arm would make your traveling more comfortable."

"I'd be pleased if you all would call me Will. And your kindness is without equal and most appreciated," said Will.

"Yes," said Christopher and Thomas in simultaneous agreement.

They all laughed at their short chorus. Then Mrs. Pierce said to Will, "Thomas can stay upstairs with you. Would you show him where it is? I'll help Joseph find some more suitable clothes." Then to Molly, "See that there's wash water in the pitcher for Thomas."

Suddenly, Christopher and Marion were alone in the room, but the moment was not as Christopher had anticipated. What he had seen from the window just minutes before made him unsure of himself and the situation. He felt very awkward and was reluctant to speak. However, Marion did not sense this and without any hesitation rushed into his arms crying, "Oh, Christopher, I've died a thousand deaths worrying about you. I was so afraid you'd never come back. What would I have done?"

Christopher reacted instinctively drawing her close to him. It felt so wonderful having her body pressed against his, the touch of her hair on his cheek, the delicate scent of her perfume. This was that moment he'd so often dreamed of. As he held her tightly but gently in his arms his concerns began to rapidly disappear, yet there remained a haunting tinge of doubt. He could not completely rid his mind of the image of Philip Wescott and the pleasantries that had exchanged between him and Marion. But, for the moment it was a moment to cherish.

At the sound of someone approaching in the hall Marion drew away, brushing the front of her dress making sure it did not look mussed. Christopher turned toward the window hoping to regain his composure before the intruder entered the room.

"Well, have you two had enough time alone?" asked Molly teasingly as she came into the room.

"Molly! I'll have you know . . . ," fussed Marion.

"Oh Sis, don't fret so. Everyone knows you two have eyes for each other."

"Maybe so, but you don't have to make so much of it!" admonished Marion.

"It's up to you two to make something of it," answered Molly as she turned and left the room giggling.

"Molly!" cried Marion angrily to the empty doorway. Then to Christopher, "I'm Sorry, Dearest. I'd better go."

Then Christopher was left alone.

Three days later Christopher announced he'd been able to arrange transportation to Newport by coach and they would be leaving the next morning. At Newport they would try to find a ship going to Philadelphia or some port not far from there. They had considered leaving Squansett Cove by sea but the chances of being intercepted by a British cutter would be considerably greater that way. It was also Christopher's hope they would meet Captain Pierce in Newport.

At dinner that evening there was a mixture of emotions as they discussed what lay ahead. Of course Thomas talked of returning to Matty and his son, Michael, while Will expressed concern over what had been developing in the Committee of Correspondence at Annapolis. Christopher was looking forward to seeing his family and home again after such a long departure but was careful not speak much about it. He did not want Marion to think he was eager to leave. In reality he was not. Although he knew he would return if she wanted him to, he was not yet completely convinced of her feelings. The specter of Philip Wescott drove daggers of doubt into his heart every time he thought about it. And because of that he didn't want to put so many miles between Marion and himself, yet something called common sense told him such a separation would test the earnestness of their relationship.

Mrs. Pierce participated in the conversation all through the meal while Marion said little and kept her eyes on Christopher most of the time. There was a certain far away look in her expression that Christopher could not exactly fathom. Molly, who usually had some remark to make in almost every situation, hardly spoke throughout the meal.

After they all had finished their dessert of custard, Will placed his napkin on the table and said, "Mrs. Pierce, that meal was exceptional. Now, if you people will be so kind as to excuse me, I'll retire to the parlor for a bit of a smoke. Would you gents care to join me?"

"Yes, thank you," replied Thomas. "Christopher?"

Christopher, deep in thought, suddenly heard his name. "What? I'm sorry."

"We're going into the parlor to have a pipe. Do you care to join us?" asked Thomas.

"Oh, thank you, no," said Christopher, "I believe I'll go out for some fresh air instead." He had some serious thinking to do and that could best be done alone.

At that, they all rose and left the dining room. Thomas and Will went to the parlor, the ladies to the kitchen. Christopher quietly walked down the hall to the back door and then outside.

There was a peaceful stillness to the early evening air. It was fresh and clear; not a leaf was stirring. The blue summer sky was softly fading into a blend of roses and yellows in the West. Only a few dark clouds to the Northeast disturbed the scene.

As he walked along the gravel path he noticed the garden was different from when he first enjoyed its serenity with Marion. It was just as beautiful, but different. Some of the flowers that were there before were now gone, and new ones had appeared. The roses were still there, as beautiful as ever, some red, some pink, others yellow. The full bloomed flowers were delicate and just as pleasant to the eye as before. There were the young buds, pointing skyward, as though eagerly waiting their turn to open and display their individual beauty. But there were also empty stems, their spent petals strewn rotting on the ground. As he strolled along, the lengthening shadows reminded him of the sun's incessant march across the sky and the never-ending passage of time. And the passage of time meant change, for the good, or for the bad. It seemed nothing ever stayed the same.

When Christopher came to the mulberry tree he remembered so well, he stopped and sat down in its lingering shade. His mind, and his heart, went back to those precious moments Marion and he had shared there. If only such moments could be frozen in time, kept forever, ever to be savored, and most of all, forever shared. But there was the gnawing fear that whatever existed between them was destined to end like the rose petals on the dark ground. Would Philip Wescott see to that, just as the coming frost would bring the final blow to every rose? Christopher felt he had so little to offer; Philip Wescott had so much. He sat there for a long time, wondering how he could possibly overcome all that was against him. Perhaps if he took to privateering he could acquire some measure of wealth. But would that be too late? Would Philip Wescott already have won her?

Christopher was so deep in thought he did not hear the swish of taffeta approaching. "My! Christopher, you seem so quiet. What is the matter?"

"Marion!" exclaimed Christopher as he started to jump to his feet.

"Don't get up, dear," smiled Marion as she moved closer and started to sit down.

Christopher rose on one knee extending his hand to help her. "I didn't hear you coming."

"You must have been very lost in your thoughts. Can you share them with me?" she asked as she sat down spreading the skirt of her dress around her.

Should he, should he dare confess his thoughts? No, it would risk too much. He might scare her away. "Oh, I was just wondering," he answered. "So many things have happened since that day I left home to visit Matty, things I never would have dreamed of happening to me. I was sort of wondering what the future had in store for me next."

"I hope it includes me," said Marion as she moved a little closer.

Christopher felt a warm glow come over him as he took her hand in his. "So do I," he whispered. He looked into her eyes searching for assurance. "But can I really hope for so much?"

"Christopher Hall!" she scolded as she drew back, forcing a frown, "You exasperate me!"

He said nothing but sat frozen in disbelief.

She leaned forward and lovingly placed her hand upon his cheek. Her smile seemed to seek a response as she spoke, "Of course you can. Don't you know I love you?"

His head was spinning. What was happening? Was all this real? "Marion . . ."

"Hush Darling and kiss me," she whispered as she moved even closer.

He took her into his arms and thrilled to the feel of her body against his. He looked into her eyes and saw the answer he so desperately sought. She loved him. She had even said so.

Time stood still as they embraced, lost in each other.

Suddenly, the spell was broken by a rush of wind followed by cold raindrops. Christopher leaped to his feet and gave Marion his hand to help her up. When she was up, they laughed and kissed again. But as the rain grew stronger Christopher said, "Come, let's get out of this." He took her hand and started toward the house.

But Marion balked. "No, the stable. It's closer."

They ran laughing through the rain to the stable that stood at the rear of the garden.

As they rushed into the building the Pierce's horse whinnied and stomped its foot. "He objects to our intrusion," said Christopher.

"No, silly. Don't you know that's a horse's way of welcoming lovers? Here, let me dry your forehead." She took her handkerchief and gently dabbed the drops of water from his face.

The loving touch of her hands and the delicate scent of her perfume were almost more than he could bear. Feelings, deep, strong feelings, were swelling up inside him. He pulled her closer and gently brushed back a wet ringlet of her hair. For a moment he just looked at her, trying to convince himself this was really happening. "Is this a dream?" he whispered as he softly stroked her cheek with the back of his fingers.

She looked up into his eyes and whispered, "If it is, I hope we never wake up. Oh, Christopher, I love you so! Can't you say the same?"

"Yes, yes, yes, I love you . . . more than words can say, but . . . ."

"Stop that and hold me tight," she admonished.

As he drew her closer she pressed herself against him and he could feel the warmth and contour of her body against his. For this moment the two of them were all that existed. Their very beings seemed to mingle into one. All the universe had been condensed to just here and now, to just the two of them, and nothing else mattered.

He gently ran his fingers through her hair as her head lay on his shoulder. Then, almost as if on its own accord, his other hand came to rest on her breast. He was instantly surprised and embarrassed at what he had done and quickly removed it. But more to his surprise, she took his hand in hers and gently put it back.

"It's all right, Christopher."

He continued to caress her and tried to picture what lay beneath those layers of fabric. But even through all that, he thrilled to the feel of the small, firm shape that was now beginning to heave passionately to his touch.

She had allowed him to come through that personal barrier of privacy. She had given part of herself to him. This meant trust and with trust comes commitment. This idea itself fostered an overwhelming feeling of intimacy. With this came a special caring and concern. Her feelings and honor must come before any of his desires. Her giving herself to him, even in this small degree, now obligated him to put her first. He could not allow this to go any further. Yet, desire was rapidly consuming him. His head was swimming in a whirlpool of emotions.

She said nothing but looked up at him with eyes of surrender. For a while he just looked into them, looked as if he were searching her very soul. He wanted her, he wanted her this moment, now, this time, this place. Yet, not this way. This moment would end and then what? Would she hate him tomorrow? Would she forever blame him for taking advantage of her? Taking her for this moment he might lose her forever. Then remembering all Captain Pierce and his family had done for him he knew this had to stop.

He took a deep breath and stepped back. "Marion, I think it would be best if we went back to the house. The rain has stopped."

She looked at him, puzzled, disappointed and somewhat ashamed, but said nothing. Straightening her bodice and hair she proceeded to the door. Christopher followed without a word.

CHAPTER XV

At last, daylight came, accompanied by an intermittent drizzling rain. But the dreariness of the gray morning was unequal to Christopher's melancholy mood. He arose mechanically, exhausted from a night filled with anxiety and despair. He was glad the struggle for sleep was finally over. His heart ached to know how Marion felt about him this morning. She had remained silent after they left the stable the night before, and had gone straight to her room when they reached the house. "Was everything spoiled," he wondered. Did she hate him for almost leading her into something she would regret the rest of her life? Or, did she hate him for rejecting her?

As he dressed, he wondered, over and over, at how things in life could change so rapidly from wonderful to terrible. What did he do wrong? But what did it matter now? What's done is done, and that was what he'd have to live with. He prayed that Marion was not hurt too much and that she would, at least, not harbor ill feelings for him. Would he see her this morning? Would he ever see her again? Then the thought occurred to him that if he did she would probably then be Mrs. Philip Wescott.

Realizing his eyes were moist, he dried them and chastised himself for falling into such a deep depression. He waited a few minutes, then went downstairs to join the others for breakfast.

Everyone was already there, except Marion, who, according to Mrs. Pierce, was not feeling well this morning. Suddenly, all of Christopher's worries rushed back to him. He tried to hide his reaction to Marion's absence and with a forced cheerfulness, greeted everyone at the table, then sat down.

"Let us pray," said Mrs. Pierce. They bowed their heads as she continued, "We thank Thee, most gracious and wonderful Father, for all thou hast provided for us. We thank Thee for this table and food, and pray that it will give us the nourishment and strength to better serve Thee. We also pray for a safe journey for Christopher, Will and Thomas and ask that they be allowed to return safely to their families. We ask for Thy mercy for those upon the sea and that Thou would bring Captain Pierce home safely again. These things we ask in the name of Thy Son, Jesus. Amen."

Christopher heard little of this for his mind was on Marion, and when the others said, "Amen," he responded, but a fraction of a second late, sounding like and echo. As the food was being passed around, the conversation began by Mrs. Pierce asking Thomas about his family. She seemed genuinely interested in all he had to say; he, of course, took great pleasure in telling it. After a while the conversation turned to Will's life at home. Being a bachelor, he talked less of home but expressed great enthusiasm for the workings of the Committees of Correspondence and their role in bringing the colonies together in a unified effort against the British.

Through all of this, Christopher said little for he was not only worrying about Marion, but he was certain Mrs. Pierce suspected something had happened between Marion and him. "She must be imagining the very worst," he thought. Several times he had caught her looking at him in an inquisitive manner. "What had she seen? What had Marion told her? What must she think of me?" he wondered.

"Christopher, are you all right?" asked Mrs. Pierce, at last, "You've been very quiet and you don't look well. Is there anything wrong?"

"No Ma'am, I'm all right. Just thinking about going home."

"Well, that's understandable," she replied, "You just remember now, this is your second home. You're like one of our very own. You must come back soon, you hear? Now, are you sure you feel all right? You shouldn't be traveling if you're coming down with something."

"Oh, I'm fine, Ma'am. Really I am." And he was, at least concerning how the Captain's wife felt about him. What a relief to know he was not going to be looked upon as an outcast. But this did not erase his worries about Marion's feelings.

Just as they were finishing the meal, Joseph appeared in the doorway. "Beg your pardon, but I just saw the coach coming down the road."

"We'd best be moving. Would you excuse us?" asked Will as he pushed his chair back.

"Of course," answered Mrs. Pierce, "are your things ready? Joseph can set them outside."

"I've already done that, Ma'am," said Joseph, "but Mr. Hall's . . . "

"Oh, I didn't bring mine down yet," explained Christopher, "I'll get it." With that, he left to go up stairs to get the small bag holding the few belongings he had acquired since Captain Pierce found him washed up on Spectacle Island. As he hurried up the stairs he could visualize the coach fast approaching and knew that within minutes he would be on it. Time was running out and he had not seen Marion yet. "She must hate me, I'm certain of it," he said to himself again. He thought she would, at least, have said, good-bye. Time was escaping him, and with it, his last desperate hope of seeing her, the only girl he ever loved. He thought once he would ask to see her. But no, it was obvious she didn't want to see him. It was useless, it's over. As he opened the door he felt as though he were turning over the last page in his life.

When he stepped into the room he was stunned as never before, for there, sitting on the bed, was Marion. She rose to meet him as he entered the. "Oh, Christopher, can you ever forgive me? What must you think of me? I . . . "

"Marion, what . . . I mean . . . forgive . . . ?" Christopher was so bewildered he had to pause to gather his wits. She came to him and he took her into his arms without hesitation. He felt the world swirling around them as he drew her closer and held her as though he were holding on to life itself. When he came to his senses, what was left of them, he said, "Marion, it is I who should beg forgiveness." But as he said it he was not sure himself whether it should be for letting them get into last night's situation or for his appearing to reject her.

She held him tightly for a moment and then backed away, looking at the floor as she spoke. "Christopher, dearest, I'm so ashamed. Last night I lost all control, you know that." She looked up at him and continued, "Darling, last night I was willing to do anything you desired, anything. No, not just willing, anxious."

"Marion, I . . . "

"Let me finish." She took a deep breath and continued, "If that had happened everything would have been spoiled. I would not have been able to face you or anyone else, ever. But you were stronger than I. You didn't let anything happen. And in spite of what you were feeling you put my well-being first. You could not have shown me any greater degree of respect or affection."

"Marion, Darling, I thought . . . "

"Never mind what you thought. I love you more than ever now, more than anything else in the world. I know you have to leave, but please come back to me, Christopher. You must!"

"Oh, Marion, yes, I'll come back. But this war . . . ."

"No, no, no! You don't have to get involved in that." She threw her arms around him and buried her head in his chest. "Something will happen to you. I just know it."

He placed his hands on her shoulders and gently held her away from him. Her eyes were moist with tears of apprehension. Even so, she appeared more beautiful than ever. "Darling, I'm afraid I already am. At first I looked at all that was happening as a spectator. But now I'm convinced we have to fight to get free from England. There's no turning back."

"But . . . ," she began to protest.

"Would you have any respect for me if I stood by and let others risk their lives for our freedom? I'd have no respect for myself; I'd have no right to expect it from anyone else. Please try to understand. Remember the poem we read in the garden? Remember the last line?"

"Yes, I remember." Then with a soft and trembling voice she repeated the line:

> 'I could not love thee, dear so much,
> Loved I not honour more.'

"Please understand. Whatever I must do, I'll do. But, I will come back. I promise . . . you mean too much to me. I love you so, Marion."

"I do understand, and I do respect you, but most of all, I love you. She was trying to smile but could not hide the worry that was in her heart. "Go now. I hear the coach outside. I'll watch from the window."

They kissed once more, as though sealing their lives together, forever. Then Christopher picked up his bag and went downstairs.

Life had begun again.

NOTES

1. In response to Great Britain's actions against Boston, Colonial leaders in Annapolis met and adopted resolutions of sympathy. They appointed an 'Annapolis Committee of Correspondence' to cooperate with the other colonies.
2. The name Rhode Island in 1775 referred only to the island on which the city of Newport is located and not the whole state as it is known today, even though the official name for the state is still 'State of Rhode Island and Providence Plantations'.
3. Dr. Joseph Warren (1741-1775), teacher, physician and a leading statesman in Massachusetts, was born in Roxbury, Mass. and studied at Harvard. He frequently wrote for the colonial cause and helped draft protests against the British. He served as president of the Massachusetts Provincial Assembly and as a Major General in the Massachusetts forces. It was Dr. Warren who sent Paul Revere and William Dawes on their famous ride to Lexington and Concord. Dr. Warren was killed at the Battle of Bunker (Breed's) Hill